WHEN WE LEFT

ELENA AITKEN

Ink Blot Communications

Also by Elena Aitken

Timber Creek

When We Left

When We Were Us

When We Began

When We Fell

Women's Fiction

All We Never Knew

Ever After

Choosing Happily Ever After

Needing Happily Ever After

Wanting Happily Ever After

Fighting Happily Ever After

We Wish You A Happily Ever After

Keeping Happily Ever After

Finding Happily Ever After

Seeking Happily Ever After

Cherishing Happily Ever After

Ever After: Volume One (Books 1-4)

Castle Mountain Lodge

Unexpected Gifts

Hidden Gifts

The Springs Series

The Springs Complete Collection - Books 1-10

The McCormicks

Love in the Moment

Only for a Moment

One more Moment

In this Moment

From this Moment

Bears of Grizzly Ridge

His to Protect

His to Seduce

His to Claim

Hers to Take

His to Defend

His to Tame

His to Seek

Bears of Grizzly Ridge: Books 1-4

Destination Paradise

Shelter by the Sea

Escape to the Sun

Stand Alone Stories

All We Never Knew

Drawing Free

Sugar Crash

Composing Myself

Betty & Veronica

The Escape Collection

Vegas

Nothing Stays in Vegas

Return to Vegas

Halfway Series

Halfway to Nowhere

Halfway in Between

Halfway to Christmas

Chapter One

WHEN SHE LOOKED BACK on it, she should have hung up on him. In fact, as soon as she saw his number come up on the screen, she should have tossed her cell phone out the window.

But she hadn't.

No. Of course not. A sucker for punishment, Cam Spears —*no*, strike that. Cam *Riley*—now was as good a time as any to go back to her maiden name—picked up her cell phone, steered her SUV with one hand and actually tried to have a conversation with her two-timing, philandering, no-good, son-of-a-bitch ex-husband. Well, he wasn't her ex yet. But he would be, soon. Hopefully *very* soon.

She'd spent way too much time turning the other way and pretending she didn't see what was going on right in front of her. Which was one affair after another.

"What do you want?" It wasn't the politest way to answer the phone, but there was no way Ryan actually deserved anything resembling manners from her anyway.

"I'm returning your call, Cam." He sighed in that way that might as well have said, "I'm far too important to deal with whatever it is you have to say."

Cam swallowed hard in a vain effort to control the wave of emotions that made her want to simultaneously scream obscenities and break down sobbing from frustration. "Right," she said as calmly as she could manage. After all, he was right. She *had* called him. "I wanted to talk to you about..." She glanced in the passenger seat at her teenage daughter. True to form, Morgan had her earbuds in, eyes closed and arms crossed. She was either sleeping or contemplating how much she hated her mother. Either way, she wasn't listening. "I wanted to talk to you about Morgan," she continued. "I'm hoping that a fresh start in a new town and a new school will be just what she needs to get her grades up and her attitude sorted out. And since no one knows her, she won't have to worry about the—"

"Right. Okay."

Cam tried to ignore the distracted tone in his voice.

"I've been really worried about her attitude lately. I mean, it's really gotten worse since the..."

"The separation?"

Cam swallowed hard and nodded. It wasn't that she was upset about the separation. Not in the way people probably expected her to be. But she was still having trouble wrapping her head around the fact that despite years of looking the other way, trying to make things work, and sacrificing her own needs and wants in favor of keeping their marriage together, it had all been for naught. The reality of what that actually meant for her and her daughter hadn't fully sunk in yet.

"Right," she said. "Anyway, I'm getting concerned that maybe she's—"

"I'm sure you can handle it, Cam."

Cam swerved slightly to the right before she corrected the steering wheel. "Pardon?"

The sigh again. "Come on, Cam. Honestly, why are you bothering me with this right now?"

"Bothering you?" She swallowed hard and struggled to

keep her emotions in check. "Because she's your *daughter*, Ryan. We may be getting a divorce, but that doesn't change things with Morgan. We agreed to co-parent."

"About that…"

"About what exactly?"

"Well, things are kind of new between me and Chastity right now and with you moving out of town…Well, I think it might be easier if you could just handle things while Morgan is with you and when she's with me, I'll handle things. Ya know?"

There was no way he'd just said that. "Pardon?"

"It would be different if you stayed in town, Cam."

Stayed? There was no way she could have stayed in Portland. Not after what he'd done. Which was basically outing his affair and announcing his love child all over local television. As the co-anchors for the local evening news, Ryan and his new, much younger co-host, Chastity Newberry had been openly flirting on-air for months. Every time Cam mentioned it, Ryan brushed it off. But Cam wasn't stupid; she'd known about Ryan's indiscretions for years. He'd always been discreet about them and considering the love between them had died long before, Cam hadn't cared. Not really. Besides, he took good care of them, and there was no point stirring things up and blowing up their lives, just because they didn't love each other.

The *ostrich* approach had worked out well for Cam, too. At least until the weatherman, on the six o'clock news, with the entire greater Portland area watching—including everyone they knew—made an offhanded comment about the *happy new family to be.* There wasn't a sandbox deep enough for Cam to bury her head into after that.

She'd been humiliated in front of everyone. When Ryan came home, and told her he was in love with Chastity, and he wanted a divorce, Cam knew there was only one place for her to go.

"You know I couldn't stay." The words came out too soft,

almost sad. She cleared her throat and tried again. "Besides," she said with a much stronger voice. "This isn't about me. It's about Morgan. I need you to—"

"You don't need anything from me. I'll always be there to love and support her and she knows that, but I can't get involved in your little parenting dramas right now. Besides, my lawyer doesn't think it's a good idea for us to be communicating. Not until the divorce is final."

Divorce. He made it sound so simple. So cold and clinical. As if almost fifteen years of marriage could be erased with a few pieces of paper. She didn't want to care, but she did because the truth was, even though she hadn't been in love with Ryan for a long time—maybe ever—there had still been a lot of positive in their relationship. A lot of good times, happy times and special memories. That couldn't just be wiped out with a few signatures on a piece of paper. *Could it?*

She ignored the feelings that tried to bubble up and tried to get back to the point. "Ryan, you're only going to see her once a month. That's hardly—"

"About that," he interrupted her. "I don't think that's very practical for me and with Morgan getting settled into a new school and everything—maybe if we did one weekend every two months instead?"

"What?"

"I'll have my lawyer contact yours."

The car jerked to the left. Cam quickly corrected it. "Wait." She struggled to wrap her mind around what he was saying. He didn't want to *see* their daughter? For everything she might have thought about Ryan as a husband, she never would have guessed that he'd be a bad father. "I don't—"

"Distracted driving is against the law, Mom."

Cam's head swung around to see Morgan staring at her, her lips pressed together, her eyes narrowed and attitude radiating from her pores. *She was awake? How much had she heard?*

4

"I'm not driving—"

"Yes, you are." Sighed with the drama that only a teenager was capable of.

"Cam, are you driving right now?"

"And there's a sign over there that says distracted driving is against the law in Washington." Morgan tapped her finger against the glass.

"I know it is, but…" She had bigger problems than holding a phone to her ear. *How much had Morgan heard her say?* "Morgan, you shouldn't have heard—"

"What?" Ryan barked in her ear. "Is she right there? Did Morgan hear you talking? Dammit, Cam. You should know better than—"

"Mom?"

"Cam. I can't believe you'd be so irresponsible."

"Me?" She slammed her hand down on the steering wheel. "*I* shouldn't be so irresponsible?" She yelled into the phone, no longer caring what Morgan overheard, at least for the moment. "Are you kidding me right now?"

"Mom?" Morgan glanced quickly behind her, but Cam barely noticed. "You should put your phone down."

With voices coming at her from all sides and her stupid emotions threatening to get completely out of control, Cam could hardly think and she definitely couldn't concentrate on the road, let alone on what anyone was actually saying. That's why when the siren sounded behind her, her first reaction was to slam on the brakes, followed by a loud, "Shit!" when she saw the flashing lights of the police car in her rearview mirror.

"Cam, what is—"

She ended the call, cut off Ryan's voice, and held the offending phone in her hand as though it were going to explode. She looked to Morgan for backup, but her daughter just shook her head and rolled her eyes.

Cam watched through the mirror as the officer stepped out of his car.

"Shit. Shit. Shit." Cam shook her head before she realized what she'd just said. As a positive example, she was doing a lousy job lately. To put it mildly. "Oh, Morgan. I'm sorry I swore. I shouldn't have used obscenities just because I was stressed out."

"Whatever." Morgan shrugged with indifference, but the satisfied smirk on her face gave her away. "I told you you should have put the phone down." She put her earbud back in and looked out the window.

THERE WERE a lot of things Officer Evan Anderson could ignore. Parking a little too close to the stop sign to run in and grab a coffee at Daisy's Diner. Sneaking up a few miles over the speed limit right at the edge of town where, in his opinion, fifteen miles was ridiculously slow anyway. Jaywalking across Main Street to say hello to a neighbor. These were all things Evan had no problem ignoring.

Driving erratically while talking on a cell phone was *not* one of those things. Distracted driving was dangerous and there was no way Evan was going to let it happen. Not in his town. Especially from someone with out-of-state plates.

With his lights flashing, he left his cruiser on the side of the road and made his way to the black SUV. Evan knew all the cars in Timber Creek, and most of the visiting family and friends too, and he certainly hadn't seen such a flashy-looking Expedition around town with Oregon plates before. Whoever it was who thought they could drive like an asshole in his town was about to get sorted out. He may not have respected Timber Creek the way he should have when he was still young and stupid, but that had changed. A lot. These days he took pride in protecting his hometown and making sure others respected it as much as he did.

He scratched down the license plate number before he made his way to the driver's side and rapped on the tinted window with the back of his hand. Evan began to talk the second the window moved down. "License and registration. Do you know why I pulled you over—"

The words died on his lips as the driver came into view. It was easy to see the woman behind the wheel was frazzled. Likely because she'd just been pulled over. But that's not what caught his attention, froze the words on his lips, and caused his heart to do a weird double flip in his chest. No, it was the familiar blonde hair—a little darker now—the profile of the nose he'd recognize anywhere because there had once been a time when he'd kissed the tip of it every single day, and then—when she turned to face him—her eyes.

Cam.

She was back? How was it even possible? He couldn't formulate a thought. Nothing coherent anyway and definitely nothing that would be remotely appropriate.

Fortunately, Cam spoke first. "Evan? Is that you?"

He blinked and swallowed hard, forcing himself to call on his army training to remain as stoic as possible and not let a damn thing show on his face. There was no doubt he was failing miserably, but it was better than nothing. "Cam?"

She smiled, but it didn't come close to reaching her eyes. "Yeah. It's been awhile. I can't believe you're a...well, you're a..."

"Cop?" He relaxed a little, seeing that she, too, was just as shocked. For sixteen years he'd dreamed about seeing her again. He'd fantasized about what it would be like to talk to her, to hold her, to—*no.* That clearly wasn't going to happen. It was still a traffic stop, after all.

Although writing a ticket was the furthest thing from his

mind. "You didn't know?" He instantly regretted it. *Why should she know what he was doing now?* She'd left town right after graduation in search of what she used to call *a future.* He'd loved her more than life itself but even as an eighteen-year-old kid, he knew he was way too much of a screw-up to give her the future she deserved, so he'd let her go. Leaving him brokenhearted. And her...well, she'd moved on a long time ago. Without so much as a backward glance.

So why was she back?

Cam shook her head. "No. I didn't know. But I think it's great." There was that *not quite* smile again. The longing to see the warm smile he remembered so well hit him with a ferocity he didn't expect. "I'm really sorry if I was driving too fast, or..." She glanced down at her cell phone that sat incriminatingly in her lap. "Morgan told me not to, but I was just in the middle of a conversation, and I know it was wrong, but I wasn't thinking. I'm sorry. I mean, I know you'll have to give me a ticket and all, but—"

"Morgan?" For the first time, he noticed the teenager sitting in the passenger seat. He'd been so focused on Cam he hadn't seen past her.

"Hey." The girl waved sarcastically, no doubt very much aware of his preoccupation.

"My daughter. Morgan."

Daughter? She had a daughter. Of course she did. He knew she had a kid. But it was one thing to *know* she was happily married and had the life and family she'd always talked about. And a very different thing to *see* it with his own eyes. But he couldn't be surprised. Cam deserved it and it was all he ever wanted *for* her. But if that was true, why was there a flash of pain at the idea that it was somebody else who'd given it to her?

He smiled and nodded his head in the direction of the girl

who looked as if she'd like to be anywhere but sitting in that car. "Nice to meet you, Morgan."

Cam's face turned red and she flapped her hands around a little, distracting him. "Here I am, not even back in town for five minutes and I'm already causing trouble."

"You're not causing trouble." He flipped his notebook closed and tucked it away in his pocket. There was no way he was going to write Cam a ticket. "What brings you back to town anyway?" He instantly regretted the question. Not because he didn't want to know. He did. Badly. Her parents moved to Arizona years ago, and as far as he knew, she hadn't been back since high school. *Why now?* That's what he really wanted to ask her, but when her mouth pressed into a thin line and she glanced down at her lap for just a second before she looked up again, her face now lined with a sadness and exhaustion that hadn't been there before, he regretted asking anything at all because the Cam he once knew slipped a little farther away.

"It was time," was all she said in response. "And we really should get going. If you wouldn't mind finishing up with my…"

"Oh." He shook his head and gave her a grin. "I'm going to let you off with a warning today. Keep your phone in your purse, okay?"

"You don't have to…I mean, you have to. Give me a ticket, I mean." She stumbled awkwardly over her words and glanced over at her daughter, who watched the entire scene with veiled disinterest. "I'm trying to teach Morgan consequences, and that means that I need to accept mine, too."

"I'm not giving you a ticket, Cam." He grinned and crossed his arms over his chest, in an effort to end the debate.

"You have to."

"No." He chuckled a little. He couldn't remember the last time anyone had begged him to give them a ticket. "I don't.

But I really would like the opportunity to catch up with you while you're in town." Once again her face shifted and he regretted his choice of words. *Dammit.* She probably thought he was letting her off the hook in exchange for a date.

"I'm not sure that's a good idea, Evan." Her voice was tight. "But if you're really not going to give me a ticket, I should get going."

"I'm not." He took a step back from the SUV. "It really was nice seeing you, Cam."

In response, she put her window up, pulled away, and drove down the road. Just as she had all those years ago. Leaving Evan standing in the dust, wondering what the hell had just happened.

EVAN. He was here. Of course he was here. It was his town. Why wouldn't he be there? Why shouldn't he?

Because he left.

He'd left her more than sixteen years ago.

Cam's head hurt with the memories that hit her with a tsunami force the second she saw those familiar eyes. She reached up and rubbed the bridge of her nose. She didn't have time for a headache. She didn't have time for anything. Especially thinking about Evan and a past that couldn't be changed.

"Who was that guy?"

Morgan. She needed to remember that just because Morgan stayed largely quiet didn't mean she didn't notice anything. In fact, it was quite the opposite.

"Who?" She tried to keep her voice light and unaffected, but her daughter clearly wasn't buying it.

"Who do you think?" Morgan rolled her eyes. "The only guy we've seen in the last few hours who wasn't pumping gas. The cop, Mom. Who is he? You know him."

She shook her head because the truth was she didn't know him. Not anymore.

"I used to," she answered honestly. "But that was a long time ago." A really long time ago and she didn't have time to consider what Evan's presence in Timber Creek would mean to her. Of course she'd known logically that he *could* be here, but Christy Thomas, her one friend who still lived in town, had never mentioned him. Likely out of concern for Cam and an unspoken understanding that Cam didn't want to know. Not really. It wouldn't do any good to revisit the past.

"I'm sure we'll run into lots of people I used to know," she said to Morgan, trying to keep her tone light and fun. Maybe if she made her return to her hometown an adventure, her daughter would buy in. It was a long shot, but it couldn't hurt to try. Lord knew she'd tried everything else to get Morgan engaged in life. She'd been chalking Morgan's behavior up to the typical teenage type of drama, but now with the added *bonus* of dealing with a public family breakdown on top of everything else, she almost couldn't blame her daughter for acting out.

Almost.

Morgan hadn't said much about her dad or the new baby, or really any of it. Whenever Cam tried to bring it up, she just clammed up. Cam was running out of ideas on how to deal with it but a fresh start could only help.

"Whatever." Morgan rolled her eyes and put her earbuds back in.

Cam tried not to sigh. There was no point starting something with her. They'd be out of the car soon enough and maybe it was best if Cam was left alone in her own thoughts and memories for the drive through town. It was always her favorite part about coming home when she was a little girl. Her parents would take her on countless trips throughout the United States, to exotic beaches, the castles of Europe, or even on her tenth birthday, to Disney World. But despite all her travels, Cam's favorite part of traveling had always been coming home. Turning the bend to see the log sign proclaiming, "Timber Creek, Home of the Timber Times Festival," had meant she was only minutes away from being in her room, sleeping in her own bed and seeing all her best friends: Christy, Drew, and Amber.

It's not that she hadn't liked traveling; she just never loved it the way her parents had. Sure, she appreciated having the opportunity to see the world and experience the things she had, but there was something about home that she couldn't find anywhere else.

Just as it did all those years ago, a familiar sense of peace came over her as she drove down Main Street, which was completely the same yet totally different all at the same time. It had taken her sixteen years, and the circumstances were less than ideal, but she was finally home.

She glanced at Morgan, who stared out the window, her lips pressed into a thin line. No doubt she'd complain about the lack of malls, the tiny streets, the small classrooms, and pretty much everything else about Timber Creek that was in direct opposition to Portland. But that was okay. Cam could handle it because whether Morgan knew it or not, Timber Creek was going to heal them. It had to, because Cam was completely out of options.

THERE'D BE plenty of time later to show Morgan the sights of Timber Creek. Not that it would take long, but for now, all Cam wanted to do was get settled so she could start thinking about her next step. A step that would need to include a job and getting Morgan enrolled in school as soon as possible. The therapist she'd sent Morgan to before Ryan cut her benefits off had suggested building a strong, structured routine for Morgan as soon as possible. If she knew there was stability in her life, she'd be less likely to act out.

Stability. Ha. The very word made Cam want to laugh and then cry. There was definitely not a lot of stability to be found, but she'd do what she could. They both needed it.

She pulled the SUV up in front of Junky's Auto Shop, looked up and let her eyes take in the grungy windows of the apartment over the shop with a faded For Rent sign in the window.

When Cam had called Christy to tell her she was going to be returning to town, she was adamant about getting her own place, something "stable" and "structured" for Morgan. When her friend finally stopped trying to convince her to stay with her and her husband Mark, she told her about Junky's apartment and because Christy was able to do some sweet talking, Cam got it at a reduced rate. Although, now that she was looking at it, she couldn't help but think it had something to do with the fact that the place likely hadn't seen a broom or a rag in years. *If ever.* And that was only what she could ascertain from the outside.

"Why are we here?" Morgan stared at her. "Is the car broken now?"

There was nothing to do but put a brave face on. "Nope," Cam said with as much forced cheerfulness as she could muster, which really wasn't much. "This is our new home."

Morgan's face screwed up in disgust. "You can't be serious. An auto shop?"

"No. The apartment above it." She pushed the button to cut off the engine, and turned to gather up her purse. The sight of a police cruiser in her rearview mirror caught her eye, but by the time she turned around to confirm, it was gone. *Evan.* No doubt he was just making sure she was getting to wherever she was going safely.

Because he still cares about you.

No.

She had no time for Evan or thoughts of Evan or anything at all to do with the past. That's not why she came home. This time, the only thing Timber Creek was going to give her was her future.

"I'm sure it's fantastic, Morgan." Cam forced herself to switch gears. Hopefully the apartment wasn't *too* bad. Even if it was, it wasn't anything a bucket of soapy water and maybe a can of paint couldn't fix. Nothing was going to bring Cam down, or deter her from starting fresh. Nothing.

"Whatever." Morgan slid down in her seat, arms crossed firmly over her chest.

"Come on, Morgan." She turned in the seat and placed her hand on Morgan's arm. To her surprise, her daughter didn't shrug her off. It was such a small thing, but when it came to dealing with Morgan lately, Cam would take whatever victories she could get, no matter how small. "I know it's not ideal and it's a little different than what we're used to."

"A *little*?"

"Okay, a lot." Up until a few days ago, they'd been living in the only house Morgan had ever known, a three-thousand-square foot mansion on the water in one of Portland's most prestigious neighborhoods. One of the perks of being married to the local news anchor. One of the only perks. Cam swallowed hard against the bile in her throat. It was a beautiful house, and she'd taken a lot of pride in making it a home over the years, but it would never be home again. Not anymore.

There was no point dwelling on things. She needed to focus. Besides, Morgan didn't deserve to be drawn into any more drama than she already had been. *Stable and secure.* That's what she needed to remember.

"Look, Morgan." She squeezed her daughter's arm gently. "I know it's not much, and it's not permanent, but it will be ours and we might actually have a lot of fun fixing it up just the way we want. We can paint it bright colors and maybe get some funky pillows and things. It'll be fun. Promise me you'll at least give it a chance."

She stared into her daughter's heavily eye-lined eyes, and hoped upon hope that something she said might be getting through to her. For a moment, she thought Morgan would close up again and shut her out, but then she nodded. "Okay."

It wasn't much, but it was all Cam needed. "Okay. Let's go find Junky." Her face split into a smile she definitely didn't feel, and she jumped out of the car before Morgan could change her mind again.

Chapter Two

"WELL, WHAT'S SHE DOING BACK?" Ben Ross, Evan's oldest friend and owner of the Log and Jam, everyone's favorite local hangout, poured Evan a beer and slid it down to him across the long bar that had been custom made out of one huge log. Everything in the pub was well thought out and custom designed. Ben had put his heart and soul into building the Log & Jam, even participating in the actual construction of the log cabin building. Antiques and various paraphernalia like old axes and saws that once belonged to the early loggers that settled Timber Creek lined the walls.

Evan stretched out his back and inhaled the comfortingly familiar scent of cedar that always lingered in the air of the pub. It had been a long shift after he'd stopped the black SUV with Cam behind the wheel. A torturously long shift. It was a damn good thing there hadn't been any important calls in the hours following because seeing his one true love had rendered him almost completely useless. All he could think of was that blonde hair—those blue eyes and the last time he'd seen them at their graduation dance the night before he'd left her without a word.

It wasn't because he didn't love her. He did. So much it hurt. But Cam deserved more than he could offer. A lot more. He was the town screw-up: the kid always getting in trouble, narrowly avoiding the law on more than one occasion—and sometimes not—barely passing his high school classes because he thought he was smarter than his teachers and didn't need to do the work. The one smart decision he did make back then was recognizing that he couldn't be the man Cam needed him to be. Not the way he was. It had killed him inside to leave town that June morning, knowing she'd be left hurt and confused. But he'd done it.

He'd gone away to try to make something of himself and he couldn't even regret it because the last time he'd been able to bring himself to ask her best friend Christy how Cam was doing, she'd told Evan how happy Cam was. Married to a successful newscaster, living the life she always wanted in Portland. That's all he'd ever wanted for her, even if it wasn't with him.

But now she was back.

"I don't know," he answered his friend. "We didn't really have a chance to chat. I was supposed to be writing her a ticket for distracted driving."

"As if you would give Cam Riley a ticket." Ben poured himself a beer and leaned against the counter. "What's she look like?"

"The same." *Only different.* She was still gorgeous. But there was a seriousness about her, too. Like she'd lived a lot of life in the years that had gone by. "And she has a kid."

"You knew she had a kid, man." Ben shot him a look because it was true, he did know that. Christy had passed on that information as well. "Right?"

"Yeah, yeah. Of course." Evan shook his head. "I mean, I knew it. But it's different than *knowing* it. Ya know?" He didn't wait for an answer. "But here's the thing. She's not so much a kid as a teenager."

Ben took a sip of his beer and tilted his head in question. "How old?"

Evan shrugged and took a swig of beer. He hadn't asked. "Fourteen? Fifteen? I don't know."

Ben shook his head with a smirk. "Damn."

"What?"

"It's nothing." He raised his hand in acknowledgment of another customer farther down the bar.

"It's something." Ben wasn't the type of guy to not say what he was thinking, and Evan knew he would speak his mind no matter what. It was one thing he could always count on from his friend. That and a buddy to go fishing with. "What?"

"Well, I was just thinking that if Cam has a teenager, it sure didn't take her long to move on, did it?"

Ben's words hit him in the gut.

"I mean, she must've gotten knocked up right after—"

"Stop." It was math Evan didn't want to do. After all, he'd already been thinking of it. At least a little. The second he'd seen Cam's daughter, the thought was there. *What if she was his?* It wasn't that far of a reach. But of course it was. He knew it was. She'd been gone a long time, and a lot could happen in sixteen years. Hell, a *real* lot could happen. He would be naive to think she hadn't been with anyone else, especially considering he knew she was married. The girl wasn't his. Even if for a split second he'd wished she was.

He took another long drink of his beer and wiped his mouth. "There's no way. I would have heard about it. Hell, she would have told me. Cam and I didn't have secrets. Never did."

Ben shot him a look before he disappeared to care for his customers. Ben might be his oldest friend, but he never did understand the way things were between Cam and him. He'd never understood anything Evan had done. But he had supported him. And when push came to shove, that's the best thing you could ask for in a friend. Ben was a rock-solid guy. Evan had leaned on him more than once over the years and with a certain blonde-haired woman back in town, there was no doubt that those days weren't over yet. Not that Evan was going to get involved with Cam again. No way. Even if she wasn't married, those days were in the past.

Weren't they?

A little voice in the back of his head chimed in.

Those days *were* in the past. Once upon a time, Evan would have fallen apart, stood up and then fallen all over himself trying to get her back. But he'd learned a lot over the years and he definitely wasn't the same person he once was. No way. Now he was a war veteran, a police officer serving and protecting the town he loved most, and a whole lot wiser than the punk-ass kid Cam once knew.

But that doesn't mean you don't still love her.

"Dammit," Evan muttered to himself. He chugged the last of his beer and slammed the glass down on the bar. He pushed up from his stool, threw a twenty on the bar and walked away.

That dammed voice never did know when to shut the hell up.

"YOU'RE GOING to love Timber Creek High." Cam forced a cheerfulness in her voice she certainly didn't feel. She'd given Morgan a few days to settle into their new place, but now with Monday upon them, it was time to move forward and start their lives. They couldn't hide in their tiny little apartment forever. Especially considering it was so small that Cam was pretty sure the close proximity to each other was doing their relationship more harm than good at the moment. She needed to get Morgan out and into society. If she could meet even one or two friends her own age, Cam had no doubt that would go a long way in helping her adjust to their new life. And Lord knew her daughter could use a friend.

"I'm sure I won't." Morgan appeared from the bathroom and Cam did her best not to react to her daughter's new look. She was only trying to get a rise out of her. There was no point taking the bait. "It's a small-town high school—what's to love?"

Cam swallowed all the comments she so desperately wanted to make about Morgan's thick black eyeliner and lips so red they, too, were almost black. She was clearly trying to make an impression on the first day of school. Even if it wasn't the one Cam would have liked to see her make. She'd learned to pick her battles, and this one was definitely not a fight she had the energy to engage in.

"The sports programs are amazing," Cam chattered on cheerfully, pointedly ignoring Morgan's scowl. "The Timber Wolves are known to be some of the strongest teams in the state. You might want to try out for—"

"I don't *do* sports, Mom." Morgan squared off in the space Cam was trying to call a living room, even if it was acting as her bedroom, having given Morgan the only room. "Have you ever known me to play a sport?"

"Well, when you were little you were a great soccer player. Maybe you could—"

"Because they have a soccer team out here in the middle of nowhere? If you wanted me to play soccer, we should have stayed in Portland."

It had been three days since Morgan made any reference to the fact that she'd moved them. Foolishly, Cam hoped she was over it, but her daughter's words stabbed her in the chest. "You know we couldn't stay, Morgan. Not after—"

"Whatever. Shouldn't we go?"

Cam put the smile back on her face and nodded. She loved her daughter, but lately, being her mother took a level of energy she wasn't sure she had. "Yes." She grabbed her purse from the counter and the folder of resumes she'd done up the night before, printing them off Junky's office printer in the shop below. As soon as she registered Morgan with the school, she was going to hit the pavement and see what she could drum up in terms of work. Ryan hadn't left much in the joint bank account; the fact that he'd left anything at all was only because he cared enough about his daughter to make sure she was fed and cared for.

Not that he cared enough to see her or hear about how she was doing.

The anger and resentment that was becoming all too familiar bubbled up to the surface, but Cam pushed it down again before it could take root. She had too much to do. She couldn't afford to let thoughts of Ryan in. Not today. Today was going to be a good day.

She looked at Morgan and couldn't help but notice that despite the heavy makeup, she'd put on her nice jeans and a clean black top. She may be trying to make a statement of some kind, but she still cared. At least a little bit. Cam reached out and squeezed her hand, trying one more time. "You know," she said. "The school also has an amazing drama program. For a small-town school, they produce some pretty impressive productions. Always have."

Morgan shrugged, but she didn't pull away, so Cam gave her hand another squeeze. It might take a little time, but they'd be okay. She knew it.

THE HIGH SCHOOL was almost exactly the same as she remembered it, down to the brick walls painted a strange, almost sickly shade of green, the trophy cases where if she stopped to look, she could probably still recognize some names, and the rows and rows of grey lockers. She smiled to herself as they walked through the foyer and the familiar feelings washed over her. She'd expected to be embarrassed to walk through those big doors again after all this time, but it was quite the opposite. She'd had some good times at Timber Creek High. Maybe some of the best years of her life.

Mrs. McReedy, the school secretary, greeted her with a hug. She'd always thought the woman was the oldest person she knew, and that was over fifteen years ago. Now, Mrs. McReedy must be at least a hundred. But she still had that sweet smile and strong arms that could either hug you or smack you depending on the situation. Although Cam was pretty certain smacking the students across the knuckles was no longer a common or accepted practice. Even for Mrs. McReedy.

She ushered Cam and Morgan into the office, where Cam signed a stack of papers, Morgan was handed a schedule and just like that, her daughter was a student at Timber Creek High. Just the way she herself had been a lifetime ago.

"Do you want me to walk you to class?"

The question was met with an eye roll and an exasperated look that Cam should have seen coming.

"Your first class is just down the hall, dear." Mrs. McReedy pointed the way. "Second door on your left. Mr. Muldoon, science. Just give him your enrollment slip here and he'll get you all settled in. If you have any questions at all, you know where to come."

Morgan took the slip, shrugged and without a backward glance at Cam, made her way down the hall. Nostalgia and a mixture of hope and anticipation filled Cam as she watched her go. She had a lot of good times at Timber Creek High. Some of the best days of her life with a group of great friends and a boy she thought she'd spend the rest of her days with. It would be good for Morgan. It *had* to be good for Morgan. Because if it wasn't, she had no idea what else to do.

The last few months had been rough for her daughter, and

that was putting it mildly. Her troubles had begun before the divorce: skipping classes, hanging out with the *wrong* crowd. Little things that mostly Cam could chalk up to typical teenage rebellion, but after everything went down with Ryan, things only got worse. A lot worse. And Cam definitely couldn't ignore the phone call from the principal when Morgan had been caught cheating on an exam, and then lipping off the teacher who busted her. The behavior was so unlike her soft-spoken, studious child, it didn't take a parenting expert to know something was up.

They'd both needed a change of scenery. A fresh start. Hopefully Timber Creek was just the place for them to get it.

"She'll be okay."

Cam was jarred from her thoughts by Mrs. McReedy, whom she'd forgotten was still standing there.

"I'll keep an eye out for her, but I'm sure there'll be no need. She'll fit right in and make friends in no time, just like her mama. Don't you worry about it."

"Thank you, Mrs. McReedy."

The older lady waved her gratitude away. "No need for that. I sure was sorry to hear about what happened with your husband. Couldn't have been easy on your girl. A little change of pace is exactly what the child needs."

The blood drained from Cam's face. "You heard? What happened with Ryan, I mean?"

"I'd reckon everyone heard, dear. At least everyone in the West Coast broadcasting district. We get the KQRZ *Nightly News* here, ya know? And knowing his connection with our little town…" She gestured to Cam in case she didn't realize Mrs. McReedy was referring to her being the connection. "Well…word's going to get out. But don't you worry. No one around here is going to judge you for a single thing. Divorce happens every day and if you ask me, you're much prettier than she is."

Cam swallowed hard. She knew Mrs. McReedy was lying, but she'd take what she could get. But one thing Mrs. McReedy was most certainly *not* right about was that no one around there was going to judge her.

Cam had grown up in Timber Creek; she knew how things worked and she definitely knew that whatever else happened, she was definitely going to be judged. Especially if word had already traveled as far east as a small, nothing town in Central Washington.

She sighed and managed a small smile and a word of thanks before she left. All Cam really wanted to do was go back to her tiny apartment, crawl back into her lumpy couch bed and forget everything. But that wasn't an option. She was running out of money fast and even though her little apartment over Junky's didn't cost much, it still cost something. Cam needed a way to make money. Fast.

As she drove away from the high school and into the main part of town, her cell phone beeped. She risked a glance at it, despite the fact that the officers in town were clearly on the watch for distracted driving. Not *officers* necessarily, but one officer in particular. *Evan.* Just remembering his smile and the way his eyes lit up when he realized it was her behind the wheel filled her with some kind of feeling she couldn't completely define. And even if she could, she didn't have time for it anyway. First things first: she needed to get back on her feet and make sure Morgan was okay. That was the only thing that mattered.

Before Cam had a chance to click open the text message on her phone, it beeped again.

Stop hiding.

Followed by, *I mean it, Cam.*

Christy.

Only one of Cam's best friends had elected to stay in Timber Creek to raise her family. The only problem was that

Christy and her high school sweetheart Mark had never actually had that family they so desperately wanted. But Christy still loved Timber Creek and everything the town had to offer, and when Cam told her she was going to be in town, she'd not only been excited, she'd prepared a bedroom and insisted that Cam and Morgan stay with them. An offer Cam had politely declined. Having their own space was important right now; they needed to heal. At least that was her excuse. It was also her excuse for not seeing Christy yet. They'd been in town three days and Cam still hadn't called her friend. She couldn't get away with it for much longer. Not without a really good reason. And she didn't have one except that she was embarrassed and exhausted plus the last thing she felt like doing was talking about her failed marriage. Even with one of her best friends. And that wasn't a good enough reason to put Christy off any longer.

Cam pulled her car into the parking lot of Daisy's Diner and texted Christy back.

I'm at Daisy's.

She half expected, and maybe hoped, for Christy to say she was busy, or maybe even at work. It embarrassed Cam that she didn't know whether Christy had a job or not. She hadn't been a very good friend lately.

Her phone beeped with a response almost immediately.

I'll be right there.

SHE WAS *NOT* GOING to love Timber Creek High. That was Morgan's distinct verdict after spending one full day in the classrooms full of kids she didn't know. Kids who definitely weren't anything like the kids back in Portland she'd gone to school with.

Nothing was like Portland.

But that was a whole lifetime away, or at least it felt like it.

As soon as the bell rang for lunch, Morgan pushed out the back door of the school into the field. There was a grassy berm with some pine trees that edged the football field, and sitting alone under a tree was a whole lot more appealing than sitting alone in the middle of a cafeteria.

Morgan moved quickly across the grass until she found a spot close enough to hear the bell that would signal the start of afternoon classes, but far enough away that she'd be able to pretend she was anywhere else.

The grass was cool beneath her when she laid back to stare up at the clouds.

For once, she didn't put her earbuds in, choosing instead to listen to the birds that chirped and flitted through the trees above her. At least Timber Creek had that going for it. It wasn't a big city.

Not that she didn't like the city, but she couldn't remember the last time she'd heard birds chirping, or seen a deer just wandering around. Well, okay, she'd never seen a deer wandering around like she had the day before.

And that was kind of cool.

If she had to be ripped out of her life, at least that part of Timber Creek wasn't too bad.

Morgan pulled her phone out of her pocket and checked again for any messages from her dad.

Nothing.

She tried not to let it bother her. He was probably busy with a meeting or something at work. She opened his contact but hesitated before calling him. Instead, she tapped out a text message.

HEY DAD. *I started school today. It's great.*

· · ·

26

IT WAS A TOTAL LIE, but her dad wouldn't know that. Besides, if she told him the truth, that she hated everything about her new school and she was miserable, he'd probably only get all defensive and tell her that it was her mom's fault they were there.

But it wasn't and she knew it.

It was his fault. He'd cheated on her mom. It was totally his fault her life had been flipped upside down.

But she still missed him.

SOUNDS GREAT! He texted back.

I MISS YOU, Dad. When do I get to see you?

MORGAN HELD her breath as the text sent. She squeezed her eyes shut until the ding that announced an incoming message sounded.

SORRY, princess. Things are kind of crazy right now, I'm not sure when I'll be able to get out there.

THE SHARP STAB of hurt hit her in the gut, but Morgan was determined not to let him see it.

OKAY. I get it.

SHE DIDN'T GET IT. Not at all.

Morgan tucked her phone back into her pocket and looked out over the field. She wasn't the only one who'd escaped the confines of the brick building to enjoy the spring day. A group of kids sat a little bit away. Far enough that she couldn't hear their conversation, but close enough so that when one of the boys looked over, he saw her looking at them.

Shit.

The last thing she needed was to stand out.

The guy waved at her, but she didn't return his greeting. Instead, she laid back on the grass, closed her eyes and waited for the bell to ring.

Chapter Three

THE MOMENT SHE WALKED IN, the smell of coffee and freshly baked bread filled the air. Cam closed her eyes and inhaled deeply. The bright and cheery diner was almost the same as Cam remembered it, with bright walls painted cheerful yellow and white tables with vases of silk daisies sitting in the center of each. The paintings and shelves showcasing local artwork were new, and Cam stopped to admire some of the pieces, before ordering her coffee.

If Cam had been hoping to slide under the radar, Daisy's Diner was the worst possible place to do it. A fact she realized about thirty seconds too late. She'd done her best, smiling and nodding and trying to look unaffected as old neighbors, class-mates, and even a handful of people she didn't remember at all greeted her with hugs, knowing nods, and sympathetic smiles. Cam knew her town and the people who called it home far too well. They may be smiling and polite on the outside, but there was no doubt that as soon as she turned her back, they'd be whispering and talking about how she'd returned home in shame.

But she couldn't allow herself to care about that. She

needed to stay focused on what really mattered. And it certainly wasn't the busybodies of Timber Creek. As soon as she could politely slip away to a table in the back of the busy diner with a newspaper and her coffee, she made her escape. She barely had time to flip to the small section of help wanted ads before she heard a familiar voice ring out across the diner.

"Cam Riley! It's about time I got to see your beautiful face."

She couldn't help it; a smile lit up her face at the sound of her friend's voice and the use of her maiden name. Christy always did know how to handle a situation. Cam pushed up from the table to meet one of her oldest, and *bestest*, friends in a surprisingly strong hug. She did her best to hold back the emotion that threatened to spill out as her friend squeezed her tight. Cam hadn't shed a tear since her life had begun its death spiral, and she wasn't about to start now. Any slip of emotion, and there was no doubt, the flood-gates would open and it would be very hard to close them again.

"It's so good to see you." Cam meant every word. It *was* good to see Christy again and for the life of her, she couldn't remember why she'd been avoiding this reunion. "You look—"

"Fat." Christy laughed and waved her hand.

"I was going to say great." She did look great. Sure, she'd put on a few pounds since the last time Cam had seen her. But who hadn't? Besides, she wore it well. Her blonde hair shone in the sunlight coming through the window, and her slightly rounder face made her look healthy and happy.

"It's okay." The women sat, Christy gesturing at Daisy for a cup of coffee. "I know I'm fat. It's all the hormones and fertility drugs they have me on. They wreak havoc on the body." There was a glimmer of something in her friend's eye, and her bright smile slipped a little. "But it will all be worth it," she said, and the smile was back in place, if not slightly forced.

Something was going on there, something Cam promised herself she'd ask about as soon as she had a chance.

"Tell me everything." Christy never was one to beat around the bush. "I mean, if you want to." She was also the one out of the four of them who was most likely to respect boundaries and feelings. Unlike Drew and Amber, their other best friends. They, on the other hand, would have already been interrogating Cam for details. It was nice to have a reprieve. Even if Cam knew it was short-lived.

"If it's all the same to you, Christy, I really don't want to talk about it. Not yet."

Christy nodded and smiled sympathetically. "I totally understand. Besides, as soon as Drew and Amber get here for the anniversary party, you'll—"

"The what?"

"The fiftieth anniversary." Christy looked at her sideways. "I know with everything you have going on, it probably slipped your mind. But Timber Creek High is celebrating its fiftieth year in a few weeks. There's a huge dance. I'm on the committee."

Hearing Christy say it out loud sparked some sort of a memory in Cam. She sort of remembered getting an invitation in the mail, but with everything going on, she'd completely forgotten. "And Drew and Amber will be here?"

Christy nodded enthusiastically. "Won't it be great? That's just what you need right now—to have all your best friends together in one place. So don't worry about telling me anything. At least not yet. You'll just have to explain it all again when they get here. Because there's no way they'll let you get away without telling them *everything*."

They both laughed, because it was definitely the truth. Daisy brought Christy her coffee, and topped up Cam's. Christy waited until the older lady, who'd been serving coffee in her diner for as long as Cam could remember, went back behind the counter, before she reached across the table and took Cam's hand in her own. "Seriously," she said. "I'm glad you're here. There's no better place to recover from a broken heart than right here at home where you belong."

Cam nodded in agreement, despite the fact that her friend was both right and wrong at the same time. There was no better place to heal, but what she didn't realize was that it wasn't Cam's heart that was broken. At least not because of Ryan. Their marriage had been broken for a long time, and although Cam had known on some level for years that there would be no happy ending for them, she certainly hadn't seen it coming the way it had. No, it wasn't a broken heart. It was a broken spirit. She'd been embarrassed, disrespected, and the friendship she thought she'd shared with Ryan, the partnership they'd built, had been completely shattered. Yes, her heart hurt for her daughter and the pain she was going through, but Ryan hadn't broken Cam's heart. That had happened years before, and not by Ryan...and she certainly hadn't stuck around to try to heal anything back then.

HE WAS ONLY two hours into his shift, and already Evan could feel the dreaded afternoon slump hitting him. The only problem was, it wasn't afternoon yet. Not even close. He really needed to get more sleep. No, what he really needed to do was to put Cam Riley out of his head. But there was no way that was going to happen, which meant Evan wasn't about to get a good night's sleep anytime soon. She was occupying every one of his waking moments, and now, when he could finally manage to drift off, his dreams, too. It had been years since he'd let her get to him like this. Clearly, time held no meaning when it came to Cam.

She was back in town. *But why now? Why after all this time?*

And without her husband. And why was she staying in Junky's apartment instead of with Christy? So many questions. None of which he had answers for. He knew he'd get some answers if he let himself listen to the gossip mill in town, but he'd never been one for gossip. It was a habit born from necessity years ago, when the mere mention of Cam's name caused him pain. So he'd just stopped listening altogether.

With his mind preoccupied, and his body exhausted, he knew he was going to need some help if he was going to make it through his shift without nodding off, he was going to need coffee. Strong coffee. He pulled his cruiser into the busy lot at Daisy's and blindly walked into the diner, focused on his goal.

"Morning, Evan." Daisy greeted him with her usual smile. "You're in early this morning. I didn't expect you until…" She tilted her head in inspection. "You don't look well, Evan. Are you taking care of yourself?"

Despite his exhaustion, he smiled broadly so Daisy wouldn't have reason to worry. The last thing he needed was the whole town thinking he was sick. It wouldn't take long for some of Timber Creek's nosier residents to piece together exactly what Evan's problem was. "Just a little tired this morning," he said. "I really could use a cup of your strongest brew to help get me going today."

"I'll make a special pot, just for you, sugar." She patted his hand. "It'll just take a minute." Daisy always knew how to take care of him. Even when he was a pain in the ass teenager, she'd always seen the good in him and went out of her way to give him an extra muffin, or extra fries with his burger.

"No rush, Daisy. Thanks." As soon as the motherly woman turned away to measure an absurdly large amount of grinds into the coffee pot, Evan turned and surveyed the room. The diner was busier than usual for a Monday morning. It was nice to see the local small businesses doing well, and it filled him with hometown pride that his little town had been one of the ones that made it through the latest recession relatively unscathed. The tables were filled mostly with people he'd known all his life, with a few tourists or visitors mixed in for good measure. He nodded and smiled at everyone, but when his eyes landed on the table in the back corner with Christy Thomas and a very familiar blonde with her back turned to him, Evan's heart stopped for a split second. His distraction didn't go without notice.

"It's nice to have her back, isn't it?"

Evan half turned so he could talk to Daisy and still keep an eye on the women in the corner. "She must be here for the big anniversary."

"Oh, I don't think she's here for a visit. You heard about that awful nastiness with her husband in the city, of course. I thought for sure that if anyone knew, it would be you, Evan."

Daisy did seem to have a way of knowing everything there was to know about everything. Why she seemed to assume that Evan would have any knowledge of Cam's life all these years later was beyond him, but he nodded.

"Just terrible what he did," the old lady continued. "But if that's what it took to get her back here, well, I'm glad for it."

Evan's curiosity was more than piqued, but he had to agree; whatever it was that happened, it was definitely good to have Cam back in town. Really good.

Before he could talk himself out of it, he tapped the counter. "I'll just be over in the corner when that coffee's ready, Daisy." And without waiting for a response, he made his way through the crowded restaurant.

"Good morning, ladies."

They hadn't seen him coming, and were clearly in the middle of some serious discussion. Evan should have felt guilty for interrupting their girl talk, but he didn't. Not if it meant seeing Cam again. And this time, not in a professional capacity.

"Morning, Evan." Christy gave him a wink, one he ignored. Instead, he focused on Cam. *Was it his imagination or did she turn just the slightest shade of pink when she noticed him?* She was never one to blush when they were teenagers, but things were different then. *They* were different then. The blush was new. He liked it.

"Sorry to interrupt," Evan said, not meaning a word. "But I saw you over here and thought I'd come by and see if…well, if you were getting settled in all right." It was lame, really lame. Especially considering he didn't even know why she was there or whether there was any settling needed to be done.

She nodded and maybe there was even the slightest bit of a smile. "I am. Things sure aren't much different around here."

"I don't know about that," he said. "I'd say some things are really different." He held her gaze until she looked away, and Evan couldn't help but wish he hadn't pushed her right away. But things *had* changed. *He'd* changed. And for a reason he couldn't seem to define, that was important for her to know.

Christy looked between them and shook her head. "Well, I'm sure it won't take long to get back into the swing of things around here. Right, Cam? Especially now that you have Morgan enrolled in school. How cool is it that she's going to the very same high school we went to?"

Evan didn't hear the rest of what Christy had to say because all he could focus on was the fact that Cam had enrolled her daughter in school. That could only mean one thing. "You're staying?" He blurted the question before he could stop himself.

Cam shifted in her chair and tapped the paper in front of her. "First I'll have to get a job," she said. "But yes, that's the plan. At least for a little while."

He could try to fool himself and say it was something else, but there was no point. Happiness filled him at her words. *Cam was staying.* He had absolutely no idea what that meant for him, or even what he wanted it to mean. He didn't have time to think about it though, because the next thing she said made his stomach churn.

"NO," Evan said. "No way."

Cam straightened her spine. "Pardon me?" *Who did he think he was? Waltzing over here in his uniform, looking sexy as all—no.* She couldn't let her mind go there. She had way too much to think about without adding Evan to the list. She needed to focus. "I don't know why you think you have a say in it." She folded the paper she'd been looking at in front of her and pulled it close when he tried to grab it from her hands.

"There is no way you're working at the End of the Road." He crossed his arms over his chest as if that were the final word on the subject.

Cam didn't particularly want to work at the sleaziest bar in the county, but according to the paper, it was the only place hiring at the moment, and something about Evan's insistence that she could not work there made her want to go down and ask for the job even more. "It's not up to you, Evan. I need a job and they're hiring. I think I'll go talk to…" She consulted the ad again and forced a smile when she looked up. "I'll go talk to Tommy. Is that Tommy Jenkins?"

"The very same. And he's absolutely no better than he was in high school."

"Worse, in fact," Christy chimed in.

Cam ignored her friend. "I'm sure he's not that bad. It's just a bar—how bad could it be?"

"Let's just say that the End of the Road is a daily stop for me, and I'm not taking in the entertainment."

"Entertainment?"

"Tommy added *dancers.*" Christy held up her fingers in air quotes and Cam raised an eyebrow.

"No," Evan said again before quickly adding, "I mean…it's not a good idea." He caught himself and his overstep the moment it was out of his mouth. Thankfully for him, Daisy chose that moment to deliver him a coffee.

"Here ya go, sugar. Nice and strong. It should get you through the day, no problem."

"Are you having trouble sleeping, Evan?" Christy turned to give him her full attention. "You should make an appointment to see Mark. Maybe he can prescribe you something to help you sleep."

Evan took a sip of his coffee, which, judging by the look on his face, was just as strong as Daisy described and shook his head. "I'm good, Christy. But thanks."

"You should probably go see Mark anyway. I didn't want to say anything, but I think it's been a little while since your last checkup." She turned to Cam and added, "Did I tell you I started working part-time in Mark's practice a few months ago? His receptionist went on maternity leave, so I'm filling in. At least until…" She drifted off, but she didn't need to finish the sentence. Cam knew Christy was only trying to fill the time until she herself could get pregnant.

While the two of them debated Evan's need for a medical checkup, Cam pulled out her tote bag and dug through the contents for her notebook. She flipped it open to a blank page, where she scratched down: *End of the Road—Tommy Jenkins.* Before she could click the pen shut, Christy grabbed the book from her hand.

"Where did you get this? It's beautiful."

"I had it made up with my photo. There's a little print shop down the road from my house…well, my old place…that does them for me."

"This is *your* photo? It's beautiful, Cam. Really."

Cam brushed off the compliment. The photo on the front of the book was one of her favorite shots of Morgan walking down the beach, her back to the camera, the ocean waves lapping her feet. So simple really, but really peaceful and serene. Her lens had captured the moment perfectly. "It's nothing."

"I don't know about that," Evan said. "I think it's amazing. I'd put that on my wall."

"You're just saying that——" She didn't finish the sentence because she couldn't think of a reason Evan would be saying that. "Well, whatever. It's just a hobby."

"It shouldn't be." Evan took the book from Christy. "This is good, Cam. Really good. I didn't know you still took pictures."

She shrugged. When they were kids, she'd gotten hold of her dad's old Canon and played around with it enough that she'd finally been able to take some decent pictures with it. Scenery shots of the mountains mostly, but she still had a few of Evan's portraits tucked away. He'd been her only human subject. At least until Morgan was born, but by then, the idea of making a career out of photography had all but disappeared.

"Seriously," Evan continued. "This is really good. This is what you should be doing for money. Forget waitressing. That's a total waste of talent, if you ask me. Never mind the fact that working for Tommy Jenkins is definitely not a good idea."

So they were back to that. Cam grabbed the notebook and stuffed it back in her tote bag, along with the newspaper. She'd had about enough of catching up with old friends as she could handle for one day. Besides, groceries weren't going to buy themselves. No matter what Evan said, she needed a job and she wasn't going home until she got one.

Chapter Four

THERE WASN'T much crime in town, but things could still be busy for one of the only officers in Timber Creek, especially when it was the last thing Evan wanted. By the time he had a chance to get out to visit Tommy Jenkins at the End of the Road, it was nearing dinner time.

No doubt he'd have reason to visit the seedy bar later on, but that would be for business, and what he wanted to talk to Tommy about was personal, very personal.

There were only a few cars in the lot when he pulled his cruiser up to the front door, and he recognized most of them as regular patrons. Tommy Jenkins's beat-up Jeep was there, too, which was exactly what he wanted.

Evan knew he had no right to do what he was about to do, but he didn't care. Even if there hadn't been a history between them, he would still look out for Cam. Just as he would any of his friends. New or old. At least that's what he kept telling himself as he pulled open the heavy wooden door and walked into the dimly lit, smoky room.

The End of the Road never failed to smell like rancid deep fryer oil, stale beer, and desperation. He tried not to wince as the odor assaulted his senses and he made his way straight to the bar.

"Rhonda." He nodded at the waitress who'd been working there for as long as he could remember, and had been the subject of more than one police call. She was a tough lady who didn't take any crap from her customers, which, unfortunately for her, also resulted in a few visits to the station from time to time. "Tommy around?"

Rhonda smiled and pointed to a table in front of the stage where a young woman with very little clothing on was moving slowly in time to the music. Evan made a note to check IDs on Tommy's dancers. "Can I get you something, Officer?"

Evan could have used another cup of coffee, but judging by the layer of grime in the coffee pot he'd seen once, he wouldn't be ordering one. "I'm good, Rhonda. Thanks."

Without wasting anymore time, Evan made his way to the table and stood over the man.

"Have a seat, Officer."

Evan assessed the chair as well as Tommy, who hadn't taken his eyes off the girl in front of him. Before he could protest, Tommy added, "I insist."

Tommy turned slowly and pulled a toothpick out of his mouth.

"I'm not staying." He set his jaw and crossed his arms over his chest.

The other man spun slowly in his chair, hitched one leg over the other and looked up at Evan. His lips twitched up in a sleazy grin. "What can I do for you?"

"I understand you're hiring." Evan didn't waste any time. "And I just came to let you know that if Cam Riley comes in here looking for a job, you need to let her know the position has been filled. Understand?"

Tommy took his time answering, flicking his toothpick around with his tongue. Finally, he pulled it out of his mouth and with a chuckle in his voice, asked, "Are you threatening me, Officer?"

"Not at all." Evan hitched up his belt. "I'm just telling you to let her know the position has been filled. That's all. I'd hate for someone to have to call the health department about your broken fume hood." He was just taking a chance that the kitchen had some sort of violation, and it likely wasn't too far of a stretch.

"Fume hood's fine, Evan."

Undeterred, Evan tried a different approach. "I wouldn't want your customers to be inconvenienced by any random compliance visits, Tommy. Every few days," he added for good measure.

With a sigh, Tommy uncrossed his legs and rose to his feet. He popped the toothpick back into his mouth and immediately flipped it with his tongue before addressing Evan again. "Well, that might border pretty close to harassment, now wouldn't it, Officer? Besides, the position has been filled."

Relief washed through Evan. He recognized the fact that he didn't have any say in what Cam did, or the decisions she made, but the idea of her working for scum like Tommy Jenkins didn't sit well with him. Not at all. If the position was filled, he wouldn't have to worry about it. *Unless*—

"I hired Cam Riley earlier this afternoon." The man grinned again. "She starts tomorrow. Grateful for the opportunity, too. Sounds like she's in a bit of a bind. I'm only too happy to help her out."

Evan was absolutely sure he was. And he didn't like it. More than that, he didn't like the smug look on Tommy's face. Evan wasn't stupid, and there was too much history between the two of them to think that Tommy's hiring Cam was anything but revenge for all the pressure Evan had put on Tommy to clean up his bar since he'd joined the force in Timber Creek.

They'd been friends once. Well, maybe not friends. Not the way he'd been with Ben. But the two of them had absolutely gotten into their fair share of trouble together when they were kids. The difference was, Evan straightened himself out. Tommy hadn't.

Not unless you counted owning the sleaziest bar in town, and conducting what Evan was positive was shady business dealings. If only he could prove it.

He shook his head and did his best to tamp down the frustration that was rising within him.

"She can't work for you."

"She starts tomorrow."

Evan glanced at the dancer who was still gyrating with a vacant look in her eyes. "No." He shook his head. There was no way Evan was going to let Cam work here. Not that he had any say in what she did, where she worked, or…well, anything at all when it came to Cam.

"She's not dancing, Evan." It was probably his imagination, but Evan caught the slightest bit of humanity in the other man's voice. "She's going to be serving drinks. The afternoon shift mostly."

That made him feel slightly better. But not much.

"I don't like it," Evan said after a moment, and then added, "If I hear of any trouble out here—"

"I know, I know, you'll shut me down." Tommy crossed his arms. "You've been singing the same tune for years, Anderson. If you had anything on me, you would have done it already. But if it makes you feel better to puff up your chest, don't let me stop you."

There wasn't anything more he could do. Except talk to Cam and convince her to find employment elsewhere, but that hadn't gone too well earlier. He turned without saying good-bye and started to walk away when Tommy stopped him.

"Maybe if you'd have been more of a man back then she wouldn't be running to me, Anderson."

It took everything Evan had not to turn around, grab the man by the neck and show him exactly who was more of a man, but he was on duty. And fortunately for him, at that moment his radio on his lapel crackled to life.

He waited until he was outside before answering the call.

"What's going on, Gladys?"

"Attempted shoplifting at Timber Trade," his dispatcher replied. "Dale Gordon caught her and is holding her until you can get there. Just a kid, from what I understand."

Evan took one last look at the seedy bar and shook his head. Talking to Cam would have to wait. But there was no doubt he'd give it his best shot. Again. There was no way a woman like her should be working in a place like that.

"I'm on my way."

It was only once he was driving down the highway that Evan realized he no longer knew what kind of woman Cam was.

CAM FLIPPED through her tiny closet one more time, this time pulling out her favorite black skirt. "It's not like I'll be wearing it anywhere else." With a sigh, she tossed it on the bed behind her and once again faced her closet.

When she'd left Portland, she'd only packed a few bags and there wasn't much in the closet that would be appropriate for her new job at the End of the Road. Not that she'd have anything appropriate if she'd brought her entire old wardrobe, anyway.

Her old clothes were more dinner party and fancy fundraiser appropriate. Not exactly what she would think of when looking for waitress attire at a bar.

A *sleazy* bar. She shuddered a little as she remembered the girl on the stage taking off her top for an audience of two. Two very indifferent men. Cam forced herself not to think about how sad it all was. Besides, she wouldn't be taking her clothes off. She was serving drinks. And even that was temporary until she could find something she was more qualified for.

She ignored the fact that she wasn't actually qualified for anything.

The last time she'd had a job was…well, long before Morgan was born. And that had only been answering phones at a car dealership part time in her freshman year at college. And even that only lasted a few months before she got pregnant.

No, Cam had traded in any dreams of her own a long time ago in exchange for the coveted position of Ryan Spears's wife. Maybe it wasn't coveted but at any rate, there was at least one other woman who'd wanted the job.

As far as Cam was concerned, Chastity Newberry could have it.

She selected a sleeveless silk blouse from the closet and then abandoned it in exchange for a simple black t-shirt. Oh yes, Cam had come a long way all right, but not at all in the direction she thought she'd be going.

"It doesn't matter." Cam moved to the mirror and pulled her hair up into a high ponytail before letting it fall down around her shoulders again. "I'm going somewhere now. Even if it is just to the End of the Road."

Cam laughed at her own terrible joke. It was better than wasting time feeling sorry for herself. And that would be way too easy to do. In her dusty little apartment, with less than two hundred dollars in her bank account, having just secured a job as a waitress, there probably wouldn't be too many people who would blame her at all if she bought a few extra tickets for the pity party merry go round.

But the truth was, despite the fact that her situation was far from ideal, she didn't feel sorry for herself. Not at all. Quite the opposite, really. Sure, there were going to be challenges—her daughter being her biggest one—and certainly it didn't sound like it would be easy to navigate a divorce, and make ends meet. But for the first time her adult life, that's exactly what Cam was going to do. And she was going to do it on her own.

She was long overdue for an opportunity to stand on her own two feet, and really, she probably should send Chastity a thank-you note for having an affair with Ryan and getting pregnant. There was no coming back from that. Not as far as Cam and her marriage were concerned. Maybe if she'd been a stronger woman, she would have been able to leave their love-less marriage a long time ago. But she wasn't. At least not then. And maybe not even now, but at least she was a whole hell of a lot closer to being the person she needed to be.

And her job at the End of the Road was going to go a long way to feed that independence. No matter what Evan thought about it.

She'd done her best not to think about Evan, or his over-protective display in Daisy's earlier that day. And she was defi-nitely not going to read too much into it either. He was just being a good friend. Nothing more. Because there wasn't anything between them. That door had shut a long time ago.

Or had it?

Even if it had been left slightly ajar, it was nowhere near the right time to even think about exploring what might be between them again.

Or still.

Not at all. Cam shook her head and left the bathroom mirror to lay out the supplies she'd gathered for the celebratory dinner they were going to have. After all, if the first day at a new school along with a brand-new job in a new town didn't call for a celebration, she didn't know what did.

She took a few minutes laying out the dishes, some pretty napkins she'd found at the grocery store, along with the rotisserie chicken and some pre-mixed Caesar salad, and glanced at the clock over the stove again.

It was already after five. Morgan should have been home by now.

Home.

She looked around the small one-bedroom apartment and shrugged. For lack of a better word, or a better place, that's exactly what it was. It definitely wasn't much, but Cam had meant it when she'd told Morgan they could spend a little bit of money to fix it up. She was sure Junky wouldn't mind if she put a coat of paint on the walls and maybe Christy would have some extra throw pillows for the sofa bed where Cam was sleeping. Or maybe she could find a lamp or area rug or something at a yard sale. Something with a little color

That's really all the place needed. A little color.

She was fully aware that she was looking at everything through rose-colored glasses, but they were the only pair she had, so she would wear them as long as she could. Or until things actually started looking brighter on their own.

It was almost five thirty when Cam started to consider going out to look for Morgan. She wasn't answering her cell phone. It was probably dead.

Maybe she'd forgotten her way back to the apartment.

That was unlikely too. It wasn't that big of a town.

Maybe she'd made a friend and was hanging out. It was wishful thinking, but stranger things had happened.

She didn't need to speculate any further, because only moments later there was a knock on the door.

"It's open, Morgan."

Another knock.

"It's open," she called again, but was also on her feet, crossing the room to open the door for herself. "It's not like

Portland," Cam started to say as she opened the door. "We don't lock our doors in—"

The rest of the sentence died on her lips when she saw Morgan and...

"Evan?"

Her eyes went first from her old boyfriend, who looked remarkably more serious than he had earlier that day, to her daughter, who stood with her hip cocked and her chin held defiantly.

A bad feeling crept down her spine, like a spider through sap.

"What's going on?" She tried to force some cheer in her voice despite the fact that her heart was sinking fast. "Did you get lost, Morgan?"

"Not unless she was lost in the aisles of Dale Gordon's store with five bottles of nail polish in her pocket."

"Dale Gordon?" Cam looked from her daughter to Evan. "Timber Trade?"

"That's the one." Evan nodded.

"Morgan, you didn't?" Cam shook her head, but she knew it was true the way that parents always knew the bad stuff even if they didn't want to believe it. "Morgan."

Her daughter shrugged. "I was going to pay."

"After you went outside?"

Morgan pulled away from Evan. "I told you I forgot."

"Which is it?" Evan's voice was authoritative and strong, and unlike anything Cam had heard from him before. If it hadn't been her daughter who was the subject of his authority, Cam may have been impressed. "You'll have to get your story straight, Morgan."

"Whatever." She shrugged down into her jacket and tried to look tough, but Cam could see she looked scared. The protective mama bear in her wanted to pull her daughter close and tell her everything would be okay. But the other part of her, the mother who was exasperated and at the end of her rope with her daughter, wanted to yell and lecture. Or at the very least get some kind of reaction out of her.

She chose to turn her attention to Evan instead. "I'm so sorry," she said. "What happens now?"

No doubt they'd have to go down to the police station and Morgan would be charged with something. *It would be a misdemeanor certainly, but still…maybe it would be enough to—*

"Nothing." Evan interrupted her thoughts. "I'll let her go with a warning this time."

There was no way she'd heard that right. "A warning?"

Evan nodded, the strong authority figure gone, replaced by the warm, approachable guy she'd known and loved. *Liked.* Known and liked. Cam shook her head and focused on the situation.

"Surely she'll have to make amends or do some community service at the very least."

Evan raised his brow and glanced at Morgan, who was doing her best to ignore the adults right in front of her. "Maybe it's best we talked about this alone, Cam."

She nodded. "Morgan? Could you go put your school bag away in your room?"

With a grunt, Morgan did as she was told, which in of itself was a miracle. The fact that she didn't have a school bag with her didn't seem to matter to anyone. As soon as she was out of earshot, Evan focused on her.

"Come on," he said. "It's the end of my shift soon and I'm going to go down to the Log and Jam. Remember Ben Ross? He's the—"

"You want me to go to the pub?" *How could he possibly think she would just forget the fact that her daughter had been caught breaking the law and go to the pub with him?*

"I'm trying to do you a favor here, Cam. Don't fight it."

"A favor?" She shook her head. "Why?"

She'd expected him to say it was because of their past history, the fact that they'd known each other better than anyone once upon a time. And she was ready for it. She didn't need his pity.

"Because it's her first day at a new school in a new town and she's clearly been through a lot. It's okay to cut kids a little slack sometimes. After all, I—"

"Are you a parent?" The words came out much harsher than she'd intended and maybe if she'd had a moment to think it over, she wouldn't have reacted the way she did. Or maybe if it was anyone else but Evan Anderson in front of her telling her what was and was not okay to do when it came to raising kids, she might have caught herself before exploding.

But she didn't.

"No," he answered in a measured voice. "I'm not."

"Then I don't think you're in any position to tell me what I should and should not do with her. And as I told you the other day, I think it's important for Morgan to learn the consequences of her actions."

"Her actions?"

"She *stole*, Evan."

"I'm aware of that. I took the call."

"She shouldn't be able to get away with that. She'll only do it again." Cam didn't know whether that was true or not but she couldn't seem to stop herself. And once she got going, she was convinced that a punishment of some kind really would be the best thing. "I need to teach her a lesson, Evan. She needs to understand that—"

"Okay." He held up his hands in surrender. "Okay. I give. I'll take her to the station. Will that make you happy?"

Cam nodded.

"Okay." He sighed, but Cam didn't miss the little smile on his lips as he shook his head. "Go get her. I'll call Judge Stewart and see what he wants to do with her."

It was the mention of the judge that gave Cam pause. But only for a minute. Being a parent wasn't easy, but what she did know was that she needed to nip this behavior issue in the bud before it got too far out of control. And she'd take whatever help she could get in that department. She was only less than a month into her life as a single mom, but already it was harder than she'd ever imagined.

EVAN SHOULDN'T HAVE BEEN SURPRISED that Cam would be the type of parent to insist that her daughter get taken in after a minor offense. Secretly, he was proud of her. Not that he knew anything at all about parenting, but it was a good decision. At least in his opinion.

In his line of work, he'd had the opportunity to see it all and he could tell from experience that the kids with strong parental support at home were far less likely to have a return visit in the back of his patrol car.

Hell, maybe if he'd had someone at home who cared enough to check on him, and make sure he was at home doing his homework instead of running all over town causing trouble, things would have turned out differently for him.

"Now, I don't want you to worry, Morgan," he said as he opened the back door of the cruiser for the girl. Underneath the eyeliner and brooding stare, Evan was struck at how much Morgan looked like her mom at that age.

Did she look at all like her father?

Ben's words flashed through his head again, taking him off guard. He'd be lying if he said he hadn't thought about Cam over the years. He had. A lot.

But this line of thinking was dangerous. He needed to stop it before it got out of hand. Particularly considering he had a job to do.

"I'm not worried." She slid out of the car and moved past him a few steps.

She had a lot of attitude, but Evan wasn't new on the job. He knew a worried kid when he saw one. And whether she admitted it or not, Morgan was worried. He took her arm gently and led her into the office.

"Judge Stewart is a very reasonable guy. He's tough. But he's fair."

"I wouldn't even be here if it wasn't for my mom."

"No." He stopped walking abruptly. Morgan jerked to a stop. "I'm going to stop you right there. You wouldn't be here right now if it wasn't for you and your poor decision to take the nail polish. Don't forget that little detail."

Chastised, she looked at her feet. Evan resumed walking down the hall until they reached a bank of chairs. A moment after Morgan took a seat, Cam walked through the front doors of the small office, followed moments later by Judge Stewart.

"Anderson, you do realize it's dinner time." The judge, an older man in his mid-sixties, nearing retirement, who resembled Santa Claus more and more every year, filled the room with his presence. "And Monday nights are pot roast. Have you ever had Mrs. Stewart's pot roast?"

"No, sir." He hadn't been thrilled about calling the judge at home. But he was even less thrilled about dragging out this little situation with Cam and her daughter for another day. "I have not had the pleasure."

"We'll have to have you over someday." The judge clapped his hands once and turned, acknowledging Cam and Morgan for the first time. "Now, what do we have here?"

He addressed the question to Morgan, but it was Evan who answered.

"This is Morgan and her mother, Cam Riley. Dale Gordon caught Morgan with a few bottles of nail polish in her pockets earlier this afternoon."

"Cam." The judge's smile was warm. "I remember you as a girl. It's nice to see you again."

Cam smiled nervously before the judge turned his attention to Morgan. He nodded solemnly and considered the girl, who, to her credit, looked suitably chastised. Maybe Cam had been right; if Evan had let her off with only a warning, the lesson wouldn't have sunk in. The angsty teenager had a much different attitude standing in the station than she had in the apartment.

"Is this the first offense?"

This time he addressed the question to Evan and turned to wait for Morgan to answer.

"Yes, sir."

Next to her, Cam nodded and worried her bottom lip.

"I see."

He nodded again and fell silent for a few long moments.

Evan was used to the judge's quiet consideration, but Morgan, obviously worried, began to fidget and shift from foot to foot.

Finally, after what must have been an eternity for the girl, the judge spoke to Evan. "Officer Anderson, what are your thoughts? Is Dale pressing charges?"

"He is not." The old shopkeeper had plenty of experience with teenagers and their sticky fingers over the years. It was a rare occasion when he was fed up enough to press charges.

"I see."

The judge gave Evan a questioning look.

"If I may, Judge?"

Judge Stewart nodded.

"Morgan is new to town, and I feel that this may have just been a bad judgment call on her behalf." Next to him, Cam made a noise of disapproval. "That being said," he continued and cast Cam a look. "I think it's important for Miss…" He realized a moment too late that he didn't actually know what the girl's last name was and hoped he hadn't offended either Cam or Morgan. "For Morgan to understand that we don't tolerate that kind of behavior in Timber Creek."

"What are you suggesting?"

He wasn't suggesting anything. In fact, after watching Morgan's reaction since setting foot into the station, he felt confident he'd made his point. But he also had a feeling that he'd hear about it from Cam if he didn't say anything, and for some reason the idea of upsetting her or disappointing her was completely intolerable to him. He took a breath. "Perhaps some community service wouldn't be a bad idea."

Judge Stewart clapped his hands. "I like it."

Evan nodded. He heard Cam sigh. And Morgan groan.

"Do you understand the severity of stealing, young lady?" Morgan nodded and twisted her hands together. "Not only is it illegal, it is immoral and does not speak well to one's character. Do you understand how important character is?" She nodded again. "I understand you are new to town, and for that, I'm willing to be lenient. However, that fact also makes it extra important that you make a good first impression. It is very hard to change people's opinions of you once you've demonstrated you are of poor moral character. Do you understand all of that?"

"I do, sir." Her voice wavered, but just a little as if she were holding back tears.

"Good." The judge smiled kindly. "In my years, I have also learned that actions go a long way in demonstrating character. Much further than words. Have you ever heard the phrase, actions speak louder than words?"

"Yes, sir." She clenched her hands so tightly, Evan could see the white fingertips.

"Well, it's true. Which is why I think fifty hours of community service will prove to the community that you are a good girl who made a bad decision and is willing to take responsibility for such decisions. Do you agree?"

Morgan didn't immediately answer. Instead, she made a gasping type of noise, followed by something that could have been a sob or a cough. Finally, she choked out the words, "Yes, sir."

"Good." The judge turned to Evan. "Anderson, you'll see to it that she completes the hours, and will act as her advisor."

It was Evan's turn to make a strange, gasping, cough-like noise. "Me, Judge?" He stared at the older man with wide eyes.

"Can you think of anyone else?" The judge gave Evan a smirk and wink, clearing holding a meaning known only to the two.

Evan could, in fact, think of someone else. He could think of any number of people who would have been better equipped to handle Morgan and her community service. People who didn't have any kind of connection, or at least not such a strong connection, to her mother. If he was working closely with Morgan, he'd be working closely with Cam. And that wasn't something he'd planned on at all.

Not that it would be terrible. Not at all. But there was a lot of history between them, and many years had gone by, changing a lot of things.

No, changing *everything*. He didn't know whether he could do it. Not with the kind of detachment that would be required.

He glanced at Cam, who, judging by the look on her face, was obviously thinking the same thing. But the judge was waiting for an answer.

"No, sir," he said. "I would be happy to oversee Morgan's community service."

"Good." Judge Stewart nodded. "And you, young lady. I don't want to see you in here again. Do you understand?"

"Yes, sir."

"I trust you will offer Dale Gordon a suitable apology as well?"

Morgan glanced at Evan, who nodded curtly. "Yes, sir," she mumbled and looked at her feet.

"Good. Now if you'll excuse me, the missus is waiting for me to watch *Wheel of Fortune*." He smiled and spoke to Cam for the first time. "She always guesses the answer before me. At least that's what I let her think."

Cam smiled. "That's a good policy, sir."

He chuckled. "It certainly is. Keeping each other happy, that's the key to a happy marriage. Life would be long and lonely without her, that's for sure."

Evan watched Cam closely, and he didn't miss the little wince and the slight dip in her smile as the judge spoke. He wondered again what had happened to Cam and her marriage. She wasn't wearing a ring, and if Daisy was right about the gossip, there'd been some sort of public scandal with her husband.

His heart squeezed. Cam didn't deserve that. She deserved everything that life could give her. Including love. Especially love.

Wasn't that why he'd stepped away all those years ago? So Cam could have everything she deserved in life and more?

He swallowed hard. Because for the life of him, at that moment, Evan could no longer remember why he'd turned his back on the love of his life.

Chapter Five

MORGAN SHOULD FEEL LUCKY, she supposed. Really lucky. If she'd been caught stealing back in Portland, there was no way she would have been let off with only community service. At least not without going to court or something. And the judge hadn't said anything about it going on her record. In fact, he'd been really cool about the whole thing.

Except she didn't feel lucky. Not even a little bit. Because if her mom hadn't opened her big mouth, the cop who obviously had the hots for her mom would have let her off the hook.

There was totally a story there. Not that her mom would tell her anything. She still treated Morgan as if she were a little kid and didn't know anything.

No doubt she thought she was protecting her, but Morgan was almost sixteen and she wasn't stupid. Not at all. Not even if her parents both thought she was. But she knew what was going on. Her dad had found a new girlfriend—hell, Chastity was only a few years older than she was. She didn't know that, but it could be true. And he'd left them.

From what she could tell, he didn't want anything to do with her at all. Her mom, fine; she guessed she could understand that. People fell out of love. It happened all the time. Half of her friends back home had divorced parents. *But how did you fall out of love with your kid?* That's what Morgan couldn't understand.

She stuffed her journal, still unopened, underneath her pillow again. She hadn't been able to bring herself to write in it since everything had happened. Which was stupid, because that was the kind of stuff she should be writing about. *Getting her feelings out.* That's what her mom would say. *It's good to get your feelings out. Don't keep them bottled up.*

But what could she say?

Morgan tapped the pen against her teeth and finally shoved it under her pillow too before flopping on her back on the little bed.

It had been nice of her mom to give her the only bedroom. Morgan knew she was trying. She should probably cut her a break. It couldn't be easy for her either, to have your marriage come apart on television in front of the whole city. Her mom probably needed a hug.

Morgan wrapped her arms around herself. Hell, *she* needed a hug. But every time she thought she might be able to reach out, her mom got that look in her eyes that she was going to cry or tell Morgan it was okay for her to cry or some other bullshit.

So she didn't.

Morgan rolled over and reached for her phone, but didn't bother picking it up. *Who would she text?* None of her friends back home cared about her. Not really. They were the kind of friends who only cared if you were there and could do something for them. *Fake friends.* She'd figured that out the second they'd driven away. *Out of sight, out of mind.*

Not one of them had returned her texts.

And she didn't have any friends in this stupid little town. At least not yet. There were a few kids who might be okay.

She reached over and flicked off the lamp. Her stomach growled and again, Morgan regretted going to bed as soon as they got home from the station. She shouldn't have refused the chicken. As soon as she'd seen the table, it was obvious her mom had made an effort with the dinner and that only pissed her off. *Why should they sit around and pretend they were a happy little family when they obviously were anything but?*

The last thing Morgan heard before she drifted off to sleep was the muffled sounds of her mom crying in the next room. Something twisted in her stomach. She swallowed hard and pulled the pillow over her head and fell asleep.

The next morning, Morgan's alarm went off before her mom could wake her. If she had to go to the stupid new school, and she obviously did, she might as well make an effort.

Not that she cared to fit in with the townies and their boring lives, but maybe it was better than sitting alone at lunch and feeling like a total freak.

This time when Morgan applied her eye makeup, she lightened up a little on the dark eyeliner. She hadn't really liked the look that much anyway, but her mom had really hated it, which was why she kept doing it. But maybe for one day she'd try it this way. *Couldn't hurt.*

Her mother insisted on driving her again, even though the school was only a few blocks away. She probably thought Morgan wouldn't go if she didn't personally see her into the building herself. Fortunately, she didn't insist on walking her inside. Morgan would have drawn the line.

Besides, of course she was going to go. *There's not like there was anything else to do in the stupid little town.*

Morgan was pulling the books she'd been assigned out of her locker and stuffing them into her book bag when a blonde head appeared around the side of her locker.

"Hey," the blonde said. "You're Morgan, right? The new girl?"

"Do you get a lot of new girls here?"

The blonde laughed. "Just you." She slid around the locker and stuck her hand out. "I'm Jess."

Morgan glanced down at the hand with its perfectly painted pink nails and looked back up at the girl. She was pretty in that all-American, cheerleader kind of way. Not at all the kind of girl Morgan would normally be friends with. Still, she took the hand.

"Hey."

"My mom used to know your mom when they were kids," Jess said. "Well, I guess she sort of knew her and her friends. She worked with your mom's friend, Amber." Jess shrugged. "Small town and all. Her name is Shelby. My mom's older, but she remembers her."

Morgan had heard her mom talk about Amber. And Christy and Drew. Apparently they were inseparable growing up. As close as sisters, her mom used to say. *Not that close if she'd been able to move away and barely see them.* But Morgan wasn't in any position to judge friendships. Not when she didn't really have any of her own.

"I've heard of her."

Jess nodded. "So what classes do you have?"

They spent the next few minutes discussing timetables and teachers. Jess moaned over the fact that Morgan had Mr. Gilman for English, but beyond that, Jess approved and they had math together that afternoon. Jess insisted that Morgan sit with her and her friends at lunch and they made plans to meet at her locker when the bell rang.

By the time Morgan made her way to first period, she felt something that she might even be able to describe as the slightest bit of happiness.

Maybe she'd have a new friend after all.

"I CANNOT BELIEVE you dumped an entire tray of drinks on Darrell Benson." Christy hadn't been able to quit laughing since Cam told her about her not-so-perfect first shift at the End of the Road.

"It wasn't funny," Cam said, which only made Christy laugh louder. "It was a huge mess and Darrell turned this weird shade of red and—"

"He's always a weird shade of red." Christy howled and clutched her stomach.

"Well, he was definitely mad."

"I can just picture him," Christy said between chuckles. "Red and mad and covered in beer."

"I'm sure glad you think it's funny." Cam shook her head and reached for her glass of wine. "I thought for sure Tommy was going to fire me on the spot."

"Tommy is not going to fire you." Mark, who'd been mostly silent on the other end of the table, spoke up.

"Why would you say that?"

Mark shook his head and looked down at his drink.

"Mark?" Christy had stopped laughing and stared at her husband seriously. "Why would you say that? Why wouldn't Tommy fire Cam?" She turned to Cam quickly. "Not that you deserved to be fired, Cam."

Cam shrugged off the comment, more interested in Mark's remark.

"It's nothing," Mark said. "Forget I said anything at all."

"Oh, I don't think that's going to happen." Christy's lips pressed into a thin line and she examined her husband before she rolled her eyes. "You might as well tell me now, Mark. I'll just get it out of you later."

With an exasperated sigh, Mark put down his beer. "All I'm saying is that hiring Cam is probably a real coup for Tommy Jenkins."

"A coup?"

"Yeah." He took a slow, careful swallow of beer. "Remember the way it was between Tommy and Evan back in high school?"

"They were friends." Cam remembered. Evan and Ben were best friends, and thank goodness for that because Ben's family more or less adopted Evan and gave him some semblance of family. Evan's mom had worked so much. But every once in a while, Tommy Jenkins would come around and convince Evan to ditch school, or get drunk in the woods, or steal a car, or…all of the above. Cam had always hated it when Evan would fall in with Tommy, and they used to have terrible fights about it that usually resulted in Evan telling her that she was too good for him, and she would be better off without him. She'd leave, crying and heartbroken, until a few hours later, or the next morning, Evan would appear at her front door, begging her to forgive him, bringing her flowers and promising he'd be the man she deserved.

Until one day he didn't.

The memory, long buried, rose up like a thorny weed in her memory, picking at her tender skin.

Mark's voice brought her back to the present. "They weren't friends so much as…well, I think we all remember."

Christy clicked her tongue and nodded. "But why would it make a difference now with Cam working for Tommy?"

"Because Tommy always wanted what he couldn't have," Mark said easily. "Especially if it was Evan's. And Cam—"

"Was Evan's," Christy finished for him with a nod.

"She was most definitely Evan's."

Cam ignored his words, but mostly she ignored how they made her feel inside. *They used to say those words to each other. "You're mine and I'm yours. Forever."*

It was another memory she couldn't afford to let herself sink into.

"But they're not friends anymore." She didn't know for

sure, but the way Evan had gotten upset when she'd mentioned trying to get a job with Tommy, it didn't seem likely.

Mark laughed. "No. Definitely not."

"Not since high school. In fact, they've been more like enemies," Christy filled in. "When he came back from the army, he was different. Grown up, serious."

"A man." Mark finished the thought for his wife with strong certainty.

"Yes. A man." Christy nodded in agreement with her husband. "He's a totally different person since he came back. At least as far as the getting into trouble. But Tommy never changed."

"He just made a career out of it. And now the two of them are constantly at odds with each other." Mark took over the story again. "So having you, the love of his archenemy's life, working for him..." He grinned. "No doubt he's probably pretty proud of himself."

The love of Evan's life?

Of course she knew that probably held a thread of truth. Just as it did for her. In fact, there was no *probably* about it.

"Well, I certainly didn't take the job to get in the middle of anything between them. I needed work and I'm in no position to be choosy right now."

"I wish I could offer you something in the office," Mark said. "But there's only so much work."

"And I'm doing it." Christy smiled, but it didn't reach her eyes.

"No worries, guys. I'm okay. Honestly."

Her friend gave her a questioning look, but thankfully didn't push. "It'll be so good when the girls get here, don't you think? Like the old days."

"Just like the old days."

They spent a few minutes chatting about their friends. Christy seemed to know more about everyone than Cam did, and that made her ashamed. She hadn't been a good friend to any of them after she left town. At the time, she told herself it was because they were all so busy with their own lives, but really it was because the memories hurt too much. If she allowed herself to go there with her friends, it was a slippery slope before she started to think of Evan and the heartache would return. And once she was with Ryan, and pregnant with Morgan, she couldn't allow those feelings in.

She'd made her choice, or it was made for her when she got pregnant. Either way, there were consequences for her actions and she'd had to live with them.

"So…" Christy leaned across the table the moment Mark went to the bar to get more drinks. "Have you heard from Evan again? I mean…I get it if you don't want to say anything around Mark, but…"

Cam didn't want to say anything around Christy either, but it's not as if she could say that. Christy would be devastated if Cam told her to mind her own business. Not that she would. Well…she *probably* wouldn't. It had been so long since Cam had a real friend to confide in, she wasn't sure she remembered how.

And that wasn't entirely true. Christy had always been her friend. She'd always been there. It was Cam who hadn't been the friend.

As if she needed the reminder.

"Well?"

Christy was clearly oblivious of the internal chaos going on within her.

"Well, yes. I have." That was an understatement to be sure, but she didn't want to lie to her friend. She also wasn't tripping over herself to tell her that her daughter had been caught shoplifting on her first day of school.

"And?"

"And…I think he's very good at his job," she said mildly.

"He's very different from how he used to be." She regretted that particular statement the moment it was out of her mouth.

"Isn't he ever?" Christy practically bounced in her seat. "So different that you might actually—"

Cam held up her hand to stave off the rest of the sentence, whatever it may be. "Don't go there." She shook her head. "Don't go anywhere near there."

"Okay." Christy sat back in her seat. "But just to clarify, would you be okay if he walked in here right now and sat down? I mean...we are all kind of friends and...the Log and Jam is kind of his place. I just don't want it to be awkward."

Like, any more awkward than it already was? Cam wanted to laugh. And not in an *it's so damn funny* way. But she wasn't worried about Evan walking into the pub, at least not on this particular night.

"He won't be coming in," she said.

"But it's Tuesday and that's trivia night."

Cam shook her head. "Well, maybe he'll be by later, but not now."

Christy tilted her head and narrowed her eyes. "And how is it that you happen to know that?"

There was no point hiding it. Besides, in Timber Creek, news would travel fast. "Because Evan is with Morgan."

"Morgan?"

Cam drummed her fingers on the table. "Helping her with her community service."

"Community service?"

"She's been assigned fifty hours of community service and Evan is in charge." She rushed the words out, hoping the details would slip by her friend.

"Evan?"

"Why do I feel like there's an echo in here?"

Christy straightened in her seat and shook her head slightly. "Start at the beginning. Morgan? Community service? Evan?"

Right then, Mark returned with another round of drinks, and Cam wanted to hug him when he set it down in front of her and said, "Judge Stewart assigned Morgan to some community service last night and Evan is the officer in charge of the case."

Both the women looked up at him with open mouths, but he directed his explanation to Cam. "Ben told me." He shrugged. "Evan was in earlier apparently and filled him in."

Perfect. It was already starting. There was no privacy in a small town. It was one of the little details about Timber Creek that Cam had not missed at all.

Christy looked to Cam for confirmation. She nodded and took a long drink of her wine. She was going to need it.

EVAN DIDN'T KNOW what to expect when he knocked on the door of the little apartment over Junky's shop. *Would Cam be home? Or just the girl?* He'd heard Cam was working her first shift earlier that day at the End of the Road and he'd made himself stay away. No doubt if he'd shown up without a legitimate reason, Tommy would make a scene and Cam would get embarrassed, or worse…mad.

He had no doubt he'd have reason enough to visit her at work sooner rather than later. He just hoped it wouldn't have anything to do with her.

But maybe Cam was home from work by now. Maybe she was there waiting for him to pick up her daughter for her punishment. The night before, he'd given Morgan the choice of starting right away, or waiting a few days. To his surprise, she hadn't put it off the way he would have expected a teenager to do.

Not that he knew much about teenagers. But when he was

ELENA AITKEN

her age, he would have done everything he could to put off till tomorrow what he could have done that day.

Finally, he brought himself to knock on the little door. Morgan answered almost immediately.

"I was wondering if you were ever going to knock." She greeted him with all the attitude he expected.

He raised his eyebrows but didn't respond. Instead, he tried to casually look past her into the little apartment.

"If you're looking for my mom, she isn't here."

"I wasn't."

It was her turn to give him a look. "Whatever." She reached behind her, grabbed a tote bag and pulled the door shut. "I guess we might as well get this over with. Unless you need to talk to my mom. Or get her to sign something or something."

"No," Evan said. "She doesn't need to sign anything. We can get going. I don't want to bother her at work."

They started walking down the steel stairs. "She's not working. At least not anymore."

"No?" He tried to sound casual, but this girl was clearly a lot more observant than he'd given her credit for, and he didn't want to give anything away. Not that there was anything to hide. Not really. He was definitely curious about Cam. And why shouldn't he be? Once upon a time, they'd told each other everything. It was only natural to be interested in her life now.

"She called after her shift," Morgan continued as he held the door of the cruiser open for her. This time, he let her sit in the front. "She's with Christy."

Evan got in the car next to her and grabbed a notebook. "Are you ready to do this?"

"You're sure you don't want to know more about my mom?"

He swallowed and shook his head. "No. Today is about you," he said. "Today and every day until you work off this

66

community service. Seems you've gotten us both a new after-school hobby."

Morgan shrugged, but he noticed her face color a little.

"So," he began again. "I think I have a bit of a plan to get us through this as painlessly as possible while at the same time, teaching you a little something. We'll do two hours a day, three days a week."

"What?" Morgan sat upright in her seat. "But that'll take forever. That'll take like three months!"

"Just over two, actually. But yes, it's not going to be finished right away." Evan flicked his pen back and forth. "You should be thankful you only got fifty hours." He gave her a look that he hoped made his point. "Let's get going." He put the car in gear and started driving to the park in the center of town. "We're going to start nice and easy with a little garbage pick-up in the park."

"Garbage?"

He shot her a look again. Apparently it was going to take a little bit for her to get the message that she was being punished for her actions.

AN HOUR into the garbage pick-up, and Evan was pretty sure Judge Stewart had been punishing him just as much as he'd been punishing Morgan. Only he couldn't figure out what he'd done to deserve the privilege of supervising a moody teenager with a garbage bag.

He could think of better ways to spend a Tuesday after-noon, like getting ready for his usual trivia night at the Log and Jam, or laying on the couch with a beer and Netflix.

Okay, maybe Judge Stewart wasn't punishing him so much as giving him a wake-up call about his boring life.

But it wasn't boring. Not really. It was…stable. Consistent.

Easy. Evan always knew what to expect. There were no surprises and no drama.

He hadn't dated anyone in over a year, not seriously anyway. At least nothing he considered serious. Stephanie might disagree.

At the thought of his on-again/off-again/not really a girlfriend/more like a booty call friend, Evan felt a wash of guilt. He hadn't called her in days. Four, to be precise. Not since he performed a routine traffic stop on a very non-routine driver.

Cam.

No one had ever been able to compare to Cam. Not before and not since. Stephanie was a nice girl, but there was never going to be anything more than a few hook-ups and the occasional night at the pub.

With a sigh, Evan pushed up from the picnic table where he'd been lounging and stretched. He scanned the areas for Morgan, who up until a moment ago had been directly in his line of sight.

He turned, and still didn't see her immediately. Finally he spotted her with a group of teenagers over by the swing sets.

For a moment, Evan debated interrupting her. After all, she was new to town; it was probably a good thing that she was getting to know some kids. But his duty got the best of him, and with a shake of his head, Evan went to break it up and get Morgan back to work.

"Officer Anderson! Hi." A boy he vaguely recognized as Tansy Butterfield's son shoved his hands in his pocket and straightened when he saw him coming. He didn't know Tansy well. She'd been five years ahead of him in school, and she'd married a guy from another town who Evan didn't really know. But the little he did know about them seemed good.

He could have laughed at himself for the way he was silently assessing Morgan's friend choices. As if it mattered to him at all.

But it did.

Even if it was only because they were stuck with each other for the next little while.

Right. That's why it mattered.

Evan pushed the annoying voice in his head away. "Hello."

"Trent, sir." The kid thrust out his hand, eager to please. "Trent Butterfield."

"Nice to meet you, Trent." He took the kid's hand and ignored the snickers from the boy's friend, who would no doubt give him a hard time later. "I see you've met Morgan."

"I was just—"

"It's okay," Evan said before she could make an excuse. "You're allowed to have a little break. But just a little one."

He saw the relief on her face and was pleased with himself.

"We won't bother her for long, sir. I just noticed her at school the other day and when I saw her today I thought I should…" Trent's friends snickered again and he jabbed one of them in the ribs with his elbow. "I just wanted to say hi." The kid looked directly at Morgan, who flushed a deep scarlet and looked at her feet. Evan did his best not to laugh.

Instead, he shook his head. "Why don't you get her number, Trent, and then you can text her later. When she's not busy," he added pointedly.

He left them alone then and went back to the picnic table, where he watched them from a safe distance.

Fifteen. Morgan was fifteen. He'd seen her birthdate on the forms Cam had filled out at the police station. About the age when he'd fallen head over heels, completely hopelessly in love with Cam.

Her daughter looked so much like she had at that age. Only…angrier. As if she were holding onto something. Cam had never been an angry teenager. Instead, she'd been filled with a longing and ambition. A dreamer, always thinking about what was next. She'd been a girl full of hope and innocence.

Morgan didn't have that about her. Instead, she seemed to be weighed down by something.

What had happened to the girl to make her so sad?

Something about her drew him to her. He wanted to protect her and heal whatever hurts she had.

It was ludicrous, really. He didn't know her. And even though he'd known her mother a lifetime ago, it didn't mean he had any right to her.

Or did he?

He couldn't deny that ever since Ben pointed out the timing, a little piece of Evan had wondered whether maybe Ben was right…Morgan was fifteen. *Was there a chance she was his?*

Of course there *was* a chance. But surely Cam would have told him. *She would have…*

Evan dropped his head into his hands briefly and scrubbed at his hair. *What would an eighteen-year-old Cam have done?*

The truth hit him like a brick.

He had no idea.

Chapter Six

DESPITE A FEW MORE MISHAPS WAITRESSING, including the original spill on Darrell followed by a dropped tray of clean glasses on her next shift and a few mixed-up orders over the following few days, Cam eventually settled into her new job and after the first few weeks of shifts, even started to get to know some of the regulars and what they liked to drink.

She still couldn't believe that a nudie bar on the edge of town had regulars, but she was in no position to judge other people or their choices, so she didn't.

When she was a teenager, Cam had a part-time job at the grocery store as a cashier, and then later, when she moved to the coast, she answered phones at a local car dealership. But that was short-lived before Ryan insisted she quit and *take care of herself*. But unlike so many of her friends, Cam had never held a waitressing job. And even though she probably wouldn't admit it, at least not to any of her friends, she kind of liked it. Especially if she could ignore what kind of bar it was that she was working in and those poor girls who stood on the stage and took off their clothes with little to no enthusiasm, day after day, for the same four faces who came in for their afternoon beer and wings.

"You're getting the hang of things, Cam." Tommy appeared out of nowhere and leaned against the bar as she cashed out and counted back her float. Distracted from her counting, she sighed but didn't let him see her annoyance. He was her boss after all, even if he did make the hair on the back of her neck stand up.

"It's coming." She smiled. "Thank you for being so patient with me, Tommy." He really had been patient with her. If it had been anyone else, there was no doubt she would have been fired after her first shift.

Cam tried not to think about what Mark had said earlier that week about things between Tommy and Evan.

"Of course." Tommy grinned and slid closer to her. "You're doing great. In fact, a few of the guys have commented on your improvement. You seem to really have an attention to detail. Are you getting settled into town again?"

She knew exactly where this line of questioning was going. It was the same every day when she was finishing her shift. The talk went from the bar to personal, and way too quickly. Not that any speed would have been okay for Cam.

Just as she did every day, she smiled sweetly, and shook her head. "You know I don't like to mix business with personal, Tommy."

"Waitressing is hardly business, Cam." He reached out to touch her arm, but she quickly sidestepped it. She was starting to get really good at avoiding Tommy but his advances were just getting more aggressive. She'd have to come up with something else.

"It's business to me, Tommy." Thankfully she finished her cash out and signed off on the clipboard Tommy kept by the till. "Besides, I should get going. I have a teenage daughter at home, remember?"

Cam hoped the idea of a teenager would be enough to be off-putting, but in fact it probably had the exact opposite effect. Either way, the fact was she *did* have a teenage daughter who was her priority.

As was keeping her job.

"And…" Cam grabbed her purse from under the bar and slipped to the other side of the stools. "I really do need to get going. I'll see you tomorrow."

Cam made her escape before Tommy could stop her again. The truth was, she really did need to get going, but not to get home to Morgan. Just as she'd hoped, her daughter had made some new friends and because she seemed to be keeping up with her homework and keeping her dates with Evan for community service, Cam had agreed to let her go for a coffee after class. The fact that teenagers went for coffee these days instead of milkshakes still made her head shake, but she was just happy that Morgan seemed to be settling in. She'd even smiled a little bit at the dinner table the night before. It wasn't much, but when it came to her moody and troubled daughter, Cam would take what she could get.

But she did have plans. Christy had called the night before and more or less guilted her into stopping by after her shift.

The friends still hadn't had a real talk since Cam had come to town. Not a drink a bottle of wine–talk all night–spill all the details type of talk. And Cam knew she was overdue for it. *Way* overdue.

Besides, it was just a quick stop before dinner. And Christy was one of her best friends. Maybe it would be a good thing. *No.* It *would* be a good thing. To get out, and not have to sit home for a few hours and worry about money and the divorce and her daughter and…everything.

But when she pulled into Christy's driveway and saw a truck she didn't recognize, she immediately began to rethink the idea. Maybe going home to worry about her life on her own was a better idea after all.

The truck is probably Mark's.

After all, she had no idea what type of vehicles Christy and Mark drove; there was no reason for her to feel anything but indifferent to seeing a car in the driveway.

But Cam also knew to trust her gut. And her gut was telling her to drive away and go home.

Unfortunately for her, she didn't listen and moments later when Christy answered the door and ushered her inside only to see a familiar face at the kitchen table, Cam was kicking herself.

She really did have to start listening to her instincts a little more.

Before she stepped into the kitchen, Cam grabbed her friend's shoulder and pulled her backward. "What is Evan doing here?" She hissed in her friend's ear. "I thought we were having coffee."

"We are." Christy looked so innocent, Cam almost believed it hadn't been planned. *Almost.* But the look on her friend's face gave her away. "With a few other people. But it's no big deal," she continued quickly. "I totally forgot I promised to host the anniversary committee meeting and with the celebrations so close, I didn't think you'd mind. Not really. Besides, you know almost everyone who'll be here."

That wasn't necessarily a good thing. Cam glanced over her shoulder into the kitchen.

"Come on." Christy grabbed her hand. "You can't leave now. It'll look... Well, it'll look like you're trying to avoid Evan."

I am trying to avoid Evan. Cam wanted to scream.

Instead she sighed, swallowed hard and made a mental note to make her best friend pay. In a very big way.

"I don't know how much help I'll be to this meeting," Cam muttered. "I'll probably just be in the way."

"Oh no." Christy's voice brightened considerably the moment she recognized her victory. "Quite the opposite, I think. We still need a few more jobs filled and won't it be a great way for you to get involved again?"

Cam was pretty sure she wasn't interested in socializing in any way, but it wasn't the time to say anything as they entered Christy's cozy kitchen and she introduced Cam to Becky, a young woman she'd never met.

"I didn't expect to see you here," Evan said when she took the empty seat next to him at the table. The *only* empty seat, she noticed.

"I was ambushed." She fiddled with a napkin for a moment. "Shouldn't you be protecting the town from—"

"Distracted drivers and juvenile offenders?" His green eyes twinkled and despite herself, Cam almost laughed. *Almost.* It was too easy to get sucked into Evan's easy way and the memories of how things used to be.

It was also very dangerous.

"Right." She looked straight ahead. "That. Shouldn't you be working?"

"They do give me some time off, you know?" His tone was light, and Cam felt bad for pushing him off. She turned back to face him. "Besides," he continued. "The anniversary celebrations are important and I like to help out in my town when I can."

My town.

"That, and Christy twisted my arm hard to get me to help."

Cam almost shook her head. The Evan she'd known hadn't even been interested in volunteering for the car wash to raise money for their graduation celebrations, let alone an entire anniversary party for the high school. In fact, the Evan she'd known had been more interested in pretty much anything else.

"You're full of surprises, Evan Anderson," she said before she could stop herself.

"And how's that?" His lips twitched up into a grin, no doubt because he knew exactly what she was talking about.

She gave him a look and was saved from answering by the arrival of another committee member and Christy joining them with a tray full of coffee and fresh baked goods.

WITH CAM SITTING NEXT to him, Evan could barely concentrate on what Christy was saying. Something about permits and road blockades. He jotted a few things down in his notepad so he could remember to get clarification from her later and spent the rest of the meeting thinking about how he might be able to convince Cam to go out with him.

Not like a date.

No. That would be...

He cleared his throat and forced himself to refocus. A date would be, well...it would be nice. Of course it would be nice. They'd had a lot of fun dating once upon a time.

That was a long time ago, but still.

He snuck a glance in her direction as she got up to help Christy clear the table of coffee cups.

The meeting was over and suddenly the idea that he would have to get up and she would no longer be sitting next to him sent a ripple of disappointment through him.

Evan had just made up his mind to ask Cam for a coffee date the moment she got back to the table when he heard the front door opening and then Christy's voice wishing her a good night.

Shit.

He jumped up so quickly, his leg jostled the table and the remaining few people seated there shot him a look. "Sorry," he muttered. "I just realized I had to get going and…"

He trailed off. There was no point trying to explain himself. Besides, it didn't matter. The only thing that mattered in that moment was getting to Cam before she got in her car and drove off.

It was ridiculous and made no sense at all, but somehow, Evan knew if he continued to let the distance between them grow, his opportunity would be lost forever.

His opportunity for what, he couldn't quite pin down, but the drive in him to see her and spend more time with her was something he hadn't felt for…years.

Evan mumbled something to Christy as he pushed past her and out the front door. He was pretty sure he heard her giggle behind him before she closed the door on him, but it didn't matter.

"Cam!" She startled and dropped her purse at the sound of her name. Evan rushed over and picked it up before she could. "Sorry," he said. "I didn't mean to scare you. I just wanted to catch you before you left."

"It's fine." She reached out and Evan noticed he was clutching her purse to his chest.

"Oh, sorry." He thrust it back to her and ran a hand through his hair in an effort to still his nerves that were quickly getting to be very annoying. He had no reason to be nervous around her. It's not as if it were the first time they'd spoken since she'd been back. And really, it's not as though she were a stranger.

"Thanks." She turned toward her car again.

"Are you in a hurry?"

She left the driver's side door ajar and turned to face him. "Sorry?"

"Are you in a hurry?" he asked again. "I was just thinking

that since you're here and I'm here and I'm not working tonight, maybe you would like to grab some dinner. I mean, it is dinner time and it's been awhile since we've caught up. I mean, properly caught up. Sorry, I'm rambling." He smiled at her and the smile she gave him in return both calmed him and made him even more nervous.

"Dinner?"

He nodded. "It's usually the meal people eat at this time of day."

She laughed then and for the first time since she'd been back in town, Evan caught a glimpse of the eighteen-year-old Cam. "I'd like to—"

"Great. Riverside has a nice—"

"But." She cut him off with a shake of her head. "I should get home for Morgan."

Right. Morgan. Her daughter. *Of course.* He nodded.

"I mean, maybe another…" She didn't bother finishing.

"It's okay. I get it," he said. "You have responsibilities and—"

Fortunately for Evan, considering he had no idea how he was going to finish his statement, he was interrupted by the ringing of Cam's cell phone.

She fished it out of her purse and glanced up at him. "Speak of the devil."

"Of course." He took a few steps away to give her a bit of privacy, but didn't want to go too far. He wasn't ready to give up on her yet. Not by a long shot.

He didn't even bother trying not to eavesdrop. *Morgan could be in trouble again.* It was bullshit, but he needed some way to justify his behavior in his head.

"You're at Jess's?" Cam asked over the phone. "Yes, I remember her mom, Shelby."

Morgan was friends with Jess Johnson. Evan nodded approvingly to himself. Jess was a good kid.

"I suppose that's okay."

What was okay?

"Do you have homework?"

Evan stared at his feet and kicked at a rock.

"Okay then," Cam said to Morgan. "No later than nine, please."

Nine? Evan's ears perked up and the second Cam ended the call, he turned around and asked, "Free for dinner now?"

He half expected her to come up with another excuse. But to his surprise, she nodded and shrugged as she tossed her cell phone back into her purse. "It looks that way."

IF SITTING NEXT to her at Christy's kitchen table was hard, sitting across from Cam at the Riverside Grill, one of the better restaurants in Timber Creek, was complete and total torture.

He wanted to reach across the table and take her hand the way he would have when they were young. He stuffed his hands under his legs to keep from doing just that.

"This is nice," he finally said after they'd ordered their drinks. A beer for him and a glass of white wine for her. "Kind of like old times."

Her face blanched a little and he immediately regretted his choice of words, but then she smiled and nodded. "It is nice."

Looking for a safe topic, Evan asked about her parents and learned they were happily retired in Arizona, spending their days golfing enjoying the heat.

"I love them and I love to visit," Cam said. "But I could never live there. It's so hot and dry and almost...lifeless in a way. Not like the forest and the mountains."

"I was wondering why you chose to come back to Timber Creek."

She stiffened for a moment, but then nodded and said, "It's always felt like home."

They lapsed into silence again and when their drinks arrived, they both drank deeply.

"I'm really glad you—"

"I wanted to—"

They spoke at the same time and Cam laughed. Once again, Evan was struck by the sound. Just as it did when he was a kid, the sound rippled through him.

"Go ahead," he said to Cam.

"I was just going to say that I wanted to thank you for being so helpful towards Morgan with everything. She seems to be responding better than I thought she would to her community service."

"She is." Evan settled back in his chair. "I get the feeling that she's caused you a bit of trouble, but she really is a great kid. You've done a great job with her."

Cam shook her head, unwilling to accept the compliment. "It's been hard. That's for sure. I mean, she was already starting to act out a little bit but with everything with her father lately…well, let's just say that it definitely hasn't helped matters."

Her father.

The words echoed in his head.

"About her father," he started. "Is he…" Evan wanted to ask her about him. What, he wasn't sure, but he felt as if he needed to know something about him. All the unasked questions died on his lips and he said instead, "He's not very involved then?"

She made a sound that gave Evan the only answer he needed. "He's too busy with his new pregnant girlfriend and the new life he wants to live to be too concerned with her. It's really hard to watch, actually."

"I bet. I mean, I'm not a father…" He shook his head a

little. It was too easy to allow himself to imagine what it would be like if he were Morgan's dad. "But I can't imagine walking away from my kid. I mean, I understand that marriages break up sometimes." He gave Cam a sympathetic nod, but she didn't seem remotely upset by his words. "But regardless…"

"You can't break up with your kids," she finished. "At least you shouldn't."

"Exactly," Evan agreed with her. "I'm really sorry, Cam."

She shrugged. "I guess I should have seen it coming."

"What? The divorce? Or…"

"All of it, really." She took another sip of her wine. "Ryan and I never should have married."

Evan's stomach did a somersault, but he didn't say anything.

"I always knew it, too. But when we found out I was pregnant and Ryan asked me to marry him, it just kind of seemed like my only option, you know? And it's not that it was all bad. It just wasn't…"

"Right."

"Exactly." She smiled sadly and for a moment Evan thought she might tell him that it could never have been right with Ryan because he wasn't Evan. Instead, she shook her head a little and leaned forward on her elbow. "But whatever I thought about our marriage, I never in a million years thought he'd turn out to be a crappy father, happy with only the slightest contact with Morgan."

"I'm really sorry to hear that."

"Actually, I'm really glad that she was assigned to carry out her community service with you, Evan." The statement took him off guard, and it must have shown on his face. She laughed. "Seriously. I mean, I probably wouldn't have said that years ago, but it's good for her to spend time with someone who genuinely seems to care about her." Cam waved her hands in front of her face. "I mean…you just seem to have a good way with her. I didn't mean that you—"

"I know what you mean." He reached out then and took her hand, squeezing it gently before lowering it to the table. "And I do care about her. How could I not? She's your daughter, Cam. And you," he continued. "I care about you, too. If you need anything…please know I'll be there for you. No matter what."

He looked deep into her eyes that were so much the same and all at once, totally unfamiliar.

"Thanks, Evan."

She didn't move her hand, which Evan took to be a good sign. A very good sign. Of what, he wasn't sure. But the only thing he was really sure of was that he wanted to spend more time with Cam. A lot more. Because the feelings she stirred in him, just by being close, were way too intense to ignore. And one thing he knew for sure…no other woman had ever made him feel the way Cam Riley did.

THERE WERE a million reasons why Cam shouldn't have been out for dinner with Evan. And a million more why she shouldn't have let him hold her hand. But for the life of her, none of those reasons came to mind as she sat across the table from him and looked into his eyes.

"You really don't need to thank me, Cam." Evan's voice was low. He held her gaze. "I would do anything for you. Always."

His words reached directly to a shuttered-off place in her heart. She believed him. Evan had been the only man besides her dad who'd ever made her feel safe and even now, after all their history and the space between them, he still had the same effect on her.

"I'm not going to lie," he said. "I'm surprised you agreed to come out with me tonight. Happy, but surprised. I kind of had the impression that you might be avoiding me."

She laughed, but it didn't sound natural even to her own ears and she pulled her hand away to pick up her glass of wine. She could have lied. That would have been the easier option to be sure, but she was exhausted.

"I was," she admitted. "I mean, I am avoiding you. Sort of."

"You are?" Evan raised an eyebrow.

"Well, obviously not right now."

"Obviously." He didn't bother trying to hide his grin. "But you were?"

She nodded. It was pointless to keep going the way they had been. She was back in town, and he was there and they couldn't avoid each other forever. Besides, Cam was realizing more and more that she didn't want to.

"It's kind of awkward, don't you think?"

Evan shrugged but finally nodded. "Okay," he conceded. "It's a little awkward. But it shouldn't be." He looked down at their hands. "At least, I don't want it to be." When he looked up, he was looking right into her eyes, and the intensity of the connection took her off guard.

"I don't want it to be either. It would be nice to be friends again." She meant what she said. Once upon a time, Evan had been everything to her. Besides her girlfriends, she'd told him everything. He was her best friend, her confidante, her...everything. Until he wasn't. "How have you been?" It was a lame question. Especially because what she really wanted to ask him was *where* he'd been. More specifically, that day she'd gone to his house and his mother had told her he'd left town and left her alone.

"I've been...good." Evan laughed. "It seems so crazy that

we think we can catch up sixteen years in only one conversation."

"Maybe the highlights then?"

"The highlights." He nodded his agreement. "Well, there's not much to tell really. After one tour, I was discharged, joined the police academy and got my assignment here in town. I've been protecting the streets of Timber Creek from the criminal types of distracted drivers ever since." He winked and she smiled. Cam hadn't missed the fact that he'd skipped over his time in the army, and whatever circumstances led him to enlisting in the first place. Maybe he assumed she knew that part. That was the part of his history that she wanted the most details on, but she couldn't bring herself to ask him. It would hurt too much to hear him say why he'd left her.

There were somethings better left unsaid.

"And your girlfriend?"

"I don't have one."

She couldn't deny the little spark of joy she felt at that. "Not at all?" Cam knew she shouldn't be prying, but she couldn't seem to help herself.

But if Evan was bothered by the question, he didn't show it. "Well sure, I've dated over the years. But there hasn't been anyone serious. Not recently anyway."

She didn't know what to say to that because as well as the little spark of joy she'd had, Cam also felt sad. A guy like Evan should be happy. He should have someone. She told him as much.

"I don't know what to tell you, Cam." Evan fiddled with his glass. "There just wasn't anyone…well, it didn't seem…tell me about you."

Cam sat back in her chair with a start. "Me?"

"Yes. You." Evan caught the waitress's attention and with a quick gesture ordered another round of drinks. They hadn't ordered their meals yet, but neither of them seemed to be in a hurry.

"Oh, I don't know." She shook her head. "I mean, there's not really much to say."

Evan crossed his arms on the table and leaned toward her. "Bullshit. I think there's quite a bit to say. And really, Cam, I'd like to hear it. Never in a million years did I think that you would one day be sitting across from me like this."

She shook her head sadly. "Neither did I, but probably for very different reasons." Cam still hadn't spoken to anybody about her divorce, or even her marriage to Ryan for that matter. It should seem strange to talk to Evan of all people about it, but it didn't. She drained the rest of her wine and sat back in her seat. "What do you want to know?"

Evan's smile was kind. "All of it. Morgan is fifteen, so I assume you…"

Those were the details Cam didn't want to get into. She did not want to sit across from Evan and tell him that when he broke her heart, she went running into the arms of the first man she met. It was humiliating. Especially because she ended up marrying him when it was the last thing she should have done.

"Ryan and I married pretty quickly," Cam said, avoiding the unasked question. "In hindsight, we never should have got married. But there was the baby and we were young, and it just seemed like the right thing to do. But it was wrong right from the start."

Evan's face scrunched into a frown but he didn't say anything so she kept talking.

"I don't regret it. Not really anyway. Ryan and I had some good times; we just weren't well suited overall. We wanted different things." Mostly Ryan wanted to live a single lifestyle, complete with all the freedom that came with it. But Cam didn't bother saying that. "I looked the other way for a long time, but it's hard to ignore when your husband openly declares his new relationship, complete with love child, on local television. Especially when he's a bit of a celebrity." Cam made air quotes and rolled her eyes. "I don't do well with public attention." Cam dropped her head. "But you know what? It is probably a good thing, because it forced me into action. Sometimes when I think about how long I stayed in an unhappy relationship, it just makes me mad. And a little embarrassed actually. Who knows how long I would've stayed, if Ryan hadn't forced my hand."

Evan reached out and took her hand again. His touch felt good. Familiar.

"You can't beat yourself up," he said. "Sometimes we just have to do the best that we can in the situation we're in."

It felt as if there were a lot more behind his words than Evan was saying. *Could he be talking about himself?*

She squeezed his hand. "Well, either way, that's in the past. And hopefully soon, I can put the whole thing behind me. I mean, as much as I can. There is still Morgan to think about." She squeezed her eyes shut and visions of her daughter's eyes filled with pain and hurt the night before when she got off the phone with her father and another cancelled date between them consumed her. "If there was one thing I could change, it would be the relationship he has with Morgan. It breaks my heart to see him pulling away from her. And it's the last thing she needs right now. I mean, even before the divorce, things were…"

"She's been a bit of a handful, has she?"

Cam laughed out loud. "You could say that."

"Well, if there's one thing I know, it's troubled teenagers. Don't forget, I was one once."

As if she could forget. His rebellious side was one of the things that she both loved and hated about him.

"Look at me now," Evan said with a satisfied grin. "You could say that I turned out all right."

"You could definitely say that. In fact, you really surprise me, Evan."

"I do, do I? And what is it that surprises you? Is it the fact that I grew into my rugged good looks? Or maybe that I'm still living in this little town that I swore one day I was going to leave. Or is that—"

"All of that," Cam said quite seriously. "And so much more."

"I'M SO glad you could stay." Morgan's new friend Jess threw her book bag on her bed and proceeded to flop down next to it. "But whatever you do, don't tell my mom you're doing community service. She would die."

Jess certainly didn't have to worry about that. The last thing Morgan wanted anyone to know was that she picked up trash for two hours a few times a week. After all, it was hard enough to be the new girl in town. She didn't need to be the new girl who was in trouble. Taking the nail polish seemed like a good idea at the time. Especially if it would piss her mom off. No doubt her therapist back in Portland would say something about not all attention being equal and she should try to get positive attention instead of negative or *blah blah blah*. *Whatever.* Who would've thought that the cop in such a backward small town would be the ex-boyfriend of her mom's? Not that she was complaining, Evan was pretty cool. She actually enjoyed talking to him during their community service hours.

"I'm actually kinda surprised my mom agreed," Morgan said. "She's been so crazy about me being home for dinner, making sure that I'm staying out of trouble and everything. She's probably just happy that I have a friend."

Jess laughed and rolled over to look at the ceiling. "You don't have just any ordinary friend," she said. "You are friends with the key to the most exciting social scene Timber Creek has to offer."

"Is that right?" So far Morgan hadn't seen much in the way of anything resembling a social scene, but she was definitely willing to explore the options. More than willing. "What kind of a social scene are you talking about? What goes on in this town anyway?"

"So much." Jess rolled her eyes. "Well, not *so* much. I'm sure it's nothing compared to Portland. But you haven't seen any of the bonfire-bush parties yet and Jason Sinclair has the best parties. *And* oh my God, I just had the best idea!" Jess hopped up from her bed, opened her bedroom door a crack and peeked out before closing it and hopping down cross-legged in front of Morgan. "You think your mom would let you sleep over this weekend?"

Morgan shrugged. "Maybe. I'll ask—oh shit!"

"What?"

"I'm supposed to be seeing my dad this weekend." Morgan groaned and dropped her head into her hands.

"That sucks." Jess looked genuinely disappointed. "But at least you get to go back to Portland, right?"

"Nope." That was the worst part. The night before, her dad had called and made some lame excuse about how it wasn't probably for the best if she came to the house. *The house.* Which meant his *new* house with his *new* girlfriend in a *new* neighborhood that would be perfect for their *new* life. A life that didn't include her.

"What do you mean? You're not going to his house?"

Morgan knew Jess was just trying to be a friend, but she wasn't used to talking about her dad. Not with anyone. Except maybe her therapist back home. But even then, she didn't like to tell her everything because even though Lucinda Davis promised there was client confidentiality, Morgan knew she was on the phone with her mom the moment she left Lucinda's office.

Morgan shrugged. "He's going to pick me up and we're going to go to some place called RiverBend for the weekend." Morgan had looked it up and discovered it was another random, small town in the middle of nowhere. But it was halfway between Portland and Timber Creek, so apparently it was some sort of *compromise* or something.

"RiverBend?" Jess made a sign of pretending to throw up. "There's nothing in that town."

"As opposed to Timber Creek?" Morgan raised an eyebrow and they both started laughing.

After a moment, Jess rolled over. "Still. That sucks. But there'll be other parties."

"Parties?" Morgan groaned again. Just her luck that there'd be a party on the only weekend she was supposed to see her dad. Not that she didn't want to spend time with her dad, but still…her life was here. That thought stopped her cold. *Her life was in Timber Creek.* She shuddered, but it was true. Her life had changed dramatically and there was no point pretending it was still something it wasn't.

"What kind of party is it?" Morgan knew she was torturing herself, but she couldn't seem to stop. She needed to know.

"It's at Jason's. His parents are out of town like every weekend. But this was just going to be small. Like only a few guys… and a few girls… You know what I mean?"

Of course she knew what Jess meant. Jason was friends with Trent. He'd only spoken to her a few times since that day in the park. But every time they did speak, Morgan got that stupid butterfly feeling in her stomach. Now she wanted to go even more.

Chapter Seven

THE MOMENT CAM walked into Christy's kitchen on Friday afternoon, she was immediately greeted by the sounds of gossip and laughter she hadn't heard for more than a decade.

The girls were there.

There was nothing quite like old friends who knew you before life had a chance to squeeze and shape you into someone else to make a girl feel like she was finally home.

"What are you doing here?" Cam's voice was part squeal, part laughter as she stared at Amber Monroe and Drew Ross, the other half of their foursome. "Christy didn't tell me you were—" She looked at Christy, who beamed.

"Surprise." She waved her arms. "They came in early."

"We thought it might be fun to have a few days before the anniversary stuff got crazy." Drew's smile lit up her face.

"Come here and give me a hug," Amber demanded. She'd always been the bossy one out of the four, a trait that served her well as a hotshot corporate lawyer in San Francisco. Cam did as she was told and crossed the room to give Amber a hug. Drew squeezed in too, and then Christy, and the four of them hugged it out the way they had so often, so many years before.

"How long has it been since we've all been together?" Drew asked when they finally untangled themselves from each other's arms and had settled into Christy's padded kitchen chairs. "Eight years, right?" She looked around the table. "At my wedding."

Cam shook her head. "No, Amber couldn't make it."

Amber flushed. "I still feel bad."

Drew waved her away. "It's all good."

"How about I promise to be there for your silver wedding anniversary party?"

Drew's smile faded a little bit, but she nodded and agreed before resuming her line of questioning. "So, has it really been since high school that we've all been together, then? Really? That can't be right."

"I think it is." Christy put a pot of tea on the table, followed by a plate of cookies and scones. "But it doesn't matter, because you're all here now and it really is the best thing. Cam, the girls are staying here with me—you have to sleep over tonight. It will be just like old times."

"I…" She looked around the table at her friends' expectant faces. "I…Morgan." But as soon as she said her daughter's name, she remembered that Ryan was supposed to pick Morgan up for the weekend. "Well, maybe I could, actually. Morgan's spending the weekend with her dad, so…"

"Perfect." Christy clapped her hands together and it was agreed on.

"Speaking of Morgan's father…" Amber never was one to beat around the bush. "What the hell happened, Cam?"

"Are you okay?" Drew reached over and grabbed a cookie. "It can't be easy to go through a divorce."

It wasn't and Cam knew she'd probably feel better if she talked about it with her best friends, but just the way she couldn't seem to deal with the divorce papers her lawyer had sent over earlier that week, it just seemed easier to ignore things.

It's not that she didn't want the divorce over and finished with. She did. It was more that now that she was in Timber Creek, and starting over, things felt...different. Like a fresh start at life. A life she didn't want Ryan intruding into. Even in the form of divorce papers.

It was ridiculous. She knew it.

"It might actually help to get it out." Christy hadn't pressed her into talking about it, but Cam knew she'd been dying to know the details. She looked around the table. Her friends clearly wanted to know what was going on.

With a sigh, Cam stared down into her coffee cup and started talking. They already knew how she'd fled Timber Creek heartbroken and how she'd met Ryan almost right away. What they didn't know was that despite what Cam had told them, she'd known from the very beginning that she shouldn't marry Ryan. It was a secret that she'd kept even from her closest friends, but she hadn't known what else to do. She was young and pregnant and if it hadn't been for Ryan, she would have been completely alone. Her parents had just announced that they were going to retire early and follow their dream of moving to Arizona. She couldn't burden them with her poor decisions. As far as she could tell, she didn't have any options besides marriage.

And it wasn't as if Ryan wasn't a good man. He was. He just wasn't the man for her. More importantly, he wasn't the man she was in love with. Now, years later, Cam finally confided in her friends the way she should have all those years ago.

She told them about Ryan's infidelities, the way Cam was left mostly alone to raise Morgan and how although he was still a good father, how he'd grown more and more distant with Morgan. She told the girls how despite the fact that they'd had their share of good times over the years, she'd always known she wasn't going to be married to Ryan forever. The divorce was inevitable, and ultimately she was okay with it. In fact, she felt better and more at peace than she had in a long time.

The women were quiet for a moment when Cam finally stopped talking. Drew spoke first. "Do you still love him?"

Cam's eyes shot up and she looked directly at her friend, who still looked as young and doll-like with her long, dark hair and beautiful brown eyes as she ever had. Drew always had a way of asking the questions that were the hardest to answer, and all these years later, she clearly still had the knack because Cam knew it wasn't Ryan she was asking about.

Still, she played stupid. "Ryan? No."

"That's not what I—"

"How is Evan these days, anyway?" It was Amber who asked.

And Christy who answered. "He's changed *so* much," she said. "Can you believe he's local law enforcement now?"

"No." Amber laughed. "I totally cannot believe that."

Cam herself was still having a hard time wrapping her head around the fact that the rebellious boy she'd known—and loved—had transformed himself into an upstanding pillar of the community.

Amber and Christy launched into a conversation about Evan and how much he'd changed that then morphed into talk about other people they'd gone to school with, but Cam wasn't listening because Drew was still watching her, no doubt forming her own, probably accurate answer to the question she'd asked.

"I'M surprised you agreed to come out here today." Ben cast his line and began the quick, methodical jerking to bring it back in before casting again. Evan had no doubt that he'd have a fish on the pole within a few minutes. Normally it was a bit of a competition to see who hooked the first one, but Evan was distracted and it was taking him forever to get his gear organized.

"You know I never pass up an opportunity to chuck some line."

Ben laughed and flicked his rod back into a graceful arc. "Right. Well, that was before."

"Before what?" Evan knew without asking, exactly what his best friend was trying to say.

"Before Cam Riley came back to town."

"Cam has nothing to do with anything." It was a lie and they both knew it. The truth was that Evan couldn't stop thinking about her and the way her eyes sparkled when she smiled, when *he* made her smile. The way her hand had felt in his and how she hadn't pulled it away but let him hold it when what he really wanted to do was pull her in for a hug and hold her close. After they'd finished dinner a few nights earlier, and Evan had walked Cam to her vehicle, it had taken all the self-control he possessed not to reach out for her, tug her into his body and kiss her.

But he hadn't. It wouldn't have been right. As much as he wanted to, and as natural as it had felt to be with her, he needed to remember that time had passed. She was no longer the young innocent girl with her whole future ahead of her. She was a single mother going through a difficult divorce and rebuilding her life from the ground up. So no matter how much he wanted Cam back in his arms, he had to remember that things were different.

He was different, too. It may have come almost sixteen years too late, but Evan had finally become the man Cam deserved. Now he just needed to convince her of that.

"Okay," he admitted to Ben. "It has everything to do with her."

His friend only raised his eyebrows in response and continued to fish.

"It's just so crazy, don't you think? That she's back here after all this time. It's like it was meant to be."

Ben tugged on his line and reeled it in before he turned around and looked at him. "Do you know what's crazy?"

Evan ignored him but he continued anyway.

"You talking like this. After all this time, it's taken you over a decade to get over her and now you're letting yourself get all worked up again."

"I'm not getting worked up."

"Bullshit. The last time I saw you like this, you were sixteen."

Evan shot him a look.

"Just remember," Ben continued. "You're not kids anymore. It's different now."

"It is."

It was very different. *That was the whole point*, Evan thought. *What if after all these years, the timing was finally right?*

"I'm not the same person," Evan said after a minute.

"Right." Ben shook his head. "But neither is she."

"IT SUCKS that you can't sleep over tonight." Jess fell into step beside Morgan as they walked together back to Junky's and the little apartment that, despite herself, was actually starting to feel like home to Morgan. "But you're going to have fun with your dad. That's cool that he's coming all the way out here to get you."

Morgan shrugged. It's not that it wasn't cool, but it was the least he could do after blowing apart their family the way he did. It's not like it was Morgan's choice for him to go and get a girl-friend who wasn't even that much older than her. Never mind the fact that they were going to have a baby. The whole thing was so gross. Of course Morgan was expected to be happy that she was going to be a big sister. She sighed and shook her head. "It's whatever. It just sucks that I'm going to miss the party."

"There will totally be more." Jess smiled and Morgan tried to smile back. She didn't want to seem high maintenance or anything. "And besides, being a little unavailable is never a bad thing. It's just going to make Trent want you even more."

Morgan blushed and looked at her feet. "He doesn't want me."

"Oh yes he does." Jess grabbed her arm and squealed. "He totally wants you. He was telling Jason about how cute you were and—"

Morgan's phone rang, cutting off whatever her friend was about to tell her. For a moment, Morgan contemplated ignoring it completely, but it was probably her mom and if she ignored her mom…it just wasn't worth it most of the time. She pulled it out of her back pocket and looked at the caller ID.

"It's my dad."

"Your dad? Isn't he supposed to be—"

"Yup." Morgan pushed the button to accept the call. "Hey, Dad."

"Hi, princess."

Morgan *hated* when he called her that. She tried not to be annoyed.

"What's up? You aren't early, are you? Because I haven't really packed yet. It won't actually take me very long, but I don't want you to—"

"No," he said. "I'm not early."

Something in his voice stopped her. She froze on the sidewalk.

"Are you going to be late?" Morgan already knew the answer as she waited the phone shaking slightly in her hand.

"Well, about this weekend…"

She dropped her head and shook it slowly back and forth. Morgan hated that she could feel the hot prick of tears at the back of her eyes. She did not want to cry in front of her friend.

"It doesn't look like I'll be able to make it out there this weekend, princess."

And there it was. The words she didn't want to hear, but had been expecting all along.

"But I haven't seen you in—"

"I'm really sorry, Morgan. I am. But it's just been kind of crazy around here with work and the baby. Chastity has been feeling really sick with her pregnancy and I don't think she should travel right now."

"Was she coming?" Morgan's head snapped up. "I thought it was just going to be the two of us anyway. Why was Chastity going to come? I want to see you, Dad." Morgan hated the way her words were coming out whiney and needy. "Are you sure you—"

"We'll do it again another weekend, okay, princess? Soon. I promise."

"Sure." She nodded in agreement because there was nothing else she could do.

"You know I love you, right?"

She didn't know that. Not really. But her dad didn't wait for an answer.

"I'll talk to you soon, princess. Have a good weekend, okay? And let your mom know for me, all right?"

"Yeah," Morgan said dumbly. "Okay. I will."

The call ended and Morgan stared at her cell phone for a moment before Jess wrapped her arms around her and hugged her. "I'm sorry, Morgan." The hug was so unexpected that at first Morgan didn't know how to react. In fact, she didn't know what to feel about anything. Of course she was upset. She wanted to see her dad. But there was part of her that didn't either. Confused, she shook her head and forced a smile.

"It's okay." She untangled herself from her friend. "I mean, he's obviously busy, so…" She shrugged instead of finishing the sentence. "But on the plus side, maybe I'll be able to sleep over tonight after all."

Jess's eyes lit up and she clapped her hands together. "Do you think so? Really?"

"Maybe. I'll call my mom."

She knew before her mom even answered the phone that she would say yes to the sleepover. No doubt, she'd feel so bad for Morgan that her dad was an asshole who couldn't be bothered to visit her that she would have agreed to almost anything. Plus, she'd been *good* lately, doing all the things she was supposed to be doing and not being a total bitch to her mom.

At least not as often anyway.

Jess waited expectantly as Morgan made the call and explained to her mom that her dad had cancelled on her. "So," Morgan said when her mom stopped trying to convince Morgan that her dad still loved her, *blah blah blah*, "I was thinking that maybe I could sleep over at Jess's house tonight instead. I mean, I'll spend the day with you tomorrow if you want, but I thought maybe…"

"Yes," her mom said. "That's a good idea. As long as it's okay with her mom?"

"Yeah?" Morgan gave Jess the thumbs-up. "I mean, it's totally okay with her mom." Jess nodded. "And it's okay with you? I mean, really?"

"Yes," her mom said again. "I think it's great that you're making friends and while I'd still really like to meet Jess, I used to know her mom and if it's fine with her, I'm sure it'll be good."

"And you won't be lonely?" Morgan wasn't sure where it

had come from, but she was suddenly consumed with worry for her mom, who hadn't spent an evening alone since the separation. It had always been the two of them. "Because if you're going to be—"

"Morgan, I'll be fine. The girls are in town so maybe I'll spend the night at Christy's and have a sleepover myself." Her mom laughed, and it was actually a nice sound to hear. It had been a really long time since her mom had laughed. *Maybe this stupid small town was actually good for both of them.*

Morgan dismissed the thought as soon as it popped into her head. Just because she didn't hate everything about the town didn't mean she had to like it.

"Okay. I'll see you tomorrow then."

"Sounds good. I love you."

She knew her mom was waiting for her to say it back. Instead, she mumbled a good-bye and hung up before turning to Jess again. "I guess you should tell Jason we'll both be there tonight."

Chapter Eight

TO CAM'S SURPRISE, sitting cross-legged in Christy's living room, drinking wine with her girlfriends, felt like the most normal thing in the world. It felt as if it hadn't been over a decade since they'd had a sleepover, or even all been in the same room with each other.

"So." Cam poured another glass of wine in Drew's glass and passed Amber the bottle. "You've heard all about my drama."

"Well, not all of it." Drew grinned. She'd made a few comments that indicated she was still waiting for an answer about what was going on with Evan, but Cam wasn't ready to talk about it, so just as she had been doing, she ignored the comment.

"I think we should hear about someone else." Cam purposely didn't meet Drew's gaze. "Amber? Have you made partner yet?"

Amber was the most career driven out of all of them and always had been. Since Cam could remember, Amber had her sights set on a high-powered law career and she'd never wavered from her plan, going right into an undergraduate degree, and then straight to law school. She'd always been top of her class and it didn't surprise anyone when she landed the job of her dreams at a top law firm in San Francisco.

"Not yet," Amber said. "But soon. In fact, I've been putting in a ton of extra hours lately because the partners are looking at everyone really closely and there's an opportunity to make partner coming up. I know they're going to pick me. I mean, how can they not? I live and breathe McLean, Paterson, and Dewitt. The spot is mine."

"Sounds like soon it will be McLean, Paterson, Dewitt, and *Monroe*." Christy held up her glass of sparkling water to toast. "That's so great, Amber. I know you've been wanting this forever."

"I have." She clinked glasses with Christy and each of the other women in turn. "And it's so close now, I can almost feel it. You know what I mean?"

Cam shrugged. She'd never wanted anything that much. Well, at least not a career. "I'm happy for you, Amber. I mean, if you're happy, that's all that matters."

"And I am." She leaned back and crossed her long, lean legs. She was still every bit as striking as she'd been as a teenager. The years hadn't touched her as far as her model-thin body and long, dark hair went. She was still gorgeous enough to be a model. But when she looked close, Cam could see the strain around her friend's eyes. She looked tired, although Cam would never say it.

"Are you *happy* happy?" Christy grinned. "Is there anyone special in your life? Come on, I'm an old married woman and I need to live vicariously through you."

There was something laced under Christy's words, but Cam couldn't put her finger on it. Christy and Mark had always been an affectionate couple. Even in high school, they couldn't keep their hands off each other and were often the source of teasing, although secretly, they all thought Christy and Mark were the very definition of relationship goals.

"I hate to disappoint you, Christy." Amber shrugged and drank deeply. "I'm not seeing anyone right now."

"Right now?" Drew prodded. "Does that mean you *were* seeing someone?"

Amber shook her head. "No. There's no time."

"There's always time for sex." Once again, there was something in Christy's voice. Cam examined her friend, but didn't say anything. "Please don't tell me that as the only one of us who's single you aren't taking advantage of that status."

Amber shrugged again, and looked into her glass. "I'm not. Really, there's no time for a relationship or…anything else," she said pointedly to Christy. "My career comes first. It always has. You know that."

"I know," Christy said. "But I just thought…well, don't you get lonely?"

Amber laughed. "No way." She reached around her back and dug into her leather laptop case that was never far from her. "Remember these?" She held up a romance novel, the kind that came out monthly in the grocery store with the sexy man chest on the cover.

Drew squealed and lunged for the book. "You're still reading these?"

When they were in high school, Amber had discovered a stash of romance books under her mom's bed and devoured them. To her delight, the stack was consistently replenished as her mom bought new titles every month. She'd shared them with the rest of the girls, but none of the others had been quite as obsessed with them as Amber. It didn't take long for the books to become a permanent fixture in Amber's presence. Mixed in along with all the textbooks she always had her head buried in were always at least a few romance novels. The sexier, the better as far as Amber was concerned.

"Books are good," Christy insisted. "But it's not the same. You really don't want to date anyone?"

Amber shook her head, but Cam was sure she noticed the slightest bit of hesitation in her. "Nope. It's career first," she said. "Besides, you know I'm not the only single one here anymore." Amber deftly shifted the focus of the conversation back to Cam, who immediately jumped up from the floor.

"Oh, I don't think so. I don't think you can consider me single. It's not the same thing." She moved to the shelf on the other side of the room and grabbed another bottle of wine and the corkscrew. "I'm not even officially divorced yet."

"But you will be soon," Amber said with an evil grin. "And then you can be the one these two look to for their illicit love affair fix."

Cam burst out laughing. "I hardly think that as a mother of a teenage girl I'll be having any kind of love affair. At least not any time soon."

"What about Evan?" It was Drew who asked. Of course it was. "What's going on there, Cam?"

"Yeah, Cam."

"Spill," Christy joined in. "I've seen the way he looks at you."

Cam spun around so quickly she almost spilled the wine. "How does he look at me?"

"Aha!" Drew jabbed a finger at her and laughed. "I knew there was something there."

Of course there was something there. It was *Evan*. Her first love. Maybe her only real love. Sure, she'd loved Ryan. But it was different. So different. And seeing Evan again after all the time that had passed felt so…natural. And completely foreign all at the same time.

"He's a good guy." The words sounded lame and completely inadequate even to her own ears. "He's changed a lot. But so have I. And I'm not looking for anything. Not right now. I mean, I have way too much going on with everything. I can't even begin to think about a new relationship. I really need to focus on myself and Morgan right now. I just can't deal with any of that right now."

"But it's not completely off the table?" Drew asked directly.

"No." A small smile crossed Cam's lips. "It's definitely not *completely* off the table."

"Oh! I knew it! I knew there was something going on between you two. It's just a matter of time before..." Christy made a kissing sound and Cam threw a pillow at her.

"Don't get too ahead of yourselves." The laugh on Cam's lips faded and she stared into her wine. "Don't forget he left me once. A girl doesn't just forget something like that."

Christy scooted over to her and put her arm around Cam's shoulders. "That was a long time ago."

"It was." She looked up into her friend's eyes. "But I still don't know why he left like that. I thought everything was perfect. We were going to get married and be together forever and then..."

He'd left. The pain in her chest was still as raw as it was all of those years ago.

"He's never said anything?" Cam only shook her head to Amber's question. "Well." Amber slapped her hand on her thigh. "I think it's way past time you asked him, don't you?"

EVAN'S SHIFT had been slow, but that wasn't unusual in Timber Creek. Even for a Friday night. Just a few routine traffic stops, a report of a domestic disturbance, and a regular visit to the End of the Road, where he'd been relieved to see that Cam wasn't working. As far as he could tell, Tommy hadn't been lying when he said Cam would primarily be working the day shifts. Evan knew the day shift probably didn't pay as well, but he was relieved that she was staying away from the rough bar during the night hours.

The urge to protect her had never gone away. If anything, he reflected, it had only grown stronger with the passing years, especially now that she was back in town.

He leaned his head back against the seat of his cruiser and closed his eyes for a moment.

Having dinner with her the other night had been something he'd never even let himself daydream about over the years. It had always been easier to tell himself he'd never see her, let alone have a date with her.

But he had.

And it had been…different. But familiar all at the same time. More importantly, she hadn't closed him out the way she had been doing. Maybe after all the time that had passed, they finally stood a chance to be together. He wasn't going to pretend that it wasn't what he wanted.

Not for a minute.

Bored, and needing to move, Evan put his car into gear and steered it through the quiet streets of Timber Creek. He contemplated stopping into the Log and Jam to grab a coffee and have a chat with Ben, but having a cop sitting at the bar wasn't usually good for business, so instead, he went to the Stop n' Shop gas station and bought one of their famously tar-like substances that they passed off as coffee.

It was a nice night, so instead of getting back into his car, Evan leaned against the hood and pulled an envelope out of his breast pocket. The letter had arrived yesterday, but superstitious and worried about the contents, he'd put off opening it.

"No time like the present." He sighed and tore open the top. He pulled the paper out and held it, expecting the worst. Evan had sent off the application form almost six months ago. He'd almost forgotten about it.

Almost.

It wasn't something he'd told anyone about. Only a handful of people even knew that Evan had applied for college. It was such a long shot, as far as Evan was concerned, that there was no point getting anyone's hopes up, especially his. He wasn't even sure that it was something he could do. School wouldn't be cheap, and taking out a student loan and managing mortgage payments probably wouldn't go well. Besides, he really did love his job. Even so, more and more, Evan was thinking that there were other things he could and should be doing with his life. Bigger things that could have more meaning.

He took a deep breath and was about to unfold the paper when his radio crackled to life.

"Go ahead, Gladys."

"I hope you're not too busy, Evan." He could practically hear the laughter in the woman's voice on the other end. They both knew there wasn't much going on, and they both liked it that way.

"I'm sure I can spare a few minutes for whatever you've got for me, Gladys."

"Well, how about a drive out to the Sinclairs' place."

"Again?" Evan sighed and stuffed his unopened letter back into the envelope and back into his pocket. It would have to wait until later. "They out of town again?"

"I'm starting to think they should either give us a copy of their travel schedule or hire a babysitter for that kid of theirs."

Evan laughed. "He's not a bad kid."

"Tell that to his neighbors. I've had two noise complaints already."

"I'm on it, Gladys," Evan said into his radio. "And you're right, it wouldn't hurt to have a talk with Scotty and Ash next week. They either don't know about these parties, or just don't care."

"I'll withhold sharing my opinion with you on that."

Evan shook his head and climbed back into his cruiser. He

knew the way to the Sinclairs' place all too well. Their teenage son, Jason, was starting to become a familiar face for his late-night weekend shifts due to his parties that were becoming a bit too frequent.

The Sinclair property was on the edge of town in a newer development where the heavily treed lots gave the illusion of being secluded, but in reality, there were neighbors right on the other side of those trees. And according to Jason's neighbors at least, the trees did nothing to deaden the sound of teenagers partying.

Evan expected to see a lot of cars in the driveway the way he normally did, but there were only a few.

Maybe Gladys was wrong. There certainly didn't seem to be a party going on.

But the moment he stepped from the car, the blast of the music hit him. He shook his head and made his way to the front door.

The Sinclairs' house was built for parties, with a beautifully landscaped backyard complete with fire pit and hot tub, and, of course, outdoor sound system. He shook his head with a laugh. If he were a teenage Jason, he could see that it would be very hard to resist the temptation to have regular parties there. He rapped on the door.

No answer.

Not surprised, he knocked again and rang the bell.

Still no answer.

It wasn't the first time. Evan had told Jason more than once that the neighbors would likely be a whole lot happier with him if he kept the music down, or at the very least, kept his little get-togethers—Jason refused to call them parties—inside where they wouldn't bother anyone.

But the kid didn't listen. Not that he would have at that age either. Evan wouldn't listen to much of anything when he was a kid. Except that one time, when not only did he hear the one thing that would change the entire direction of his life, but he listened.

It had always been his hope that one day he might have the same type of impact on a kid just like him.

Somehow, he didn't think it was going to be Jason Sinclair. At least not on that particular night.

Evan left the porch and followed the pathway to the backyard. Just as he'd expected, the party was taking place outside.

But what he hadn't expected was the number of kids. Instead of the usual twenty to thirty, there were only a handful. First glance told him they were paired off in couples.

Perfect. It was *that* kind of party.

Evan hadn't been noticed yet, so he took a moment to scan the yard, looking for the host. The kids were all about Morgan's age and the question crossed his mind if she'd ever be at a party like this one. It wasn't totally off base. After all, Timber Creek was a small town, and just as when he'd been a kid, there wasn't much to do to stay entertained. Of course, if he ever found Morgan in this situation, he'd—

What? He'd what? It's not as if Morgan were his daughter. It wasn't his job to tell her what she should and should not be doing. It was his job to break up parties, regardless of who was attending.

And that's exactly what he was going to do.

With a sigh, Evan locked onto the boy who was in the hot tub. Jason Sinclair. He might as well go directly to the source. Of course Jason had a female companion, but it wasn't until he got closer that the kid moved to the side and Evan could see the back of a female head. A head that looked very much like Morgan's.

Before Evan had time to fully process what he was doing, he'd closed the distance between him and the hot tub and had both hands on Jason's arms. "Get your hands off her." With a strength that should have been impressive, he hauled the kid out of the hot tub and spun him around.

Jason took one look at the enraged cop in front of him, and the cocky look slid right off his face. "Officer Anderson? I... you...we were just—"

"You need to..." The words died on Evan's lips as he glanced to the girl in the hot tub.

It wasn't Morgan.

He released his grip a little and let that fact sink in. *It wasn't Morgan.* Evan took a breath. He needed to pull himself together. "I'm getting more than a little tired of paying you visits, Jason."

"I'm sorry, Officer Anderson. I didn't realize the music was so loud." Behind him, the girl who wasn't Morgan was climbing out of the hot tub and wrapping herself in a towel.

"We weren't doing anything wrong, Officer." The girl, who he now recognized as Jess Johnson, Morgan's friend, came to stand next to Jason. She handed him a towel, which he took the second Evan let him go. "We were just hanging out."

"I've had a number of noise complaints, Jason." Evan focused on the boy because it was the only way he could calm the temper that had exploded inside him at the idea that some teenage boy had his hands all over Morgan. "Turn it down. Now."

Jason, with Jess in tow, ran off to turn the stereo down. Evan took a deep breath and began making his rounds, checking for alcohol or drugs. Either the kids had seen him coming, or they really weren't doing anything wrong as Jess had insisted because he found nothing more than a few bottles of beer, which he made a show of pouring out. He turned toward the fire pit that was set back into the yard at a distance. He could make out the silhouettes of a couple by the flames. They obviously hadn't noticed the commotion or the fact that the music had stopped.

Evan made his way across the grass and once again, heat flared through his veins at what he saw.

———

MORGAN COULDN'T BELIEVE her luck. Sure, she hadn't been thrilled that her dad had bailed on her. Not at first anyway. But later, when they took Jess's little brother's old bikes out of her garage and snuck out to Jason Sinclair's house, it had all been worth it.

Jess was right. Trent was totally into her.

It was clear from the moment they got there that it was a *couples* party. There were a few other kids from school who Morgan only vaguely knew, Jason of course, and Trent. But they were all couples. Except for her and Trent.

"At least not yet," Jess had whispered to her before taking off with Jason to go to the hot tub.

She wanted to call after her friend not to ditch her, but she didn't want to look like a total loser. Besides, Trent had already noticed her and had waved at her. She stood at the door like a moron for a minute before finally working up the courage to walk into the kitchen where Trent was getting some drinks out of the fridge.

"Hey," he said. "I'm glad you made it."

"Yeah. I didn't think I was going to, but…" She didn't want to talk about her dad. "It worked out," she finished with a shrug.

"Cool." He reached into the fridge and pulled out two bottles of beer. "Want one?"

Morgan had never had a beer before, and she didn't particularly want one now, but something about the way Trent held it out to her changed her mind.

"Sure."

He nodded and smiled and Morgan was absolutely sure

her heart was going to explode in her chest. He was so cute and maybe Jess was right. Maybe he *was* into her. "You've never been to Jason's before, right?"

She shook her head, even though they both knew she hadn't.

"Let me show you around." Trent took her hand as though it were the most normal thing in the world and led her through the kitchen first into the living room, and then out the sliding doors onto the most amazing back deck. There were a few more kids she recognized from classes, and a few she'd met. But it was definitely not like any party she'd ever been to before.

"This is so nice," Morgan said before she could think about how stupid it sounded. "I mean, this deck is huge and the back-yard...well, it's...never mind."

She blushed and was glad for the dim lighting outside so Trent couldn't see how embarrassed she was.

"No," he said. "I totally agree with you. This deck *is* huge. His backyard is killer. You should see my yard—it's nothing like this."

"Ha." Morgan laughed. "I don't even *have* a yard." It was the first time she'd ever laughed about her living situation. Usually she tried not to bring it up at all because it was completely mortifying to live over an auto shop.

"That's right," Trent said. "But I bet you have a super cool apartment."

She stared at him with an open mouth. He wasn't making fun of her. "You think it would be cool to live over Junky's?"

Trent nodded and grinned. "Totally. All the access to cars and stuff. It would rock."

She laughed again and instantly felt relaxed with him. "I suppose if you're into cars and all that stuff," she said. "But yeah, it's not really that bad. My mom's tried really hard to fix it up."

It was the first time she'd actually considered the fact that her mom had been trying her best to make her feel at home over Junky's. The thought had come out of nowhere and she shook it off. The last thing she wanted to do was think of her mom with Trent standing next to her.

"Hey." Trent leaned in, so she could hear him clearly over the music. "Do you want to go throw some logs on that fire? I can't believe no one is sitting out there." He pointed out into the yard where a neglected bonfire was burning down.

Growing up in the city, Morgan hadn't spent much time camping or around bonfires or anything like that, but standing there with Trent, the idea was appealing. *Very* appealing. "For sure."

With the music from the party as a backdrop, it felt as if Morgan and Trent were in their own little world next to the fire. Trent put a pile of logs on, and used a poker to stoke up the flames until the bonfire was once again roaring. With the heat coming off the logs, it wasn't remotely chilly, but Trent sat close enough that their knees touched.

"Here." Trent took her still unopened beer bottle out of her hand and with a swift turn, popped the top off and handed it back to her.

She'd never tasted beer before. The few times where friends back in Portland had experimented with alcohol, it was usually wine coolers or hard iced teas they'd found in their mom's fridges. It was bitter and sour on her lips, but she did her best not to make a face.

But Trent noticed anyway. "It's okay," he said. "It's not really for everyone. I can get you something else if you like?"

"No!" Morgan shot her hand out over her mouth. "I mean, no. Thanks. I'm good."

He grinned and slid even closer to her. "It's nice sitting here with you like this."

She nodded, unable to control the smile that she knew dominated her face. "It is."

"I really like you, Morgan." He ran a hand through his hair and it flopped over his eye. "I'm glad you moved to town. Things were boring before you got here."

"And they're more exciting now?"

"They could be." He leaned in then until he was only inches away from her.

Was he seriously going to kiss her?

Morgan was sure he would be able to hear her heart beating. Or worse, that she would pass out and fall off the log bench she was perched on.

But when his lips touched hers, she forgot all of those things because there was no room for thinking. It was over almost before it began, and when Trent pulled away, it took her a moment to catch her breath.

Heat raced through her.

"I hope it's okay that I kissed you?"

Unable to properly form a word, Morgan nodded. Finally, she muttered, "Yes."

"Can I do it again?"

Morgan didn't have time to answer him before his hand cupped her cheek and pulled her gently toward his lips. This time, the kiss was a little deeper, more intense. The noise of the party completely faded away until it was just the two of them and the crackling of the logs on the fire.

She couldn't have said how long they were kissing, but as far as Morgan was concerned, it could have gone on forever. And it might have, too, if it hadn't been for the deep, booming voice that startled them apart.

"Excuse me."

Trent pulled away from her and jumped up before Morgan even realized what was happening. Her fingers floated to her lips and reluctantly she looked up into the face of…

"Evan?"

"That's Officer Anderson, Morgan." He didn't smile. "I'm on duty." His eyes flicked to the beer bottles laying discarded on the ground. "And by the looks of things, it's a good thing I am."

"No, Officer. This isn't what it looks like." Trent took a step forward, but when Evan turned to face him, he froze in place.

"It looks like you're drinking underage and about to take advantage of a young girl."

"What?" Morgan cried and jumped up. "No! That's not at all what happened."

Evan didn't turn around but took another step toward Trent. "You aren't twenty-one, are you, son?"

Trent shook his head.

"But you are a junior and Morgan here is a freshman."

"No." Trent shook his head, and his eyes widened. "Nothing was happening here, Officer. Really. I mean, we were drinking. Well, not really. I mean—"

"Evan." When he still wouldn't turn around, Morgan grabbed at his sleeve. *What was actually happening?* She'd never seen Evan mad. They'd been working together for weeks and he'd always been friendly and joking. Of course, she'd never had a reason to make him mad. Not even when he took her in for shoplifting had she seen him look like this. "Trent didn't do anything wrong. Listen to me, please."

Slowly, Evan turned around and stared at her as if he were looking at her for the first time.

"He wasn't taking advantage of me. I promise," she said quickly. "And I only had a sip of the beer, really. I didn't like it. And it's not like—"

He silenced her by lifting his finger and turned again to stare wordlessly at Trent.

It felt like an eternity, but finally he turned back to Morgan. "Let's go," he said. "I'm taking you home." He started walking away before Morgan could say anything. She looked to Trent for help, but he only shrugged, looking as startled as she felt. "Now, Morgan," Evan called without turning around.

"I'll call you," Trent whispered before she could go running behind Evan like a chastised child.

MORGAN REFUSED to sit in the front seat of Evan's cruiser, so together with Jess, who'd changed quickly back into her clothes, she sat in the backseat like a criminal for the second time since moving to Timber Creek.

Now that they were away from the party, Morgan was feeling a little braver. "You can't take me home." She crossed her arms over her chest. "My mom is at Christy's for the night and I'm sleeping at Jess's."

He seemed to think about it for a minute before saying, "Fine. I'll take you to Jess's."

Morgan and Jess exchanged a glance, and Morgan knew exactly what her friend was thinking. "You're not going to tell our parents, right?" She glanced at Jess quickly. "I mean, it's not like we were doing anything wrong."

Evan was quiet for a few minutes and Morgan was beginning to think he hadn't heard her. Finally he said, "No. Not this time."

Like there would be a next time. But Morgan didn't think it was wise to say that. Satisfied, she sat back in her seat and waited until they pulled up to Jess's dark house. The second Evan opened the back door, Jess slid out. Morgan followed quickly, but Evan stopped her before she could escape into the house.

"I don't like to see you like that, Morgan."

She stared at the officer who'd come to feel a little bit like a friend in their time working together. She was confused by this new version of Evan. He was acting as if he were her father.

But he wasn't her father and even if he was, her dad never behaved like he had. "Like what?" She crossed her arms. She knew she should scale back the attitude but she couldn't seem to stop herself. "Like a *teenager*? Like I was having fun instead of doing community service all the time? God forbid."

"That's not what I meant, Morgan." He almost looked sad and Morgan almost felt bad. *Almost.* "I just meant that I don't want to see you get into a situation you can't handle."

"I can handle myself just fine." She turned away from him, ready to storm up the pathway, but before she left, she spun around one more time. "And it's none of your business anyway. You're not my dad."

Chapter Nine

SPENDING the night with her old friends had caused a shift inside Cam. She couldn't really explain it, but when she left Christy's house the next morning, with a promise to stop by the next day to help with the final preparations for the anniversary dance the following weekend, she felt good. *Really* good.

Maybe all of this time, all she really needed was some quality time with the people who knew her best.

They'd talked late into the night over more bottles of wine than they should have. But despite drinking too much, Cam didn't wake up with a headache. Quite the opposite. She felt invigorated and renewed. And not just about herself.

The conversation had circled back to Evan more than once, and finally Cam had admitted to her friends that the old familiar feelings were still there. In fact, not only was the spark back, it was more intense than it ever had been.

She was still terrified to see where things could lead. If anywhere. After all, he'd left her once.

But she was also excited because talking to her girlfriends had given her the idea that maybe everything had happened the way it had for a reason, and maybe, just maybe this meant that after all the years between them, she and Evan were being given a second chance.

Cam laughed at herself as she drove home to change for her shift at the End of the Road. She'd felt lighter than she had in months, maybe even years. So much so that instead of grabbing a quick shower, she pulled her hair up into a messy bun, changed her clothes and grabbed her camera as she rushed out the door. By saving herself a few minutes, she'd finally have time to capture some shots of that log fence on the edge of town. There was nothing particularly remarkable about it except that it was a broken-down old fence made the traditional way with hand-cut logs. She'd driven past it on her way to work more times than she could count and every single time she did, there was something new about it that she noticed.

Sometimes it was the way the sun reflected off the grass around it, or the way the fence cast shadows as the sun set. More than once, Cam had considered stopping to take a few shots but she never had her camera bag with her. Besides, it had been so long since she'd taken any photos, she was a little afraid of how they might turn out.

But she wasn't scared today. She was excited.

Cam pulled her car to the side of the highway, checked her camera and the settings, and hopped out. She was careful as she picked her way through the tall grass until she was close enough to capture the angle she wanted. She knew she only had a few minutes or she'd be late, so she moved quickly, changing positions and viewpoints. She was still laughing at herself, high from the effort of doing something that filled her soul, when she arrived at the bar twenty minutes later.

"You're in a good mood," Rhonda, who'd been waitressing for longer than Cam had been alive, or so it seemed, noticed with a smile. "Don't tell me you and Officer Anderson finally—"

"What?" Cam almost dropped the tray she'd only just picked up. "No! That's…why would you think that?" She didn't bother objecting too hard. After all, she'd definitely considered the idea herself once or twice, especially in the last twenty-four hours.

Rhonda laughed. "Everyone knows you two are a thing, sweetheart. It's just a matter of time."

"We're not…I mean, we haven't been…"

"Oh, I know the story, sweetheart." Rhonda winked at her and finished loading her tray full of drinks. "I think everyone in town knows your story. Even Stephanie Olsen."

Something about the way Rhonda said the other woman's name made Cam's radar go up. "Stephanie?"

"She works down at the Crop Shop," Rhonda said, completely oblivious of the effect her words were having on Cam. "She's really good too. A total miracle worker with my grays."

"Your grays?" Cam repeated dumbly.

"Oh yeah." Rhonda used her free hand to twirl a few strands of her hair. "You wouldn't even know it, right? Steph really is amazing."

"And why would she care about the history I have with Evan?" She should have known better than to ask, but she couldn't stop herself.

The other woman grinned innocently and hefted her tray of drinks up to her shoulder. "Because she's been dating Evan for years."

Rhonda's words rang in her ears, long after she'd disappeared to the other side of the bar to deliver her drinks.

Years?

Dating?

Evan said he wasn't dating anyone. Of course, she hadn't asked about his dating history. And it made sense that he'd have a history. It's not as though Cam could expect him to stay single all those years. It's not as if he was promised to her. After all, she'd left town.

Because he left you first. The little voice in her head reminded her.

Cam took a deep breath and straightened her shoulders back. "It doesn't mean anything," she said out loud. "Everyone has a past."

A past, yes. The problem was, by the sounds of things, Evan may have a *present.*

She pushed the idea from her head. Evan was a grown man. If he was dating someone else, she wouldn't get in the way of that. But she also wasn't about to let anyone, girlfriend or not, get in the way of rekindling a friendship with him. And maybe that's all it should be? A friendship.

She glanced around and grabbed her phone from her purse and sent a text.

DINNER TONIGHT? *I'm cooking. As a thank-you for helping Morgan.*

IT WAS A FEEBLE EXCUSE, she knew it. But as she sent the text to Evan, she didn't care. Cam needed a few questions answered because now that he was back in her life, even in a small way, she thought she might like to keep him there.

"SO OPEN IT."

In an effort to procrastinate the ever growing list of projects his mother had for him over at her old house, Evan had stopped in to see Ben at the Log and Jam for a game of pool to blow off a little steam after his shift the night before.

Morgan's words were still ringing in his ears. *You're not my dad.*

How could he tell the kid that there was actually a chance, no matter how remote and totally off base, that he might be her dad?

He couldn't.

Evan may not be an expert in child psychology, but he knew that much. If he even mildly suspected it, which clearly he did if last night was any indication, it was a conversation he was going to have to have with Cam, not Morgan. The trick would be finding the right time to bring it up. Their relationship, or friendship, or whatever it was, was still developing. Too much time had gone by. They needed to rebuild things between them before he could go asking questions like, "Is Morgan my daughter?"

"Open what?" Evan blinked at Ben and shook his head. "What are you talking about?"

"The envelope." His friend rolled his eyes. "You must have it bad. I swear, you can't even have a conversation for a full five minutes before you're off in la-la land thinking about her."

"Who? Cam?" Evan lifted his pool cue and lined up to make the shot. He was stripes.

Wasn't he?

Shit.

He couldn't remember.

Instead of asking Ben, and proving his point, Evan took a wild shot that hit all the balls and mostly scattered them. If Ben noticed, he didn't say anything. But of course he noticed. He was Ben.

"Um…yeah. Cam. You're clearly all twisted up over her again and as far as I know, you haven't even kissed her." He raised his eyes in expectation.

Evan shook his head. No. He hadn't kissed her. But not

because he didn't want to. Damn, did he ever want to. "It's not like that with us," he said, and it was the truth. There was still a distance between them. A big one.

But it was getting smaller every day. And if the dinner invitation he'd received earlier was any indication, maybe he was finally closing in on things with her.

"Well, whatever," Ben said. "You're going to need to figure that situation out. *And* the school situation. Why don't you just open the envelope?" He pointed to the bar table where their beers sat, as well as the envelope that Evan had started to open, but hadn't quite gotten around to looking at the night before. "Don't you want to know if you even got in to school?"

"Of course I want to know."

"Then why don't you look and find out?" Ben asked his question and turned to make his shot. He easily sank the blue two in the corner pocket. *Good, so Evan was stripes.* "Or are you afraid?"

"Why would I be afraid?"

Ben missed his next shot, and it was Evan's turn. He lined up and easily sank the twelve. Vindicated, he moved onto the next one, sinking the fifteen before missing again.

"What if you get accepted?" Ben lifted his bottle of beer to his lips and grinned as he took a sip. "You'd have to move. Away from Cam. Right after she got back."

Shit. His friend knew him too well.

The thought had definitely crossed his mind. More than once.

He glanced at the envelope on the table and reached over it to grab his beer. "That's only if I get in," he said. "And that's a very big *if.* Never mind the even bigger *if* of Cam." He took a deep slug of his beer. "And that's the biggest if of all."

Ben laughed. "I don't doubt that for a minute," he said. "The two of you always were…well…" He shook his head and sunk his shot.

"We were what?"

"You were…big," he finished.

"Big?"

"Yeah." Ben sat across from Evan and slid the envelope toward him. "You guys were always big. Like you would suck the air out of a room when you walked in together. Every head would turn. The way you would look at each other as if there literally was no one else in the world." He shook his head, as if remembering the two of them in high school. "The two of you were just…big. Everything about you."

Evan thought about it for a minute and finally nodded. "I guess you're right. We were big. Because everything I ever felt for Cam was so huge that I couldn't even explain it back then, and I'll be damned if I can explain it now. But it's still there, man. It's still so very much there."

"I figured as much. But you know what that means?"

"What?" Evan blinked and looked at his friend. "What does that mean?"

"It means you're going to have to decide what to do about school, buddy." Ben waved the piece of paper he'd withdrawn from the envelope without Evan even noticing.

Evan stared at his friend for a moment before the reality of what Ben said sank in. "I got in?"

Ben nodded.

"I got in?"

"You got in." Ben grinned and held the paper out to him. "You are the newest member of the School of Social Work at the University of Washington. Congratulations, man. You're going to change lives. I just know it."

Stunned, Evan reached out and took the letter from Ben. He scanned it once, then twice before looking up. "Holy shit," he said. "I never thought I'd actually get in." He couldn't have wiped the smile off his face if he'd tried. Ever since he'd started thinking about doing something different, helping kids the way he'd once been helped, it had been a pipe dream. Something he never thought he'd actually realize.

Until now.

Chapter Ten

CAM DANCED AROUND THE KITCHEN, fully aware that she was acting more like a teenager than her own, actual teenager, who had been glaring at her from the kitchen table for the last thirty minutes. Cam had done her best to ignore Morgan, who was obviously upset at her for something. Sadly, it wasn't unusual, and for the life of her, Cam couldn't think of anything she'd done wrong.

Unless letting her have a sleepover at her friend's house was the wrong choice. Instead of getting into it, Cam turned up the dial on her radio and danced a circle around Morgan.

"Seriously?"

"Yes," Cam said, straight-faced. "Seriously, you need to shake off whatever funk you're in this afternoon."

"Why?" Morgan crossed her arms and leaned back in her chair.

"Because life is too short to be so serious. It's a beautiful day, the sun is shining, and things are finally looking up."

Morgan lifted an eyebrow. "Are they?"

Cam realized a moment too late that her daughter might have been more affected by her dad bailing on their plans than she'd let on. Morgan said she was fine, and she'd rather spend time with her new friend anyway, but maybe she was just putting on a brave face.

Dammit. She should have known better.

The smile slipped off Cam's face.

"I thought things were looking up." She sank into the chair next to her daughter. "But I forgot that things didn't go as planned last night with your dad." She took Morgan's hand and squeezed. "I'm really sorry that—"

"It's fine." Morgan jerked her hand back and tucked it under her legs. "I don't care."

She was lying, but Cam didn't push. She could have killed Ryan for cancelling his weekend with her. Not only that, but he was too much of a coward to even call Cam and let her know himself. No doubt because he was afraid of what her reaction would be. And with good reason, too. She would have torn him a new one if he'd been brave enough to tell her. As it was, Cam was having a hard time keeping silent when what she really wanted to do was call Ryan and tell him what a jerk he was being when it came to Morgan.

Never mind everything else.

But she'd promised her lawyer not to make things worse by contacting him directly. She still hadn't looked at the divorce papers. Cam let her eyes travel to the stack of books and magazines that still sat on top of the offending envelope. She glanced back at her daughter and made a private promise that she'd look at them the next day.

But she wouldn't ruin her good mood today and the fact that Evan had agreed to come for dinner by letting Ryan intrude on her thoughts more than he already had.

"Well, even if that is true, you know you can talk to me whenever you need to. Right?"

Morgan blinked and for a minute, Cam thought Morgan might actually start talking to her. But whatever she'd seen flash through her daughter's eyes was gone as quickly as it showed up.

"Yeah," Morgan said. "Whatever."

Not going to be deterred so easily, Cam wrapped Morgan in a quick hug and released her before she had a chance to protest. "I love you."

"Yeah. I know."

Cam jumped up from the chair, but before she walked away, she tried one more time to lighten the mood. She took her daughter's hand and pressed a kiss into the palm the way she used to when Morgan was a little girl.

To Cam's surprise, Morgan didn't pull away. She closed her fingers slowly and smiled. As far as Cam was concerned, she might as well have won the lottery. She winked and went back to dancing around the kitchen and pulling ingredients out of the fridge. "I'm making lasagna tonight."

"What's the special occasion?"

"Nothing really." It was a lie, but the last thing Cam needed was to try to explain something to Morgan that she couldn't even explain to herself. "I've invited Evan over for dinner. As a thank-you," she added quickly.

"A thank-you? For what?"

Morgan's face shifted and the color leached from her face, causing her eye makeup to look even darker. The effect was more than a little alarming.

"Are you okay?"

"What are you thanking him for?"

"For being so great helping you out with your community service." Cam examined her daughter. "Are you okay?"

"I'm fine. Is that all?"

She nodded. "Yes. Should there be more?"

"No." Morgan slammed her textbook closed and gathered up her things. "I think I'm going to finish this in my room."

Cam watched her go and shook her head as the bedroom

door closed. She was never going to understand teenagers. Whoever said newborns were hard had obviously never parented a hormonal teenage girl. It was a wonder any of them survived to adulthood, as far as she was concerned.

"YOUR PARENTS DON'T KNOW anything, right?" Morgan kept her voice down and glanced at her bedroom door before pressing her phone closer to her ear. "They haven't said anything to you, have they?"

"About last night?" Jess questioned. "No. I don't think so. I mean, if they do, they haven't said anything. And if they knew that Officer Anderson dropped us off, they would have flipped out."

"So you don't think he said anything?" Morgan wasn't convinced. Maybe it wasn't a totally far reach to think that her mom would have him over to thank him for the community service, but still it seemed…a bit of a stretch.

"Why are you so paranoid?"

Morgan flopped backward on her comforter. "He's coming for dinner."

"No!"

"Yes." She sat up again. "See what I mean?"

"Totally. But it's not like your mom is having him over to grill him on what teenage parties he's broken up lately, right? I mean, they're friends or something, aren't they? My mom said they were pretty serious in high school."

Morgan knew that they'd dated once, but obviously it wasn't too serious because they'd broken up and she hadn't given it more thought than that. It was gross to think of her mom dating anyone, especially Officer Anderson.

"Maybe they're dating again," Jess said.

"Gross."

"I'm just saying…"

"Don't say anything." From the other room, Morgan heard the knock on the door, followed by Evan's voice. "They're not dating. They're just friends." Even as she said it, she wasn't sure. "Besides, my mom isn't even divorced yet."

"I'm not sure that matters."

Morgan squeezed her eyes shut. Jess was right. Marriage didn't seem to matter. At least it hadn't for her dad. "Ugh. I can't talk about this right now."

"So tell me about Trent. Did he text you today?"

Not only had Trent texted Morgan, he'd called her right after she'd gotten home from Jess's early that afternoon and they'd talked until her mom got home from the grocery store. Morgan had never had a boyfriend before, not really—not that Trent was her boyfriend. But he sure felt like he could be. The girls talked for a few more minutes as if they hadn't just spent the night together talking until the early hours of the morning. They made plans to go to a movie at the local theater later that night, and when Morgan's mom called from the other room, they said good-bye with the promise of seeing each other in only a few hours for the movie.

She walked out into the living room hesitantly, still unsure whether Officer Anderson was going to keep his word and not say anything about dragging her out of the party the night before.

"Hi, Morgan." He waved casually and smiled when he saw her.

"Hey." She shrugged and shuffled from foot to foot.

"Kiddo, I was hoping you could make a salad to go with dinner."

Kiddo? Morgan rolled her eyes. Her mom hadn't called her kiddo in years.

"Is that a yes?"

She shrugged, went to the fridge and started gathering

ingredients. Making the salad for dinner had always been her job, and she didn't mind. She used the opportunity to watch her mom and Evan on the couch. *Was it her imagination, or was he sitting a little closer than he needed to? Did her mom just put her hand on his leg?*

Maybe Jess was right—maybe they *were* dating.

She shook her head and sliced a tomato. It was too strange to wrap her head around.

But when they were all sitting around the table, plates of cheesy lasagna in front of them, and her mom was laughing at something Evan said, Morgan couldn't take it anymore. "Why did you guys break up?"

Her mom dropped her fork and Officer Anderson choked on his wine. "Pardon?"

"Why did you guys break up?" Morgan asked again. "Everyone says you two were pretty hot and heavy in high school. So what happened?"

"Who's everyone?" her mom asked.

"Jess's mom."

"That's everyone?"

Morgan shrugged. "Close enough. So why did you break up?"

"Well...I...it was..."

"Sometimes things don't work out when you're eighteen," Evan finished.

Her mom stared at him, and for a moment the two of them shared a look that made Morgan feel bad. *Maybe she shouldn't have asked.*

"We were young," her mom added.

"Are you dating now?" She tried to keep her voice light. After all, it was an innocent question. Or maybe it wasn't. Either way, she wanted to know.

Morgan knew she was probably pushing her luck and her mom was going to lose her shit on her later, but it seemed like a good opportunity to get some answers, and if she could keep them talking about themselves, maybe she could guarantee that Officer Anderson wouldn't say anything about the party the night before.

"No. We're not dating now," her mom answered quickly. Too quickly. "We're just friends."

"Good friends."

Morgan rolled her eyes and shoved the last of her lasagna in her mouth. "Whatever you say. Hey, is it all right if I don't help clean up tonight? Jess and I wanted to go to the eight o'clock show. Her dad said he'd drive us home because it will be late."

"Are you asking me, or telling me?" Her mom challenged her with her eyes and Morgan realized her mistake. Some days she could push it. Maybe today wasn't one of those days.

"I'm sorry," she said quickly. "I was going to ask but things were busy and then Officer Anderson came over and I just kind of forgot." She was careful not to meet his gaze. "I should have asked. Is it okay if I go to a movie with Jess tonight?" Morgan couldn't imagine the answer would be no, especially considering they were very clearly trying not to act like they were dating when it was so obvious that they were. Either that, or they would be soon.

"I suppose it will be okay," her mom said after a minute. "Her dad will drive you home?"

Morgan nodded.

"Is it just the two of you going?"

Morgan whipped her head around to stare at Evan. Her mouth fell open but she closed it quickly. "What?"

"I was just wondering if it was just you and Jess going to the movie or if there was a group of you?"

She knew exactly what he was asking, and it pissed her off. He may have kept his promise not to say anything about the night before to her mom, but that didn't give him the right to interrogate her about who she was spending time with. Besides, it's not as if he had any right to ask anyway. He wasn't her dad. She shot him a look, but aware that her mom was watching them, Morgan finally said, "Well, I'm sure there will be other people at the theater. We're not renting it out."

She grabbed her plate and took it to the sink where she rinsed it with a little more force than was probably necessary.

"Morgan. You don't have to be rude," her mom said behind her. "Sorry, Evan. I don't know what—"

"It's okay," he said. "I was just curious. But she doesn't have to tell me."

Guilt washed through her. He really wasn't a bad guy and she did owe him one. "It's just Jess and I tonight." She looked him in the eye. "Sorry I was rude."

"All good. And don't worry about cleaning up." He smiled at her. "Your mom cooked, so I'll handle the dishes. You have fun and say hi to Jess for me." He winked at her and she almost laughed. Instead, Morgan shook her head, gave her mom a quick hug, and got out of there before her mom changed her mind.

"I'M SORRY ABOUT MORGAN." Cam took the sudsy plate from him, rinsed and dried it before putting it away and reaching for another. It was nice having someone to do dishes with her. Someone besides a moody teenager that was. "I don't know what's going on with her lately."

"She's a teenager."

"Oh, don't I know it. It's so hard some days."

"Don't worry about it. I can't even imagine how difficult it would be to raise a daughter. You're like some kind of super-hero." *A really cute superhero*, he thought. Cam always looked good, but that night, there was something different about her.

It was as if for the first time she seemed relaxed and comfortable around him. He'd caught a glimpse of it when they'd gone out for dinner, but this was different.

Her long blonde hair was pulled up in a ponytail that reminded him of an eighteen-year-old version of herself. She had a little makeup on—not that she needed it; she never had —but the light pink slicked on her lips made them look even more kissable than normal. Instead of the t-shirt he usually saw her in, she was wearing a silky red blouse that was unbuttoned just enough to show off a hint of cleavage.

"Right." She laughed. "I guess my cape is at the cleaner's right now."

Evan put the dishrag down and reached for her hand as she spun around to take the next plate from him. "Seriously," he said when her eyes locked on his. They were wide in surprise that he was touching her. Truthfully, he was surprised too. But ever since they'd held hands across the table at the restaurant, he'd wanted to touch her so badly it burned inside him. This time, holding her hand wasn't going to be enough. He pulled her close until she was pressed up against his chest.

"You are the most amazing woman I know," he finished his sentence. "And you definitely don't need a cape to prove it. You're doing an amazing job with her."

She shook her head, but didn't pull away. "I don't know about that. Some days I can hardly keep my head above water with her."

"Amazing," he repeated. "Really."

He stroked his soapy finger down her cheek, leaving a tiny trail of bubbles on her skin. "Cam, I know there's a lot…it's been a long…"

Screw it.

Unwilling to continue the game of trying to justify his actions, Evan took the chance he'd been wanting to take almost since the moment she rolled back into town. His hand slipped under her chin and he lowered his lips to hers.

The taste of her was familiar but new at the same time. Her soft lips yielded the way he'd known they would and a small sound slipped from her. Taking a chance, Evan deepened the kiss, his other hand coming up to cup the back of her head.

Kissing her was *everything*.

It had been sixteen years, but their lips remembered each other immediately. Nothing had ever felt so right.

Finally, when Evan pulled away a little, he was shy and a little unsure, which was ridiculous. But when he saw the small smile on Cam's lips, he knew it was okay. "I've wanted to do that for a long time."

"Over a decade?"

He nodded, not bothering to deny it. "I've missed you, Cam. More than I even knew."

"I've missed you, too. But...I need to ask you something."

He took a step back, needing the distance to keep from pulling her back into his arms. "Anything."

Her eyes clouded and she glanced down at her hands before looking up again. "I won't get involved with anyone who's in a relationship," she said quickly. "I've been on the receiving end of that, and I just can't do it."

Confused, Evan stepped forward and tried to reach for her hand, but she pulled it away. "Relationship?" he shook his head and tried to make sense of what Cam was saying. "I told you, Cam, I'm not dating anyone. I'd never do that."

She stared directly into his eyes. "Stephanie?"

What had she heard? A million possible scenarios flew through his head, but there was only one thing to tell her. The truth.

"We've dated on and off," he said. "But it's been off for a while. We're not together, Cam. It's never been serious with Steph. At least not for me. She knows that."

Whether she chose to accept that or not was a different

question. But Evan had always been upfront with Stephanie about who and what they were to each other. And serious had never been part of the conversation.

"You're sure?" She took a tiny step toward him. "Because I can't be part of anything that will hurt another person. Not intentionally." Her eyes were so big, so open, so full of emotion, it took all his restraint to keep from kissing away all her worries.

But first, he needed to be sure she understood him. "I know," Evan said. "And please believe me when I tell you that I'd never put you in that position, or anyone else. I'm not that guy, Cam. It's just you. It's always been you."

"I believe you." The concern on her face melted into a soft smile and he knew it was true. "There's just one more thing I need you to know."

Evan waited.

"Things are kind of complicated right now."

He knew that. He nodded.

"With Morgan and the divorce and…I just don't know if I can…"

"Hey." He held her cheek until she looked at him. "I'm not asking for anything more than you can give. I just know that this…us…it's…well, I'm not going to pretend that it's any small thing." He remembered what Ben had said. "Because you and I are anything but small, Cam."

This time she kissed him, and there wasn't anything soft about it. Her kiss was laced with years of built-up emotion. She wrapped her arms around his neck and pulled him down to her. His hands traveled the length of her back, up her neck and into her hair. Gently, Evan tugged her ponytail and let her hair cascade in soft waves around her shoulders.

They lost themselves in each other and even Evan was surprised when he realized he'd backed her up until they were pressed against the wall. He couldn't get enough of her.

Touching her through her clothes wasn't going to satisfy him. He wanted to feel her skin on his, feel the heat of her body on his, the connection he'd missed for so long.

He pulled away. "Cam, I—"

"I do, too." She answered his unspoken question and it was all he needed. Complicated or not, they both knew what they wanted. Evan bent and scooped her up easily in his arms. He looked down at her face, flushed with the heat of their kiss, her chest heaving and straining against his, and he almost came completely undone.

He took a few steps out of the kitchen, then stopped, unsure.

"The couch," she said. "I don't have a bed." Her voice was laced with an apology, but none was needed. She was in his arms, and as far as Evan was concerned, it didn't matter where they were—that was the only place he needed her.

He kissed her again and crossed the room, putting her down as gently as possible before losing himself totally and completely in Cam Riley, just the way he had all those years ago.

———

CAM LAY TANGLED in Evan's arms, staring up at the water-stained ceiling of her tiny apartment with a million questions going through her head. She hadn't intended to sleep with Evan, not really. But the second his lips touched hers, it just felt so right.

She laughed a little at herself and the childish romanticism of it all.

"What's so funny?" Evan shifted a little bit so he could look at her.

"Nothing." She snuggled closer into him. "I was just thinking how silly I was."

"Silly?" It was Evan's turn to chuckle. "Sweetheart, what we just did was anything but silly."

"I know." She squeezed her eyes shut and tried to decide whether she could confide in him what she was thinking. Decision made, she said, "It's just that I wasn't really planning on that happening tonight. That's not why I invited you here."

"I'm okay with it."

"I'm sure." She grinned. "What I'm trying to say is…" Cam hesitated, unsure how to put her feelings into words. "It just felt right. Does that make sense?" She didn't wait for an answer. "Just being with you…it was…"

"Like home." It wasn't a question, but it didn't need to be because Evan was exactly right.

"Yes." She sat up and looked down into his eyes. "And I laughed because it's kind of hokey, don't you think?"

"It may be hokey." He reached up and stroked her arm. "But it's true. I feel the same way." Evan pushed up to a sitting position and pulled her onto his lap. "And that's all that matters."

She let him hold her, his hand drawing circles on her back, because it was exactly what she needed and her body craved Evan's touch with an intensity she didn't know she was capable of. But despite her happiness, something still troubled Cam. Morgan's earlier unanswered question rang through her head. *Why did you break up?*

They'd still never talked about it.

At the risk of shattering the moment, Cam had to know. "What happened, Evan?"

His hand stilled. "What?"

She pulled back. "What happened? Why did you leave me?"

His face twisted in pain. "Sweetheart, I didn't leave you."

"You did."

"No." He reached for her again. "I left myself."

"That doesn't make any sense."

"You deserved the world, Cam. You still do." She shook her head, but she didn't say anything. "And I couldn't give it to you. I was just a small-town kid with a chip on his shoulder and a bad attitude. I wasn't going to amount to anything. Not ever."

"That's not true. You did—"

"The only reason I made anything of myself was because I made a choice. It was the hardest thing I ever did, but it was the only option I had."

"I don't understand." Evan shifted her off his lap, wrapped a blanket around her and stood. She watched while he tugged on his jeans and moved to the kitchen to get her a glass of water. He didn't sit down again, but instead started pacing, and talking.

"Do you remember when Tommy and I got busted vandalizing the wall behind the general store? It was right before graduation."

She did remember. For a while, there'd been a rumor that Evan and Tommy would be charged and wouldn't be able to attend graduation. Or worse, jail. Evan was already eighteen, and Tommy was just shy by a few months. In the end, Tommy never went to the graduation celebrations, and to Cam's knowledge, may not have actually graduated. But to Cam's relief, Evan was permitted to go and somehow managed to earn his diploma. He'd never spoken about it. Not even to her.

When she nodded, Evan continued. "Judge Stewart saved my life that night."

"Judge Stewart? The same Judge Stewart who gave Morgan community service?"

"The one and only." Evan nodded. "Obviously it was a long time ago. But he saved my life. And I don't mean physically, but in every other way." He scrubbed a hand over his face. "I don't think I'll ever understand why he chose me to try to make a difference with, but I'll be forever grateful that he did. Tommy and I were caught red-handed. Literally. The paint we used was red." He grinned a little, but there was no humor in his words. "There was no denying what we'd done and Judge Stewart had every reason to ship us both off to juvie. Hell, I probably would have. We were little shits who caused nothing but trouble. Instead, he did something I never saw coming."

"What's that?" She was shocked to hear what was coming out of Evan's mouth because he'd never told her any of it. They'd been closer than two people could be, and yet, he'd never shared this with her. Cam couldn't pretend it didn't sting a bit, but she wanted to hear the rest.

"He gave us a choice. He could charge us, which for me would have meant jail time, or…we could change our lives. We had to make a choice, right then, on the spot. I'll never forget that night. He'd never once said anything about all the shit we got into. He never tried to lecture us or tell us we could do better—nothing. But the judge looked straight into my eyes and told me that this was my moment. I could make a change for the better. Enlist in the army and learn a thing or two about life, and what it was all about, or…keep doing what I was doing. Which would mean, no more leniency. He told me that I was better than the way I was behaving. I could have more. I could have a wife and kids, and a respectable job, and it wasn't too late for me to have everything I wanted. As long as I made the choice."

"Wow." It seemed like a dramatic understatement, but it was all Cam could think of to say. "So you chose."

Evan nodded. "I chose. And just like I promised Judge Stewart, the day after graduation, I enlisted."

Pain, fresh and hot as if Cam were experiencing that day all over again, seared through her. "But you didn't say goodbye," she whispered. "You didn't tell me." Tears dripped down her face as she remembered how it felt to stand on his mother's porch and hear that he was gone and not coming back. That he'd left her. Without so much as a word. "You just left."

Evan dropped to his knees in front of her and grabbed her hands. "I had to," he said. "I was afraid I wouldn't go if I told you. I knew you'd be hurt and I couldn't bear to see it in your face, so I chickened out and left. But the first time I got leave, I came to tell you what I'd done and that I'd done it all for you. For *us*. Because you deserved better than what I could give you. You deserved the life you wanted. The career, the house, the kids. Everything. And I was finally in a position where I'd be able to give it to you. But…"

"I was gone."

He nodded. "Christy told me you'd gone to Portland and met a guy and—"

A sob ripped through her, cutting him off. He pulled her into his arms and held her tight. "It doesn't matter anymore. None of it does. Because you're back, and I'm here and we're together. It doesn't matter."

But it did matter. Their whole life could have been different, if only… *Everything* could have been different.

Chapter Eleven

THE NEXT FEW days passed in a blur of happiness unlike any that Cam had felt in years. It amazed her how easily Evan had slipped back into her life. As if he'd never left at all. But he had, and the other night, talking about the real reason why they'd broken up, was the only dark spot on what was otherwise a very bright new beginning.

After Evan told her his story about what had gone down all those years ago, they'd made love again and cuddled together on the couch, catching up on the last few years. She'd told him all about her years in Portland and shown him photos of Morgan as a baby. He'd spoken about his time in the army, and how once he was discharged, he hadn't quite known what to do, so he'd joined the police academy and come back to Timber Creek to give back the way Judge Stewart had done for him all those years ago.

The only thing they hadn't discussed was how when Cam had gone to his house the day after graduation, it was his mother, a woman she'd cared about, who'd shattered her heart completely. Lorraine Anderson had come to the door, a cup of coffee in her hand, and Cam could still remember the way her mouth had pressed into a thin, hard line when Cam asked for Evan.

"He's gone, honey." Her voice held none of her usual kindness. "Left this morning."

"Gone?" Her voice shook, but still Cam hadn't realized what she was hearing. "Where did he go?"

"Wouldn't say." Lorraine took a long sip of her coffee before speaking again. "But one thing is for sure. He's not coming back. Not for you, at any rate."

"Did he say that?"

"Not in so many words, honey. But I know my son. As much as you loved him, it wasn't the same for him. He needed to spread his wings. High school's over. It's time to grow up."

Cam didn't remember much after that. Somehow she'd made it home and fallen into her bed, where she'd cried for days until her parents made her get up and go to Portland with them. They were still hoping there was a chance she might register for college, even though she'd put it off because not only was she not sure what to take in school, she mostly wasn't willing to leave Evan. With the recent developments in her relationship, her parents had a renewed hope that she'd attend classes, or at the very least, enjoy a little vacation to take her mind off of things.

She went.

Met Ryan. And that was it.

She didn't tell Evan any of that; it hadn't felt like the right time and besides, what would it change? They were together again, and that's all that mattered. Despite the fact that Cam told him she wasn't looking for anything serious, and that her life was complicated, that didn't seem to matter. Not to either of them. Besides, there'd been no talk of the future or what was going to come next. As far as Cam was concerned, that was perfect.

Cam examined herself one more time and last minute,

decided to pull her ponytail out and wear her hair down. She brushed it out quickly, put a slick of lip gloss on and was about to rush out of her apartment for her afternoon shift when her cell phone rang.

She glanced at the caller ID and her stomach flipped just the way it always did when she saw her daughter's face on the screen. "Morgan?" She answered as cheerily as possible. "What's going on? Shouldn't you be in class?"

"I have a problem."

Cam's stomach tightened in a knot but she refused to panic. There hadn't been any major issues with Morgan in a few days. Maybe this was finally a turnaround. "A problem? What's going on?"

"I forgot my science binder in my room."

"That's the problem?" Relief washed through her and Cam almost laughed at how worried she'd been. "That doesn't sound like a problem."

"You don't understand! If I don't hand in my homework, Mr. Muldoon is going to freak out."

Cam held the phone out from her ear and shook her head. "Well, I guess you do have a bit of a problem."

"Mom!" Morgan's exasperation oozed through the line. "I *need* you to bring me my binder."

It was the third time in the last few weeks Cam had received a similar call. She'd told Morgan the last time that she refused to act as her messenger service any longer. She was going to have to get more organized. It wasn't Cam's job. She repeated as much to her daughter and said, "I'm on my way to work. I can't run to the school right now. I'm sorry. You'll have to run home at lunch."

"You're such a bitch!"

It took Cam a second to process what Morgan had just said. "Pardon me?"

"All you care about is yourself. It's not like I'm asking for much," Morgan yelled into the phone. "It's just a binder. You'd think you would *want* to help me after ruining my life."

"Excuse me, Morgan?" Cam's voice shook with barely contained anger. She couldn't afford to lose control. "You cannot talk to me like that," she said through clenched teeth.

"Whatever." Morgan spat out the word and the line went dead.

Cam was left staring dumbly at her phone. *What had just happened?*

CAM'S SHIFT kept her busy, and fortunately for her, Tommy wasn't at the End of the Road so she didn't have to deal with his almost constant advances. Evan popped in briefly under the guise of a routine check on local businesses, but when he snuck her a kiss before heading out, Cam knew the real reason and his attentions kept her going until her short shift was over.

She was still only working lunchtime shifts and occasionally a late afternoon or evening, but Tommy still wouldn't let her work the night shifts. She'd asked about it more than once because that's where the good tips were and she knew it. It definitely wasn't her dream job to be serving drinks while naked women gyrated behind her, but it was paying the bills at the moment and it would be nice to have a few extra dollars in her wallet to buy Morgan the new jeans she knew she wanted, or maybe even get something nice for the dance that weekend. Despite the fact that her daughter had just gone off the rails with her attitude, it would pass and maybe it wasn't the best parenting move to reward her behavior, but it felt like it had been so long since there'd been anything positive between them. It probably wouldn't hurt.

At any rate, Tommy hadn't budged on letting her take a

late shift, and Cam was pretty sure she knew why. *Evan.* His concern was sweet, sure, but it wasn't helping her pay the bills.

Before leaving the bar, she checked her phone and wasn't surprised to see a text from Morgan.

SORRY I FREAKED OUT.

IT WAS PRETTY MUCH how things went lately. A freak-out by Morgan, followed by an apology, usually because Morgan needed something. In this instance, that something was a new outfit for the anniversary party this weekend. Cam had promised her weeks ago that if she agreed to go, she'd buy her something nice to wear. She hadn't really expected her daughter to either agree to the dance, or accept the offer of a new outfit that wasn't completely black, but that was before Morgan had met her new friends. Obviously there was some peer incentive to go to the party.

Not that Cam was complaining. Despite Morgan's unpredictable mood, she did seem happier generally and Cam was pretty sure it had a lot to do with the kids she was hanging out with.

IT'S OKAY. *Try to remember your books aren't my responsibility.* Cam texted back.

I KNOW. *I'm sorry.*

CAM SMILED and tapped in another message.

· · ·

STILL ON FOR SHOPPING?

IF THAT'S OKAY?

JUST LEAVING WORK. Cam responded. *Meet you downtown in 5?*

SHE TUCKED her phone in her purse, counted her tips one more time and did some rough calculations on how much money she had left for the rest of the month. There should be enough to get Morgan something nice. She hoped.

"IT IS NOT *CUTE.*" Morgan grabbed the top her mom was holding out and stuffed it back on the rack. "And don't say cute."

"Okay...it's *cool?*"

"Mom!" She rolled her eyes and stormed to the opposite side of the store. Shopping with her mom was such a pain in the ass. Well, most of the time anyway. Sometimes it wasn't so bad. But Morgan couldn't remember one of those at the moment. She shoved a rack of black silky tops to one side. At least she might get something new to wear out of it.

If she could find something.

There were only like three stores in Timber Creek and from what Morgan could tell, none of them had anything worth even trying on.

Except maybe that last top her mom had picked out. But there was no way she was going to go near it! Not if her mom liked it.

Morgan tried to swallow her anger and take a breath the way her therapist in the city had told her. It wasn't her mom's fault that she couldn't find anything. Not really.

Still.

"I'm just going to be over here," her mom called from the other side of the store where the slightly dressier clothes were. If her mom thought she was going to get anything like that, she was crazy. Morgan refocused her efforts on the racks in front of her. There may not be much to choose from, but she had to find something. After all, it would be her first dance in Timber Creek. Hell, her first dance ever. She'd never bothered to go to the dances at her last high school, they were so lame.

But this one was different because Trent had asked her a few days ago if she'd be there. Jess answered for her before Morgan could tell him that she hadn't really thought about it.

"Of course she'll be there," Jess said. "The whole town is going to be there."

"Cool." Trent nodded and then turned to smile at Morgan. "I'm not a very good dancer, but that doesn't stop me."

"Same here." *Same here?* Morgan still couldn't believe she'd said that. It made her cringe every time she replayed it in her head. Which had been a lot.

Still. Trent was going to be there. Which meant, she was going to be there. And she was going to look *good*.

She picked up a black tank top that looked like most of the black tank tops she already owned but put it back when her phone beeped.

Hey. Whatcha doing?

Her stomach did a little flip. She responded to Trent right away, not caring whether it seemed too eager.

Shopping.

FOR THE DANCE?

. . .

HOW DID YOU KNOW? Morgan grinned. *Are you watching me?*

NOPE. Lol. Just a guess.

"MORGAN? FIND ANYTHING YET?" Morgan lifted her head from her phone to see her mom standing with a woman she vaguely recognized from some old photos and shook her head. "Well, keep looking."

"As if there were another choice," she muttered. An idea popped into her head, and she quickly texted the question before she could chicken out.

WHAT'S YOUR FAVORITE COLOR?

THERE WAS no response for so long Morgan started to think she might have made a mistake. *Maybe it was too forward? Too much to ask. She didn't want him to think that she—*

BLUE. Like your eyes.

IF MORGAN WAS A SQUEALING type of girl, she might have done just that. But she wasn't. Instead, she did a little dance on the spot and refocused her search for an outfit.

"Just grab a few things to try on," her mom called. "I won't even give you my opinion."

She shot her mom a look across the store, but she either

didn't notice or didn't care—she was too lost in her conversation with her friend.

Whatever. The sooner she found something, the sooner she could get out of there and away from her mom. She tucked her phone into her back pocket and went on a mission through the racks, until she found a silky royal-blue tank top. She normally would choose the black, but…Trent had said blue. She snagged a pair of skinny black jeans and headed for the changing room, completely ignoring her mom as she walked by.

CAM DID her best not to be annoyed by her daughter's attitude. After all, it was almost always how shopping trips with Morgan had gone for the last few years. If Cam suggested something, even if she *knew* without a doubt it was something her daughter would like and look good in, Morgan would avoid it as if it were a floral, paisley, plaid combination and not the basic black Cam knew her daughter preferred.

Most of the time she didn't even bother offering an opinion, but sometimes she forgot herself.

"Is she okay?" Drew asked after Morgan stormed past them into the changing room

Cam laughed and nodded. "Be thankful Austin is still little. And a boy," she added. "I obviously don't know, but I can't imagine boys are ever this hard on their mothers."

"I sure hope not. But we have a few years before the hormones will hit."

"At least you'll have Eric to help you out," Cam said. "I think a partner in solidarity would definitely help."

The light in Drew's eyes dimmed and she turned away. Cam put the skirt she was looking at back in the rack and touched her friend's shoulder. "Hey? Is everything okay with you and Eric?" The store wasn't really the place where Cam wanted to talk about Drew and what she'd guessed were some marital problems, but Cam had been meaning to say something. The other night at Christy's, she'd noticed how Drew had avoided talking about Eric or answering any real questions about him. It wasn't too obvious, but Cam had picked up on it and considering that next to Christy and Mark, Drew and Eric were the cutest and most completely in love couple she'd ever known, there were all kinds of red flags going up.

Drew ducked her head and picked a dress off the rack. "What do you think of this one?"

"Drew?" Cam reached out and gently pushed the dress to the side. "Is Eric going to be coming for the dance?"

Her friend's eyes filled with tears and she shook her head softly.

"Oh, Drew. I'm so—"

"Here." Morgan crashed between her and Drew and shoved an arm full of clothes in Cam's hand. "I like these."

"Morgan!" Cam took a step back from her friend and spun to face her daughter.

"What?" Morgan shrugged, exasperation all over her face. "You told me to pick out an outfit. I did."

"That's not what I was talking about." Cam glanced over at Drew, who'd averted her gaze and was pretending to look through some dresses. "I was talking to Drew. You interrupted."

"I interrupted? Well, *excuse* me."

Cam knew well enough to know when to pick her battles, and it had already been a touchy day with Morgan, but she could not excuse her daughter's rudeness to her friend. Especially when Drew was clearly going through something. "You're not excused, Morgan. Get back here please."

Morgan had already reached the other end of the store

and had her phone out in her hand. She paused and stared at Cam.

"I'm not sure what you're so upset about today, Morgan. But if this is about me not bringing you your books when you asked, you need to—"

"That's not what I'm upset about."

With great restraint, Cam held back the sigh of frustration. More and more, dealing with Morgan's unpredictable moods tested her patience in ways she never could have imagined. "Then what, Morgan? What did I do? Because I don't deserve to be treated this way."

"You don't deserve it?" Morgan shoved her phone into her back pocket and crossed the distance between them. Her eyes flared. "Do you think *I* deserve this?"

"What are you—"

"Do you think I deserve to have my whole life uprooted, to move to this shitty little town? My dad doesn't even want to see me and it's all *your* fault."

Cam's heart ached for her little girl. Despite the fact that she was raging and yelling at her, she knew Morgan was hurting and it killed her. But she needed to be strong. "You know it's not my fault, Morgan. That's not fair."

"It is your fault, Mom. You had to go and ruin everything. It's always about you. You never think about how I'm going to feel. Not about anything." Morgan jabbed a finger toward Drew. "You can't even go shopping with just me. Even that has to be about you, too." Morgan was yelling now, with tears streaming down her face.

Cam couldn't decide whether she was angry, upset, completely mortified at the public teenage tantrum, or simply exhausted.

She shook her head. "That's not true and you know it." She took a deep breath and stepped forward. "You need to calm down right now and get home. This is totally unaccept-able behavior and not the time or—"

"It's never a good time for you." Morgan's jaw was set, anger radiating off her in waves.

What had Cam done to cause her daughter to hate her so much? Not for the first time, she wished she had the answers.

"Morgan, go home."

"No."

Anger was the emotion that finally won out. "Go home right now or you'll be grounded." The words came out through clenched teeth.

Morgan opened her mouth to say something, but obviously thought better of it. She closed it again, squeezed her eyes shut for a brief moment and took a few deep breaths before opening them again. Tears flowed down her face and Cam longed to wipe them away and take her baby girl's pain away. But when Morgan opened her mouth again, it was like a thousand knives to her heart.

"I hate you."

It wasn't the first time Cam had heard the words, but they never failed to have an impact. A fact Morgan surely knew. She knew the right thing to do, the thing all the parenting books she'd read told her to do. Morgan was only crying out for help. She knew logically that Morgan lashed out at her because she felt safe with Cam. She knew her mom wouldn't leave her. But knowing that didn't make her outbursts any easier to deal with. Cam should reach out and try to pull her into a hug. Or at the very least tell Morgan that she loved her. But she couldn't bring herself to do any of those things.

Instead, she nodded solemnly. "I know you do."

CHRISTY AND MARK'S house had become the unofficial party headquarters for the big anniversary party, so Evan wasn't surprised when he pulled up to see their driveway full of vehicles. His stomach flipped and his mood only got better when he saw Cam's SUV.

They hadn't talked about going public with their relationship. Or even if it was a relationship. In fact, they hadn't talked much at all about what was going on between them beyond the fact that something was. Not that Evan needed to put a label on anything.

He lugged the giant helium container he was there to deliver from the back of his truck and up the front stairs to Christy's house. He didn't bother knocking, but walked in and called out, "Your hot air is here!"

Christy greeted him almost at once with a laugh from the kitchen. "You can leave it in the hallway."

He did as instructed and went in search for the women, or more specifically, Cam.

He found Christy first.

"What's going on today? I didn't expect there to be so many cars out front." He looked around, trying not to be obvious in his search. "Who all is here?"

Christy gave him a look that told him she wasn't buying his innocent act, but she didn't say anything. "Just the girls."

"Hey, Evan," Drew greeted him on cue as she walked into the kitchen, an empty wine bottle in her hand.

He raised an eyebrow at the bottle and gave her a hug. "Don't tell me you're day drinking? Isn't that a sign of a problem?" he teased, but Drew didn't smile.

"It's been a trying day," she said. "At least for some of us."

"What's going on?" Evan looked between the women. "Everything okay?"

Drew exchanged a glance with Christy, who only shrugged. "It's Cam," she said finally.

Evan's body responded instantly. "Is she okay? What's going on? Where is she?" He was about to push past the women to find her, but Drew's hand on his arm stopped him.

"She's just having a rough time with Morgan is all."

Most of the tension drained from his body hearing she was generally okay. "What type of rough time?"

"There was an incident downtown at the shops." Drew quickly gave him the overview of what had happened in the store and how Morgan had yelled at her. "I think she's mostly just drained. Parenting can take a lot out of you at times, and I think parenting teenagers is just that much harder."

"Teenagers aren't easy." He almost laughed remembering the hard times he'd put his own mother through, but neither of the women were laughing. "It could always be worse, right?"

Drew nodded, but hesitantly. "What's going on with you two anyway?"

It surprised him that the girls didn't already know all the details, but he tried not to show it. The teenage version of Cam would have told them everything as soon as she had a chance, but that didn't mean that grown-up Cam would. He took a breath and tried to decide how much to say. "We're getting to know each other again."

"Right." Christy rolled her eyes and laughed a little.

"Hey, Drew?" Cam's voice called from the other room. "Don't worry about that other bottle. I should really get—" Her words died on her lips when she walked into the room and saw Evan. "What are you doing here?"

He took a step toward her and pulled her into a hug, stopping before giving her a kiss. "I was just delivering helium for the balloons. I didn't expect to see you here."

She smiled, but it didn't reach her eyes. "I didn't expect to be here, either. I just needed a bit of a break before I went home. It was...well...it's not been a great day."

"I heard." He nodded sympathetically.

"You did?" She gave Drew a look, but her friend only grinned.

"I did." He could see the stress on her face, and the need to make things better for her was intense. "But don't worry. It's normal teenage stuff."

Cam's back stiffened and she gave him a sharp look. "Normal?"

Next to her, Evan vaguely recognized Christy and Drew make their escape into the living room, Christy shooting him a look of warning as she went. *But warning of what?* Evan knew teenagers. He'd worked with them for years as local law enforcement. And he knew Morgan. After their time doing the community service, he knew she was just a normal kid who had some typical angst to deal with. Cam didn't need to worry about anything. He told her as much.

"You have no idea." She shook her head and turned away from him.

Determined to cheer her up, Evan took a step closer to her and because there was no one watching, wrapped his arms around her and kissed her neck.

Cam shrugged him off and stepped away. "Stop it."

"Stop what? I'm trying to cheer you up." Again, he stepped in close.

She spun around and pushed him back with one hand. This time, Evan held back from reaching for her again. "Cam? What's wrong?"

Her mouth fell open. "You're serious?"

He shrugged.

"Nothing about this is normal, Evan." She waved her arms to encompass the kitchen, but Evan was smart enough to know she wasn't talking about Christy's house. "It's a total mess. My *daughter* is a total mess. She hates me, Evan."

Evan shook his head. "We all used to hate our parents, Cam. Don't you remember how—"

"No." She squeezed her eyes. "This is different. You have no idea."

No. He clearly didn't. But if she'd let him, he wanted to find out. "Cam, it can't be that bad. Morgan's a good kid."

Cam turned around and stared out the window into Christy's yard. "She's hurting so much and I'm afraid she might be right."

He risked putting a hand on her shoulder because he just couldn't *not* touch her while she clearly needed a hug. "Right about what?"

"Maybe it is all about me. Maybe I haven't been putting her first the way I should be."

"Cam, you're a great mother."

She shook her head.

"Let me help you," Evan said. "What do you need from me? I can talk to her. I can—"

"No." She turned and he saw her tear-streaked face. "I don't think you can help. It's just a lot. *She's* a lot. She always was and that was before this big mess with her dad. I need to deal with it on my own."

"No." He didn't know why, but he could feel her slipping away and he desperately needed to prevent that from happening. "You don't need to deal with it on your own. There's no reason you should be alone in all this, Cam."

"You're right." She scoffed. "Her dad should be helping me."

I should be helping you.

"You're right," Evan said. "He should be."

"But he won't," she said. "In fact, he doesn't want anything to do with her. It's breaking my heart but I can't even call him and tell him what's happening because he'll just tell me how I need to handle it because she's with me, and I don't need to go running to him all the time." She dropped her head into her hands. "Her own father doesn't want to deal with her. How can I ask you to get involved with this?"

The conversation took such an unexpected turn, it took Evan a moment to catch up. "What?"

"Maybe she's right," Cam continued as if he hadn't spoken. "Maybe I am being selfish. I can't ask anyone else to be part of this. Not when I don't even—"

"Cam." He grabbed her wrists and forced her to look at him. "What are you talking about? What do you mean you can't ask me to be a part of this? Of what?"

"Of *this*, Evan." Tears streaked down her cheeks. "I mean, I don't even know what's going on with us. Everything is such a mess."

He pulled her close. "We're not a mess, Cam. I've got you." He felt her relax a little against him so he continued to murmur reassurances in her ear. She might not believe it right away, but he really was going to be there for her. No matter what. "I'm not going anywhere." He repeated the words over and over while he stroked her hair until her tears were exhausted.

Chapter Twelve

"SO THE BIG DANCE IS TOMORROW."

Morgan was finishing a shift of her community service hours with Officer Anderson, and something about it felt weird. No doubt her mom had told him all about her freak-out at the store a few days earlier. It was such a pain in the ass living in a small town where everyone knew everyone. Especially if they knew her mom.

"And?" She dipped her brush into the paint can and slapped it onto the boards in front of her. With every hour she completed, Morgan was more and more sure that community service was just code for free child labor to get odd jobs done around town. Like painting the gazebo in the town park.

"Are you excited?"

Morgan almost laughed. *Almost.*

"I guess."

"That sounds like a yes."

She turned and looked at him where he sat on a nearby picnic table. "It's neither a yes or a no. It's an *I guess.*"

He grinned. "It's okay to be excited about it. The whole

town is. I've never seen everyone so jacked up about something."

She turned back to her job. "Are you? Excited about the dance, I mean."

"I am." Behind her, she could hear him jump off the table and walk closer.

"Is that because you're going with my mom?" Morgan wasn't stupid and after hearing about how hot and heavy the two of them were when they were kids, and then seeing them together when they were trying to act like they didn't care about each other, she was pretty positive they were dating. She'd thought a lot about it and Morgan had decided that she didn't care. In fact, if anything, it was a good thing. Maybe.

To her surprise, he answered her honestly. "Yes. Is that okay with you?"

She nodded. "I guess."

"Are you going to the dance with Trent?"

The question came so far out of left field that her cheeks flamed to life.

"Your mom said she bought you a new outfit."

Morgan's cheeks flamed again, this time because she remembered what a bitch she'd been to her mom at the store and then she'd come home to see the bag with the outfit she'd picked out. Her mom had bought it for her despite her tantrum. It had almost made Morgan feel worse.

"Yeah," she said after a minute. "She didn't have to do that."

"Because you freaked out on her?"

"Jesus." She dropped the brush into the paint can and stalked off to the picnic table. "You just don't care, do you?"

"About what?" Evan stood in front of her. "About confronting you on your shit?" He shook his head. "No. And yes, I just said shit."

She couldn't help it. That made her smile. But just a little.

"But yes," he continued. "I'm not going to ignore the fact that you've had some pretty major meltdowns lately. Want to tell me about it?"

She shook her head.

"Then maybe you should get back to work?"

Her head shot up and she glared at him. "Can't I take a break?"

"Only if you're going to talk."

"That's blackmail."

He shrugged and smiled. "Maybe."

She picked at a drop of paint on her shoe for a minute and finally said, "I don't actually know what to say. It's not that I don't like it here. I kind of do." She looked up. "Don't tell my mom that."

"Promise."

"It's just different and I'm just kind of mad I guess."

"At your mom?"

She nodded. "But mostly my dad."

"So why take it out on your mom?"

Morgan was quiet for a minute. Finally, she looked up. "Because she's there."

"There?"

"Not like there-there. But more like *there there.* Does that make sense?"

Evan sat on the picnic table next to her and for a minute she thought he might put his arm around her. She decided she would probably be okay with that. "It makes perfect sense. Your mom's always there for you. So it's safe to be mad at her because she's not going anywhere. Right?"

When she looked up again, there was a tear in her eye. "Yeah. But I guess that's not very fair, is it?"

"No," Evan agreed with her. "But it makes sense."

They sat in silence for a few more minutes before Morgan sat up. "Thank you." He looked as surprised as she felt to be saying it, but she continued. "For listening, I mean."

"You're welcome. It's no big deal."

"Wrong." Morgan jumped up and started to walk back to the gazebo. "It's a very big deal."

CAM LOOKED at the price tag on the dress and for the fifth time, calculated how much money she didn't have. She couldn't justify it. Instead, she turned to the rack with the sale items and picked up a cream-colored blouse. She could pair it with one of her black skirts that she'd been wearing to work. Maybe with her red heels it would even look a little dressy.

"There's no way." Amber took the blouse out of her hand and shoved the dress she'd just been admiring at her. "This is what you should wear. It'll make your eyes look crazy awesome."

"Crazy awesome?" She laughed at Amber. "And no." She shook her head slowly. "I can't afford it. Not right now."

"My treat." Amber started to push her toward the dressing room. "Seriously. Pretend it's for all the birthday presents I forgot to send. And then, after you try it on so I can confirm how hot you'll look in it, we're going over to the Chop Shop for a little pampering. I booked appointments for all of us. Christy and Drew are meeting us there. And I don't want to hear any complaining because I want to do it. So don't make me feel bad about doing this for us."

Amber had always had a generous spirit. Cam gave her a spontaneous hug. "I've missed you. So much." It was true. She hadn't even realized how much she'd missed her friends but now that they were back, even temporarily, she didn't want to let them go.

"Yeah yeah." Amber protested, and tried to act tough the

way she always did, but Cam saw the shimmer in her eye. Most people didn't know it, but Amber had a secret soft side. "Now go and try it on. We only have a few minutes."

Twenty minutes later, after Amber confirmed how great Cam looked in the dress, paid for it, and begrudgingly let Cam treat them both with lattes from Daisy's, they both walked through the door at the Chop Shop and were immediately greeted by Christy and Drew. The shop was buzzing with activity as people clambered to look their best for the big anniversary party.

"I've never seen Timber Creek like this," Cam told Christy as they waited for their names to be called. "You've done such a great job with everything. The whole town is excited."

"It's nothing." Christy waved away the compliment. "It's kept me busy and given me something to focus on."

"As if you don't have enough to keep you busy with helping out at Mark's clinic and everything."

"Right." She snorted. "Like Mark wants me there."

Shocked, Cam stared at her friend. "What are you talking about?"

Christy tried to act as though it were no big deal, but Cam could see the thread of hurt right beneath her bubbly surface. "Mark would rather have me home with all the kids we don't have. But since that never happened, he gave me the job to keep me busy more than anything while we wait for the fertility treatments to work."

"I'm sure that's not true."

"Oh, it is." She shrugged. "It doesn't matter. But working on the anniversary committee has definitely done one thing for me. At least we're not in each other's faces all the time now. It's been kind of nice not seeing Mark all the time."

Concern for her friend filled her. "What do you mean? I thought you guys liked working together."

"Right now we don't like doing anything together." Christy

tried to keep her voice light, but Cam caught the shake in her words. She looked Cam in the eye. "Like *anything.*"

"*Anything* anything?"

"*Especially* anything." Christy rolled her eyes.

Cam wanted to ask her what she meant by that, but before she could, Christy gestured behind her and Cam's name was called. She glanced at the lady who held out a smock for her to slip over her clothes and back at Christy.

"Do you want me to—"

"You know what, Cam." Christy put her hand on Cam's arm, interrupting her. "Why don't I take this one and you can take my slot?"

"That's okay. It looks like you're next anyway." Another stylist stood next to the first one. "We'll go together."

"Let's switch." Christy's eyes filled with concern and her lips pressed together. "It's no big deal. If we just—"

"Why?" Cam laughed. "You're being silly. Come on."

It wasn't until Cam was sitting in the stylist's chair with the smock fastened a little too snugly around her neck that she understood her friend's strange behavior. "So *you're* the famous Cam Riley?"

The stylist's voice was laced with something Cam couldn't quite place. She tried to laugh. "I wouldn't say that."

The woman picked up her long blonde hair and let it drop onto her back again. "Oh I would definitely say that." She met Cam's eyes in the mirror. "I'm Stephanie."

Stephanie.

Cam quickly racked her brain for where she'd heard that name and why it should be of relevance to her. The moment she made the connection—this was Evan's ex-girlfriend, or at least the woman he'd dated—her eyes widened. Especially considering Stephanie clearly knew exactly who Cam was.

"Hi. It's nice to meet you."

Stephanie ignored her. "I've heard so much about you."

She didn't like the tone in the other woman's voice.

"I can't imagine you've heard that much," Cam tried to joke. "I haven't lived here for so long I'm sure no one remembers me."

"Oh, he remembered you quite well."

He?

"Look, Stephanie." Cam twisted around in the chair so she could look at the other woman easily. "Whatever you've heard about—"

"Oh, it's fine." Stephanie's face transformed into a sweet smile. "It's really old news, isn't it? I mean, it's not like Evan and I were ever really serious." Her voice was light, but Cam wasn't sure she could trust what she was saying. Regardless, the woman did have scissors poised over her head. "Now, what are we doing today?"

———

"I'M SO SORRY." Christy had been apologizing ever since they'd left the salon. "I tried to switch with you, I did."

"It's no big deal." Cam touched her now *much* shorter hair and tried her best to smile. "I needed a trim."

"You did *not* need that." Amber shook her head with disgust. "Totally unprofessional."

It had been unprofessional, but Cam couldn't dwell on it. She had no idea how much Stephanie knew about her, or her past relationship with Evan, or more importantly, her *current* relationship with him. And she didn't want to get into it. But it had become clear quite quickly that the stylist didn't like her, nor was she going to listen to what Cam did or did not want done to her hair.

"Honestly," Cam said again. "It's fine. And it's no one's fault. It's just hair."

"Well, I think it looks cute." Drew smiled, ever the optimist. "A shaggy bob is a good look for you."

"It is cute." Cam shrugged. It really was just hair and if it hadn't been for everything else that had happened lately, she probably wouldn't be upset at all. As it was, she wasn't going to let her friends see that she was upset. Besides, it wasn't the worst thing that could happen.

No. That happened a moment later as she was waiting outside Daisy's while the others went inside to order more coffees.

"Mrs. Anderson?"

Cam hadn't seen Evan's mom in years, not since that day she'd gone looking for him. The day she'd told her how Evan hadn't loved her. But she couldn't mistake the bright-red hair, now streaked with more gray than there'd been all those years ago, but still unmistakable.

The older woman turned around. The smile fell from her face the moment she saw Cam.

"It's me," Cam said, as if she didn't already know. "Cam Riley." She took a few steps toward Evan's mom, who clutched her purse to her chest and took a step back. "How are you?"

Despite the memories of the last time they'd seen each other, Cam couldn't forget all of the good times either. Lorraine had welcomed her into her home and treated her like a daughter simply because she loved her son.

Lorraine shook her head. "I heard you were in town."

"I meant to come and see you." It was a lie and they both knew it.

"It's been a long time."

Cam nodded, no longer sure what she should say. She shuffled from foot to foot. "Lorraine, I was meaning to ask you—"

"I don't think that's necessary."

"But you don't know what I was going to—"

Evan's mom took a step closer so she stood directly in front of Cam. "I may be an old lady," she said. "But I'm not yet forgetful and I remember very much what things were like once between you and my son."

Something in the way she spoke told Cam she wasn't referring to all the good times.

"You were a good girl, Cam. And I'm sure you're a good woman now. But sometimes that isn't enough."

"I'm not sure I know what you're talking about."

"You're a mother now." It wasn't a question, but Cam nodded. "And I assume you'd do anything to make sure your child has the best opportunities." A trail of ice slid down Cam's spine, but she nodded nonetheless. "I thought so," Lorraine continued. "So you can understand how I will always look out for Evan, no matter what?" She didn't wait for Cam's acknowledgment before she continued. "Which is why I knew you'd only hold him back." Cam gasped a breath as if she'd been punched in the gut. "Just the way I know it now. Not everyone saw it in him when he was a boy, but Evan was always destined for great things. He's achieved a lot, but he's not done yet."

"No," Cam said with a nervous laugh. "I'm sure he's not."

"Exactly." Lorraine nodded curtly. "Which is why he needs his freedom. He's worked too hard. It's not the right time for him to be tied down. It wasn't then, and it isn't now. Do you understand what I'm saying?"

Confusion swirled through her head. Cam gripped the side of the building to keep the ground from spinning around her. She shook her head. "No," she managed to say. "I'm afraid I don't."

"You're a good girl, Cam. It's not personal." Lorraine's face was a twisted mess of emotions. "It never was."

Before Cam could react, Lorraine turned and walked away. A moment later, her friends rejoined her. She tried to look past them to see where the woman had disappeared to, but she couldn't spot her.

"Was that Evan's mom?" Drew handed her a cup of coffee. Cam nodded.

"I bet you haven't seen her in ages."

Cam shook her head. "That was the strangest thing." She stared down the street and blinked hard as she tried to process everything Lorraine had said.

"What was?" The women had started to walk back toward Christy's house, just off the main street of town.

"I don't even know how to explain it." Cam took a sip of her coffee and let the liquid warm the chill that had settled over her. She shook her head again, and cleared the negativity. "It's nothing." She forced a smile to her face. "Let's go take care of the balloons. I still can't believe you ordered so many."

Chapter Thirteen

AFTER HIS AFTERNOON WITH MORGAN, Evan was on top of the world. He knew he still had a long way to go, including a ton of education, before he could properly counsel kids, but his breakthrough—or at least what he felt was a breakthrough—with Morgan could only be a good sign. He was on the right track.

Working with kids was his calling.

He loved being a police officer, but working with kids... making a difference...that would be something else.

"You should have seen it," he told Ben. They were stringing an endless amount of helium-filled balloons into arches. Christy had somehow sucked them into the job, which, judging by the quantity of balloons that kept coming into the high school gymnasium, could potentially go on well into the night. "It was a real moment."

Ben chuckled. "I'm not even going to pretend that I understand. The last time I had a real conversation with a teenager, I was one."

"You'll understand one day." Evan handed Ben a blue

balloon. "We need more blue on that row. Don't you ever think about it?"

"About teenagers? I'm not following this conversation anymore."

"No." Evan laughed. "Well, yes. I mean kids in general."

"Like having them?"

"Yeah." Evan rolled his eyes. "Like having them." It had been something he'd been thinking of more and more since Cam had come back into his life. It had been in the back of his head, definitely, but despite the timeline, he didn't believe that Morgan could be his. Not really. Cam would have told him. He knew that in his heart. But it didn't mean he couldn't be there for her now. He *wanted* to be there. For both of them. And maybe…one day…kids of his own.

"No way," Ben said. "It's not for me. Never was."

Evan eyed his buddy. They'd been best friends their entire life, and Evan had never known Ben to date. Not really. He'd had a few short-lived relationships through the years, but there'd been no one who'd captured him. Not since high school and Drew Frederick. She'd been the only one to turn Ben's head. Ben was secretly in love with Drew from the time they were in the second grade, but as far as she was concerned, he'd never been more than a good friend. He would have done anything for her back then. And he did. Including promising her that he'd tell his older brother Eric that she had a crush on him.

Evan remembered the day well. He'd been sworn to secrecy. It was Valentine's Day in their junior year when Drew came to Ben and begged him to tell Eric, who was two years older, that it was her who'd left the little stuffed teddy bear on his desk in homeroom. Ben did it, even though Evan knew he would have rather punched his brother in the face. That night Eric called Drew, asked her out and they dated until finally, a year after Drew graduated, he asked her to marry him and Ben had lost his chance forever.

"Have you seen her?" Evan asked his friend now. "Drew, I mean."

"I know who you mean." He snatched the balloon out of Evan's hand and shoved it into the display before reaching for another one. "And no. I haven't. Eric called the other day, but I didn't answer."

Although it had never been spoken of, Eric's relationship with Drew had driven a wedge between the brothers. After the new couple had married and moved south, Ben had let their relationship all but drop off.

"I don't think Eric came."

That caused Ben to look down, but he didn't say anything.

"All of that was a lifetime ago," Evan said. "And you never know what the future can bring. It's never too late for love. Look at me and Cam."

Obviously eager for a subject change, Ben asked, "What's going on there? What did she say about school?"

Evan swallowed hard.

"You haven't told her yet, have you? You're such a chicken shit."

"It's not that."

"No?"

"I'm telling her tonight. In fact, I should get going. I promised her I'd pick up a pizza and bring it over. Apparently she met Steph at the salon today and well...I hear Cam got a new haircut."

Ben laughed and climbed down from the ladder. "No shit? I bet that didn't go well."

"Steph was never going to be..."

"Cam?" Ben punched him in the arm. "Go. I'll finish this. But make sure you tell her." Evan started to walk away, but he didn't miss Ben calling after him. "I mean it, Evan. Tell her."

CAM'S DAY couldn't get much worse, so with a few minutes before Evan had promised to come by with pizza, and Morgan tucked into her bedroom doing whatever it was she did in there with her earbuds shoved into her ears, Cam finally reached under the stack of books and magazines where she'd hidden the divorce papers.

She stared a long moment at the yellow manila envelope that contained the paperwork that would signify the end of her marriage. She sighed and dropped her head.

It was an indescribable feeling to hold such papers. She didn't know what she was supposed to feel.

Things hadn't always been bad between her and Ryan. When they'd first met, she'd been swept up by his charm and charisma. Everyone would turn and look when they walked into a room. When he spoke, he commanded the attention of everyone in the room and everyone wanted to be around him, be friends with him and just bask in the glow of who he was. And he'd chosen her.

Those early days, Cam had felt so loved and protected and...*wanted.*

It was everything she'd needed. She probably shouldn't have rushed into a relationship right away, and it wasn't really her intention. Not at all. But she also hadn't intended to get pregnant. After that, there hadn't been a lot of choices. Besides, things could have been worse than marrying an up-and-coming journalist with his sights on the news desk. And *he* wanted her.

Evan didn't.

That was how she'd justified her choices anyway. She'd been young, scared, and heartbroken. Ryan came along when she needed him and then there was Morgan.

Cam ripped open the envelope and drew the papers out

slowly. She took another deep breath and sat at the table. She'd been avoiding her lawyer's calls for weeks. It was time to get it finished up.

She flipped through the first few pages of the document that outlined their marriage: the date, location. A wave of unexpected sadness hit her and a tear dropped to the page, leaving a wet stain.

Cam had never intended for her life to turn out like this. Divorced in her thirties, a single mom. It didn't seem real.

But it was.

And she knew it was the right thing. Besides that, it was the only thing.

She took a deep breath, wiped her eyes and resumed reading.

Cam read through everything once. Then, with her hands shaking, again.

And then she picked up the phone and called her lawyer.

"I've been trying to reach you."

"He can't do this."

"He can."

"No." Cam shook her head and stared at the papers she'd shoved to the other end of the table as if they were radioactive. "He can't do this to her." She glanced at the closed bedroom door.

"We can set it up like a regular doctor's appointment, Cam. She doesn't have to know."

Cam's heart fractured into a million pieces at the thought of her daughter ever finding out that her father was demanding a paternity test before he'd pay child support. It would break her. She shook her head and dropped her face into her free hand.

"But that's not everything, Cam. You need to be prepared for what will happen if Ryan is not the father."

"He is!" Her head snapped up and she lowered her voice.

"Of course he is," she hissed into the phone. "I would never have…no. Ryan is the father."

Once upon a time, she'd tried to convince herself that he wasn't the father and Evan was. It was a game she'd played with herself on the lonely nights when Ryan was working late, or…doing whatever he was doing. She'd rock baby Morgan, stare into her eyes and try to will them to be the same beautiful shade of green that Evan's were. She'd stare at her perfect little face and wish for something that could never be because it wasn't true.

She was sure of it.

"How could he even think something like that?"

But even as she spoke the words, she knew exactly how Ryan might have drawn that conclusion. It had never been a secret that Evan was her first love and Ryan knew the timeline was tight. She'd never tried to hide it. But she would never have deceived him. Or Evan.

"Bring her in," her lawyer said. "We'll set it up." Cam wrote down the lawyer's instructions and appointment times, and tucked the piece of paper into the envelope along with the offending papers.

She'd been right to ignore them.

"THIS WAS NICE."

Evan wrapped his arm around Cam on the couch and pulled her close. He'd brought over pizza, just like he'd promised, and a bottle of wine for good measure. Morgan had joined them to eat, and happily, her good mood from earlier had continued into the evening. She'd even cracked a few jokes over the table. But despite the easy atmosphere, Cam had seemed distracted and distant.

He was pretty sure he knew why, and he'd been waiting

ELENA AITKEN

until Morgan retreated back to the privacy of her bedroom before he said anything. He kissed the side of her head. "I like your hair."

She shook her head. "I'll be honest, it's not exactly what I was going for. But it's not terrible."

"It's not terrible at all." Evan leaned forward and grabbed the bottle of wine so he could top up her glass. "She may not be good at hiding her jealousy, but she is a good stylist."

That made Cam laugh. "True. I think she was trying to piss me off, but in the end, her pride at doing a good job won out. Lucky for me."

"I really do like it," he said truthfully. "I hope it wasn't too strange to run into her. I probably should have warned you."

"Warned?" Cam raised an eyebrow. "Like, is she unstable or something? Will she come after me with her scissors again?"

"No." He laughed. "Nothing like that. It's just...Steph always thought we were more serious than we ever were. I was always really upfront with her, but I think secretly she was hoping that one day I'd change my mind and..."

"You'd get married?"

He shrugged. But that was exactly it. He'd never thought of Stephanie as more than a fling. He liked her and they had a good time together, but it had never been serious. Not for him anyway. There was only one woman he would ever have considered marrying, and she was sitting in front of him.

He didn't tell her that.

"Anyway, it was never a big thing. And it's totally over. "

"Well, I hope so." She smiled, but it still didn't reach her eyes. "Considering that..." She used her finger to gesture between them. "But really, it's all good. I'm not bothered by it. I think I can handle an ex-girlfriend. I'm a big girl."

"You are." He kissed her and let his lips linger on hers for a moment before he pulled away. "Are you okay tonight? You

174

seem a little distracted. I thought maybe it was the whole haircut thing, but...is everything okay?"

"It is." She smiled. "It was. But it's fine. I'm fine. Honestly. It's just been a really crazy few days."

Evan sat back and examined her. There'd been a time when he would have known just by looking at her whether she was keeping something from him or not. That was no longer the case. But it was still early days in their rekindled relationship, so he wouldn't push her.

"Well, it doesn't have to be crazy right now. Come here." He gestured to the space between his legs so she could position herself for a shoulder rub. She snuggled in and Evan went to work releasing some of the tension from her shoulders. Cam closed her eyes and every once in a while there was a moan of pleasure when he hit a particularly tight spot.

He rubbed and massaged for a few minutes until he could feel her muscles relax. Her head dropped low and Evan looked past her to the coffee table and a stack of photos. "Are those yours?" He paused his rubbing and reached out to pick up the pictures.

Cam's eyes opened. "They're nothing. I was just fooling around with some new techniques I've been wanting to try."

"They're beautiful." He meant it. "I honestly never would have thought to photograph that old broken-down fence like this. You have a real eye for it."

She shrugged, but he could tell she was pleased. "Can I show you something else?"

"Of course."

She hopped up from the floor and retrieved her camera bag from the closet. "I haven't had these ones printed yet, because I didn't think I should. At least not yet." Cam powered up her camera and set it to the slideshow function so Evan could flip through the shots.

He didn't say anything right away, looking first through all the pictures, and then flipping through them again quickly until he landed on his favorite. "These are amazing, Cam. I didn't know you took portraits."

The camera was full of pictures of people, most of whom Evan recognized from around town. She'd captured her subjects in a wide array of human emotions. Some were laughing, some crying, some just looking pensive or deep in thought. The one thing Cam's subjects had in common, however, was that they didn't know they were being photographed.

Evan turned the camera so that Cam could see his favorite picture. "This one is stunning."

She smiled sadly and nodded.

"She's so beautiful." The picture was one of Morgan sitting at the kitchen table. Her head was tipped down, looking at whatever books were in front of her. Her hair fell over her face, partly shading her from the camera and although she looked to be studying, it was clear that she wasn't. The look in her eyes was what caught Evan's attention. At the young age of only fifteen, she looked like she'd already lived a lifetime.

"She's hurting so much," Cam said. "I wish I could take it all away."

Evan put the camera down and pulled her close. He knew that feeling well. He'd seen the hurt in Cam's eyes. The same pain and struggle that she saw in her daughter and more than anything, he wished he could take it away for her.

They stayed that way for a few minutes. "Have you ever thought about doing this professionally? I mean, I know you talked about it as a kid, but..." He gestured to the camera on the couch cushions next to them. "You're so talented. I think you could really make a go of it."

"Honestly? I have."

"Really?"

She nodded and in that moment looked so young and

excited, it brought back memories of the Cam he'd known so long ago.

"When Morgan was born, Ryan bought me my first digital camera and I just couldn't stop taking pictures. She was the perfect subject. And of course as she got older, I learned more and I didn't just take pictures of her. I mean…" She laughed. "I took a lot of pictures of her. But I also started messing around with landscapes and macro images. I guess I always kind of dreamed that maybe I could sell some prints or even take pictures of other people's babies. I love it. It's felt really good to pick up my camera again. It got so busy with the move and everything, I kind of forgot how much I loved taking pictures."

"Why don't you do it then?"

"I am doing it." She pointed to the camera and gave him a *duh* look.

"No." Evan sat up, excited about the idea that was coming to him. "I mean, like really do it. Why don't you take pictures for a living? You could set up a little studio and show your work. I bet people would—what?"

She was shaking her head and laughing. "You can't really be serious, Evan? It's not that easy."

"Sure it is." He was on his feet now. "You already have the talent. That seems to me like it would be the hard part."

"And where would I display my pictures? Where would I set up this *studio space*?" She used her fingers to make air quotes. "Never mind the time. I'm doing it in my spare time now, but that's not always so easy to come by. I have to work. I have bills to pay."

"But that will come, Cam. If you start following your passion, you won't need to work as much. Not as a waitress anyway. You're an amazing photographer." He was pacing now, getting more and more worked up at the idea of Cam following her dream and becoming a photographer. *Why couldn't she see that not only was it an option, but it was the only option?* "Just think about it, Cam."

"I have thought about it." She laughed and reached out an arm for him. "It would be amazing. Of course it would. And maybe if I was young and not a mother and…well, a million things. But it doesn't matter."

He sat next to her again, but he was far from finished with the conversation.

"I'm not giving up on this." He kissed her on the cheek. "I think it's important to chase your dreams."

Was that it? Was he so excited about the idea of Cam pursuing her passion because it would make it easier for him to pursue his? He swallowed hard. It was time to tell her about his acceptance to college. "Have I ever told you about my dream?"

Chapter Fourteen

AFTER THE LAST few days she'd had, the very last thing Cam wanted to do was get dressed up and go to the anniversary dance at the high school. She'd managed to avoid all of the other meet-and-mingle events by picking up a last minute shift at work, but there was no way she'd be able to get out of the dance. Not without her friends descending upon her.

Now that she was home from what turned out to be a very slow shift—it seemed everyone was partaking in the festivities and not in the local skin show—all she really wanted to do was put her sweatpants on, climb into bed, and forget all about everything. Instead, she had a quick shower, blew out her now, much shorter hair, and slipped into the dress Amber had so generously bought her.

"Wow, Mom."

Startled, she turned to see Morgan standing in the bath-room door, looking pretty wow herself.

"Oh, Morgan." She brought her hand to her mouth and willed herself not to cry at the image of her daughter in some-thing besides a black t-shirt, ripped jeans or a hoodie. "You look so…well…oh."

She pulled her daughter into a hug and for the briefest moment before Morgan pushed her away again, reveled in her closeness. The moment was gone all too soon and Morgan slipped from her arms.

"I really like you in blue." Cam had been surprised when she'd seen the outfit Morgan had picked out, but pleasantly so. The blue tank top brought out the brilliant color of her eyes and the skinny black pants complemented her curves perfectly.

Cam leaned against the doorjamb and watched as Morgan ran a brush through her hair and proceeded to apply makeup. She bit her tongue from suggesting that she go a little lighter on the eyeliner.

Morgan shrugged at the compliment.

"Hey." Cam stood up straight. "I just had an idea. Stay right here."

"As if I had anywhere else to go."

Cam went to the front closet and dug out a box she'd shoved at the back and pulled out a pair of black strappy heels. She was going to wear them, but she had another pair that would go just as well with her dress. She took the shoes to the bathroom and held them out for Morgan. "Do you want to wear these tonight? I think they'll look really good with—"

"Really?" Morgan spun around and moved to grab the shoes, stopping short as if Cam would snatch them back at the last minute.

"Yes," she said. "I think they'll look great on you."

Morgan's face split into a smile. "Yes. I totally want to wear them."

She slipped them on right there in the bathroom and at once stood inches taller than Cam. "They're perfect."

Cam blinked back a tear. "No, baby. You're perfect."

HER MOM MADE her drive to the dance with her, but to her surprise, Morgan didn't mind. Not really. Besides, the second they pulled up, Christy hijacked her mom so she was saved from the mortification of actually walking into the school with her. The whole idea of a high school anniversary party was still so completely lame to her, but really when there wasn't much going on in a backward town, in the middle of the sticks, maybe a fiftieth anniversary of a school was celebration worthy.

As far as Morgan was concerned, it just meant that her school was old.

But it probably wouldn't be too totally lame.

Not with Trent there.

She tried not to be all girly and freak out at the idea of seeing him and kissing him again. They hadn't kissed since the party at Jason's house. He'd held her hand and hugged her and…she assumed that meant they were *dating.* Or whatever.

"Holy shit, hottie!"

Morgan turned so quickly on her heel that she stumbled a bit. Fortunately she caught herself as Jess ran toward her. "Whatever," Morgan said. "Look at you."

"It's true." Jess did a little pivot and flicked her long hair back over her shoulder. "We're totally smoking. These guys aren't going to know what hit them."

"Where are they?" Morgan looked over the parking lot, which was full of students, past and present. Again, she was surprised by the sheer amount of people who'd come back to town just to celebrate an old school. "I thought Jason might have picked you up."

"Nope. My parents wanted to drive and *blah blah blah.* Let's go in. We need to put in our appearance."

"Appearance?"

"Oh yeah. You didn't think we'd be staying here all night, did you?"

She had, but she wasn't about to tell Jess that.

"Oh," Jess said. "I almost forgot." She dug into her purse and pulled out a flask.

"What's that?"

"Just a little party juice." She took a sip and handed it to Morgan. "Tonight is going to kick ass."

Morgan took the flask but hesitated before putting it to her lips.

"Have you ever had coconut rum before?"

Morgan shook her head.

"It's delicious and I promise you're not going to get drunk. Just a little buzz. It makes everything a little more fun. Have a sip and we'll go dance. You'll totally see."

What the hell. It wasn't as if anyone was going to notice if they had a few little sips of rum. Their parents were totally caught up in having their own reunion; nobody seemed to care at all about what they were doing. *And a few sips weren't going to hurt.* Especially if they made her less nervous around Trent. And Jess did say it would make things more fun.

She lifted the flask to her lips and took a drink.

THE GYM HAD BEEN COMPLETELY TRANSFORMED with more balloons than Cam believed possible. Even at their graduation dance there hadn't been so many balloons. Christy and her committee had done an amazing job. And she'd tell her that too, if she could find her friend. She'd lost track of her after running into her in the parking lot. The second they'd gone inside, Christy was off to tend to one task after another. Cam had done her best to help out, but after making sure the name tag table had fresh markers, she begged off and went in search of Amber and Drew.

"Isn't this insane?" Drew shook her head in wonder. "I think the last time I was in here was when we graduated."

"That for sure was the last time I was here," Amber said. "And it still smells the same."

Cam laughed because it was true. The underlying odor combination of dirty gym socks and sawdust that was uniquely the Timber Creek gymnasium still lingered in the air.

"I guess not much has changed." Drew shook her head. "Can you believe we were once as young as those kids?" She pointed to a group of students and they all shook their heads in disbelief. It seemed like a million years ago and at the same time, just yesterday.

"I can't believe so many people came back for this." Cam looked around again, pointing out Brenda, who'd been the class president, although Christy was convinced the vote was rigged and she should have won. Standing in the corner was Franklin, who'd played the tuba and never actually spoke to anyone except that one time he'd asked her out and she had to turn him down. He'd never made eye contact with her after that. And there was Grant, dancing with a man she didn't recognize. He'd pitched the winning inning of the state baseball championship and had secured himself as the hottest senior at Timber Creek High, with every available girl vying for his attention for the rest of the year. Cam was probably one of the few people who'd known back then that he was gay. He'd confided in her one day while they finished up a lab assignment. She'd kept his secret, even from Evan. It filled her with happiness to see he'd obviously found happiness.

"Hey," Amber said. "I ran into Ben Ross. Did you know he owned the Log and Jam?" She aimed the question at Drew, who nodded.

"Of course I knew. He's my brother in-law."

"He and Evan are still best friends," Cam offered. "Have you seen him yet?"

Drew shook her head. "No." A sadness clouded her eyes. "Things between Eric and Ben haven't been very good in a long time. And right now it's...well, Eric tried to reach out before I came and...it doesn't matter."

"That's too bad." Amber put her hand on Drew's arm. "I'm sorry they're not close anymore."

"Me too."

"And it's too bad he couldn't come. He should have been here, too."

"He would have liked to, it's just that...well...things are—hey, who is that?"

Amber and Cam both turned to see who she was pointing at.

Cam's mouth fell open.

Amber let out a low whistle that only the three of them could hear. "Whoever he is...holy shit. He looks like he could be on one of the covers of my books."

"Oh my God, yes!" Drew agreed.

The man in question wore a black button-up shirt that hugged his clearly defined muscles underneath, with equally well-fitting pants.

"Hey." Christy slid up behind them. "What are you guys staring at?"

"Who is that?" Amber wasn't shy about pointing directly at the man. "Because whoever he is, I think I may need to meet him."

Cam shot her a look of surprise. She'd never heard Amber talk like that about a man. Ever.

"You know exactly who that is."

"No, I assure you, I do not."

"That's Logan Myers."

Cam almost choked on the sip of punch she'd just taken. Drew gasped and Amber's hand shot out and smacked Christy on the arm.

"Ow."

"Sorry. But seriously. Logan Myers? As in, Junky's kid? No way."

Christy laughed but took a half step away from Amber. "He grew up all right, didn't he?"

"Wasn't he like six years younger than us?" Drew shook her head. "Little Logan?"

"He certainly doesn't look little now."

"No he doesn't." Evan appeared next to them. He slipped his hand into Cam's and squeezed.

"What's he like?" Amber directed the question to Evan.

"You should go introduce yourself and find out, Amber." He winked at Amber and turned to Cam. "Will you dance with me?"

"Of course."

The song was slow and when Evan wrapped his arms around her and started moving her around the gym floor, Cam felt all the tension ease out of her. She rested her head on his shoulder. When she closed her eyes, she could almost imagine they were seventeen again, with the cheesy love song in the background, the sweaty throng of people all around them, and Evan's familiar embrace.

"This is nice."

"Kind of like old times." He kissed the top of her head. "How many times did we dance like this over the years?"

"Too many to count." She smiled against his shoulder. "But this time Mrs. Hesterman isn't jabbing her ruler between us, telling us to back up two inches."

In response, Evan pulled her closer. "I'd like to see her try."

Cam's eyes flicked open. Across the dance floor, she could see Stephanie watching them, a sour look on her face. "Maybe there'll be someone else who wants to get between us."

He turned to look and then back to Cam. Evan smiled and immediately danced them to the far side of the gym. "Nothing will come between us, sweetheart. Especially not Stephanie. She'll be fine. Her feelings are just a little sore, but she knows as well as I do that she and I were never serious. Don't worry about her."

Oddly, Cam wasn't worried about Stephanie. But there were other things on her mind. She'd tried to put Ryan's outrageous claims and their impending trip back to Portland to prove herself out of her mind. But it wasn't just Ryan that was troubling her. Every step she and Evan took on the dance floor felt more and more like graduation.

Everything had seemed perfect that night. She'd never felt closer to him, more in love, more excited about their future. But the entire time they were dancing and partying, Evan kept a secret from her and he'd left her the very next day. For a future.

What about the future he was looking forward to now? She'd tried to be excited when he told her about his application to college and that he'd been accepted. And she was happy for him. She really was. But more than that, she was terrified.

Lorraine's words rang in her ears, like an echo that wouldn't fade. *"He's worked too hard. It's not the right time for him to be tied down. It wasn't then, and it isn't now."* No matter what, Cam would never keep Evan from living his dreams.

"Hey." Evan tipped up her chin so she was looking at him. "Relax. Everything is perfect tonight."

Perfect. She wanted to believe that. She really did. But if she told Evan what was really worrying her, about what his mom had said…and about the paternity test…well, she just couldn't. It wasn't fair. And it definitely wasn't perfect.

"Have I told you how gorgeous you look?"

She smiled. He had, at least a dozen times.

Everyone was having a good time. Cam didn't want to bring drama into what was otherwise a fun day for everyone. And judging by whatever was going on with all her friends, it was a day they all needed to cut loose and relax. She forced a smile on her face and let Evan spin her around the dance floor as the song changed to something more upbeat.

When the song changed again, and they slowed their pace once more, Evan pulled her in close and kissed the top of her head. It was hard to imagine there had ever been a time when they hadn't been close this way. Being with him in their old high school gym, it was as if all the years didn't matter. And maybe they didn't. Maybe none of it mattered. If she closed her eyes, she could pretend that everything really was perfect.

"I could stay like this forever," she murmured into his chest.

"Mmmm."

"Cam?" A voice that sounded vaguely familiar intruded on their peace. "Cam Riley?"

Chapter Fifteen

EVAN RELUCTANTLY LIFTED his head to see Shelby, Jess Johnson's mom, next to them on the dance floor. He took a step back.

"Cam Riley?"

"Yes." Cam looked from Shelby to Evan, clearly unsure of who she was.

"Cam, you remember, Shelby, Jess's mom. Morgan's new friend."

"Oh my goodness." Cam's face split into a smile. "Of course. It's been so long, I'm sorry. I should have—"

"It's nice to see you, Cam." Shelby wasn't smiling. "And I'm so sorry to interrupt, but I was wondering if you'd seen the girls."

"The girls?" Cam turned to scan the room. "I'm sure they're just dancing—"

"They're not." Shelby shook her head. "I've been looking for Jess. I wanted a picture of the two of us under the—it doesn't matter. I can't find her and she's not answering her phone."

Cam dropped Evan's hand and looked around the busy gym in earnest. "I don't see them…but I'm sure…"

"Why don't you call Morgan's phone?" Evan began to lead the women to the edge of the dance floor, but Cam had already pulled out her cell phone.

"It's going straight to voicemail." She looked directly at Evan. "Why would she have her phone off?"

Evan's senses were on full alert, but he wasn't yet worried. Not really. "Have you seen Jason Sinclair or Trent Butterfield?" He directed the question at Shelby. "I'm willing to bet the girls are with them."

"With Jason?" Shelby shook her head. "I didn't think they were dating anymore. Jess told me—"

Evan nodded. He remembered his promise not to tell the girl's parents about the party the weekend before, and maybe he still didn't have to. "I think they might still be seeing each other," he told Shelby. "And I'm sure they've probably just all gone—"

"Gone where?" Cam grabbed his arm. "Why would they have gone anywhere, Evan?"

"Because they're kids." He looked at the mothers, who clearly were working themselves up. "Don't you remember what—"

"No." Cam interrupted him. "You and I were very different kids, remember? I never would have gone off from a school dance."

It was true. He'd tried more than once to convince her to join him at a party at the lake instead of staying at the school dance, but Cam was a rule follower. A trait that Morgan clearly hadn't inherited.

"Okay, but—"

"Jess would." Shelby nodded. "She definitely would have gone if there was a party somewhere. Especially if she's dating Jason again. Damn kids."

Cam's eyes widened.

"I see Scotty and Ash," Shelby said. "I bet they know something. Hell, they probably bought the beer for him. I'll go ask them if they've seen Jason."

Evan shook his head. "That's probably true."

The minute Shelby was gone, Cam spun on him. "What do you mean that's probably true? Who are these kids, Evan? Parties? Beer?"

Evan put his hands on Cam's arms and squeezed. "It's fine, Cam. They're just being kids and I wouldn't worry about the beer. Morgan wouldn't drink it. She didn't have any last weekend and there's no—"

"Last weekend?" Cam took a step backward and Evan realized his slip. "What happened last weekend?"

"It's nothing."

"It's obviously something. What didn't you tell me, Evan? Was Morgan at a party?"

Trapped, he had no choice and nodded. "But she wasn't drinking," he said quickly. "And it was a small party. Just a few couples and—"

"Couples?"

Shit.

"What the hell, Evan? I'm her *mother.* You are supposed to tell me these things."

"Calm down." He tried to lead her out to the hall, but Cam shook her head.

"Don't tell me to calm down. Do you have any idea what it's like to be a parent? You have no idea what it's like to deal with this shit. And then to think you're making progress with your daughter only to hear about a whole other..." She waved her hand. "You don't get it. I can't believe you didn't tell me that this has happened before."

"This hasn't happened before." He leaned in and took her

hand, but she only pulled it away again. "And I'm sure she's fine, Cam. We'll find her. Don't worry."

She opened her mouth, but before she could say anything else, Shelby was back, a meek-looking girl in tow. "Tell Officer Anderson what you told me, Jann."

Faced with two angry, upset mothers, Evan decided it probably wasn't a good time to point out that he wasn't on duty.

The girl looked between the adults, clearly intimidated.

"You won't get in trouble," Evan said encouragingly. "We just need to know if everyone is okay."

"No," Cam interrupted. "We need to know where the hell the girls are."

Evan put his hand out to try to calm her, but it was a losing battle and he knew it.

"There's a party in the woods," Jann said. "Out by Ghost Lake."

Evan wasn't surprised. Ghost Lake was a favorite hangout for teenagers.

"What else, Jann?" Shelby urged the girl.

"They're going to kill me." She swallowed hard and looked at her feet. "They were drinking something. I don't know who was driving."

EVERYTHING WAS SPINNING, including the backseat of the car Morgan knew she shouldn't have been in. *Jason's? Trent's? No. It wasn't Trent's car; he was sitting next to her.* She had no idea whose car she was in.

But Trent was next to her. He had his arm around her. That felt good.

Really good.

She'd been having a good time at the dance and hadn't really wanted to leave. Dancing with Trent was nice.

"It'll be more fun to go to the lake," Jess had convinced her. "We always do it."

She'd handed her the flask of rum they'd been sharing all night and Morgan had taken another deep drink. Only it wasn't the same. Whatever was in the flask now stung her throat as it went down.

Jess laughed and told her Jason filled it up for them.

Morgan didn't want anything else to drink. She just wanted to get out of the car and make it stop spinning.

Finally, the door opened, and the shock of the fresh, spring air hit her face.

It felt so good.

Morgan was vaguely aware of leaning over Trent to get closer to the fresh air, and then he was moving and holding her hand, taking her with him.

"Come on, let's go sit by the fire."

Fire?

She remembered the fire. The last time they'd sat by a fire together, he'd kissed her. She wanted to do that again.

They were walking and she was trying not to stumble over the rough ground in her mom's high heels.

Mom.

She'd be so pissed at her if she knew she left the dance.

But she didn't have to know.

Jess promised they'd go back before it was over so that their moms never found out.

Morgan pushed aside any thoughts of her mom and focused on the moment. The moment that included Trent. That was a much better thing to focus on.

She threaded her arm through his and laughed as she tripped over a branch. He held her tight and led her to a grassy spot by the roaring fire.

"You look really nice tonight." Trent smiled and Morgan's heart did a weird little flip. She'd never had a boy look at her like that. Hell, she'd never had a boy interested in her at all before. "I like the blue. It's my favorite color."

She giggled then immediately slapped a hand over her mouth so she didn't sound stupid. "I like you."

Too late for not sounding stupid.

But if Trent noticed he didn't seem to care. He leaned in, cupped her cheek and kissed her, and the world was spinning again. Only this time it was for a completely different reason.

Morgan had no idea how long they kissed, or when another drink got put into her hand, or how long they'd been by the lake. The time passed in a swirl of laughter and alcohol. She couldn't remember ever having such a good time. When Jess appeared in front of her, extending a hand down to where she sat, Morgan grabbed it and was pulled up into a hug from her new best friend.

"Let's go swimming," Jess announced.

"Swimming?" Morgan's head swiveled around to stare at the lake. "In there?"

"Of course, silly. It's the only place to go." Jess was pulling at her. Morgan waved good-bye to Trent as she was pulled closer to the water's edge. "Let's leave our clothes here."

"Clothes?"

"You don't want them to get wet, do you?" Jess laughed and Morgan joined in, the idea of her clothes getting wet suddenly hilarious. Of course she didn't want them to get wet.

Together the girls stripped their clothes off down to their underwear, left them in a pile and then, hand-in-hand, went running into the water, screaming and laughing the entire time.

It might be almost summer, but the mountain lake was still freezing cold and it took her breath away, but with Jess yelling encouragement, Morgan moved a few more steps before she let go of Jess's hand and dove in.

As soon as she broke the surface, Morgan gasped and

shrieked out. "It's so cold! Holy shit!" She laughed and splashed around to keep herself warm.

It took her a few moments to realize that Jess wasn't laughing and splashing with her.

Jess wasn't there.

Morgan spun in the water and scanned the surface for her friend. "Jess? You chicken," she called toward the shore. She must have chickened out at the last minute and let Morgan run in by herself. "Get in here."

But Jess wasn't on the shore. The shoreline was empty, the pile of clothes a dark, shadowy lump where they'd left them under a tree.

"Jess?" Morgan's voice was little more than a whisper and then, as she realized what might have happened, louder. "Jess! Jess!" She splashed and screamed for what felt like forever, trying in vain to find her friend.

Finally there were more voices. More yelling. More splashing.

And then arms around her, pulling her out of the water and wrapping her in a coat before holding her tight. A hand stroking her wet hair. "It's okay, Morgan. It's going to be okay." Soothing words being muttered in her ear.

A familiar voice. A comforting voice.

Unwilling and unable to accept what was happening, Morgan squeezed her eyes shut and let her mom hold her.

CAM WAITED until she was sure Morgan was asleep before backing silently out of the hospital room. The paramedics had insisted on bringing her in for observation, a fact Cam was grateful for. She wrapped her arms around herself and leaned against the wall.

She'd never been so terrified in her whole life than when she'd heard her daughter's voice screaming out in the night.

Evan had driven them out to the lake in his truck. There were kids everywhere. Music played from a car stereo. A giant bonfire illuminated the scene, and the lake beyond. They'd only just started looking for Morgan, when Cam heard her scream out Jess's name.

Evan had heard it too. After that, everything happened in a blur. Cam followed Evan to the water's edge, where he immediately ran into the water—understanding on some sort of level that must have been instinct exactly what was going on.

Morgan was still screaming and splashing and Cam didn't hesitate. She splashed through the shallows and pulled her daughter to her before leading her out to the beach, where someone handed her a jacket to wrap Morgan in.

In the few moments they'd been there, everyone, it seemed, was now on the beach. People were yelling. Shelby, Jess's mom, was crying. It was all a blur. Cam stood and watched everything unfold as she held tight to her daughter, shielding her from everything.

Evan pulled Jess from the water and began CPR.

The police showed up, along with an ambulance. Thank God Evan had called in the party on their way to the lake.

Shelby fell to her knees in the sand when Jess coughed and spat out water. Cam's heart hurt for the other mother, and she wanted to go to the woman, but she couldn't leave Morgan. Thankfully, Jess was loaded into the waiting ambulance and together, mother and daughter were whisked away.

Morgan had been assessed at the hospital, and despite having a blood alcohol level that was way too high for a girl her age—not that *any* level would have been acceptable—she was going to be fine.

Cam hadn't had a minute to digest everything that had

happened. She needed to process, but she knew if she did, she would fall apart. And she couldn't do that here. Not now.

She dropped her head to her chest. Cam didn't see Evan until he spoke. "Hey. How's Morgan?" He wrapped his arms around her and Cam let him hold her for a moment. It felt good to be in his arms. To not have to hold herself up, even for a moment. It had been a whirlwind after they left the lake. Evan had driven her to the hospital, following the ambulance. After they arrived, he volunteered to deal with the police officer who had a few questions, and they'd been separated ever since.

"She's fine." Cam nodded. "She's going to be fine. I haven't heard anything about Jess." She brought her hand to her mouth and swallowed back a sob. She couldn't lose it. Not yet.

"Jess will be okay." He released her from his embrace and took her hand. Evan led her to a nearby bench. "She hit her head when she dove into the lake and because of the alcohol in her system, she didn't react the way she should have. She took in a lot of water, but she'll be okay."

The impact of what Evan was saying crashed through her. "Oh my God. She could have—" She shook her head. "That could have been Morgan. We're so lucky. We're just all so lucky. They never should have been there, Evan."

"They're just kids." He shook his head. "They were just doing what kids do."

He still didn't get it.

"No!" She yanked her hand away from his. "Not all kids do that, Evan. You can't keep saying that. You can't excuse their behavior because they're kids." She couldn't sit anymore. Cam paced in front of the bench. "You just don't get it, Evan. And maybe you'll never get it. You think that's how all kids behave because it's how *you* acted. And even if that was true, it didn't have to be like this tonight. You should have told me about the party last weekend. You never should have kept it from me. Maybe if I had known, none of this would have—"

"Cam, that's not fair."

"It isn't?" She stopped in front of him. "What do you know about fair? Do you think pulling your drunk fifteen-year-old daughter out of a lake while her friend almost dies next to her is *fair*? Because that isn't fair. You couldn't possibly understand, Evan."

He jumped to his feet. "Why can't I understand, Cam?" He gripped her arms and forced her to look him in the eye. "Why can't I understand how horrible everything was tonight?"

"Because you don't have children."

He dropped his hands, releasing her arms and took a step back.

"Don't I?"

Cam blinked hard. And then again. "Pardon?"

"Don't I have children, Cam?"

"I don't know what you're talking about." But she did, and the realization of what he was asking her made her stomach roil. *He thought the worst of her, just like Ryan did.* She'd hoped that Evan was different. She'd hoped and *believed* that he knew her better and knew she'd never in a million years keep something like that from him. But he wasn't different. All this time, he hadn't said a word, but he thought that she was capable of letting another man raise his baby. She stood in front of him, but could no longer feel her legs beneath her.

"Is Morgan mine, Cam?"

The second he said the words out loud, her blood roared in her ears, drowning out the sounds of the hospital around them. Her legs wanted to buckle. She couldn't feel her fingertips. Somehow, unbelievably, she stayed standing.

"How could you ask me that?"

His voice was quiet, but firm. "Tell me the truth." He swallowed. "The timing…after you left…everything…is she… could she be…" His eyes pleaded with her, searching for something he wouldn't find.

"Do you really think that?" Her voice broke. "Do you really think that I would keep something like that from you? That I would keep you from your daughter?" Her heart squeezed and cracked. It hurt to breathe. "Is that what you think of me, Evan? Really?"

He didn't answer, but he didn't have to.

"I was young, and I made choices that I'm not proud of. Choices that led to the life I have now." She wished more than anything that Morgan *was* his daughter. She deserved a father that loved her, that wanted her and cared about her more than anything in the world. If Evan was her dad, things would be different. *A lot* different. Everything would be changed. The idea that he thought even for a minute that she could keep that from him, broke something inside her. She shook her head in a vain attempt to clear her thoughts.

"Cam. I—"

"No," she said softly. "Morgan is not your daughter." She looked into his eyes, at the man she thought she knew so well. But she'd thought that once before, too. And she'd been wrong then too. "So you can go." Each word she spoke caused a new and fresh pain in her chest. "There's nothing tying you down here, Evan. You have all the freedom you need."

His hand reached out to her, but then fell to his side.

"Leave." Her voice was barely a whisper, laced with a hurt she could hardly process. "Just like before." Cam turned and silently walked back into Morgan's room because there was nothing left to say.

Chapter Sixteen

THE SUNLIGHT CUT through the half-broken metal blinds that hung across from Morgan's bed, just as it'd done every morning for the last few days, as if the world outside with its blue, sunny skies had no idea that her entire world had ended.

She pulled the pillow over her head but it was immediately pulled away.

"Nope," her mom said. "Not today."

Morgan groaned and rolled over on her side.

"I mean it, Morgan. You need to get out of bed."

"I have a headache."

Her mom laughed. She *laughed*. As if it were funny that she'd drank too much and her friend had almost died. She shot straight up in her bed and almost told her mom what an unfeeling, heartless bitch her mom really was. But she didn't.

"Mom, please."

Cam sat on the bed, the flimsy mattress sinking a little. "Hey, I know it's been a rough few days but you can't hide forever." She stroked Morgan's arm over the blanket. "Besides, we need to leave for Portland this morning. Remember that doctor appointment I told you about?"

Morgan groaned. "I was literally just at the doctor."

"Different doctor."

Her mom wouldn't look at her. When she'd first told her about taking a trip to Portland, Morgan hadn't really thought much of the lame story she'd given her about needing Morgan to have her yearly checkup at some sort of specific doctor. She probably could have pushed for more details then, but she didn't really care. She cared even less about it now, except for the fact that it meant she had to get out of her bed.

"Come on. We leave in an hour. Besides, I know you want to get out of bed because that means you'll get your phone back."

Her mom grinned at her because she knew she'd won. Morgan had been asking for her phone ever since coming home from the hospital. Her mom had been holding it hostage. "Really?" She eyed her mom suspiciously. It seemed too easy.

"Really. But you have to be showered, packed for an overnight and in the car."

Morgan groaned again, but the second her mom left the room, she rolled out of bed.

———

"AS PROMISED." Forty-five minutes later, as they pulled away from the curb, her mom handed Morgan her cell phone.

Morgan stared at it for a minute instead of immediately powering it on. She already knew from her mom that Jess was okay. She had a concussion and she was grounded, but she was okay.

Thank God.

Morgan didn't remember much from the night of the dance. Only snatches of memory came to her.

The taste of the rum. The light of the fire. The cold of the lake water. The sounds of her own screaming.

She squeezed her eyes shut and tucked her phone away. She'd check it later.

Her mom squeezed her thigh. "It'll be okay."

Morgan nodded. "I know." But nothing felt as if it would be okay again. Or at least, nothing felt as if it would be the same. She rested her head against the window and pretended to sleep for the four-hour drive.

She must have actually fallen asleep because when Morgan opened her eyes again, they were pulling into a parking lot she didn't recognize. Her mom smiled and babbled on about health checkups and other stuff that Morgan knew was complete and total bullshit. She didn't know why they were there, but she had a pretty good idea and she was going to find out.

As soon as they were seated in the waiting room, Morgan asked outright. "Why are we here?" Her mom opened her mouth, but Morgan stopped her before she could continue. "Please don't lie to me, Mom. I think after everything that's happened, I can handle a little bit of truth, don't you?"

Her mom squeezed her eyes shut and dipped her head. Finally she nodded and looked up. "Yes," she said. "I think you can. And you're right, Morgan. I shouldn't lie to you. I think I struggle sometimes with how much is okay to tell you."

Morgan nodded. "I'm not a kid anymore. Not really."

"I know." Cam smiled and took her hand. "Your dad just wanted some tests done before we signed our divorce papers."

Morgan let that sink in. She wasn't a fool, and she'd watched enough late-night television to know what kind of tests her mom was talking about. "Okay," she said after a minute. "But it's kind of a big waste of everyone's time, isn't it?"

Her mom shot her a look, obviously surprised that she wasn't upset. "I sure think so."

Morgan nodded. "Me too. After all, I have his eyes."

"Sweetheart, I'm so sorry all of this is happening." Her mom took her hand and Morgan could tell she was trying not to cry.

To her surprise, Morgan didn't feel sad about it the way she should have upon discovering that her father wanted a paternity test. *Shouldn't she be upset? Or hurt? Or…something?*

"It's okay, Mom. Really. I guess just with everything that's happened, this doesn't seem so important." She shrugged. "You know, in the big picture, it's not a big deal."

Her mom shook her head and smiled. "Sometimes you really surprise me, Morgan." Her mom squeezed her hand in hers. "You really are growing up. That was a really mature thing to say."

Morgan dropped her head and stared at her hands.

"None of this is fair to you, Morgan," her mom said. "I'm so sorry. I wish things could be different. But it'll be over soon and then you and your dad can…"

Her mom trailed off and Morgan didn't bother trying to finish the statement, because she didn't know how either.

EVAN HAD some vacation days banked up, and no better time to use them. He couldn't even think straight after everything that had gone down with Morgan and Cam, so he did the only thing he could think of. He went fishing.

For two days straight, he got up at dawn, went to the river, and walked mile after mile, chucking line and thinking.

Fishing never failed to sort out his thoughts, but after the second day, his feet hurt, his arm was sore, and he still didn't have anything sorted out.

Morgan wasn't his. He'd *known* that. Of course he did. He still couldn't believe he'd even asked her. It just slipped out.

Maybe it was because of the heightened emotion of the

night, or maybe it was just wishful thinking, but he'd never intended to ask Cam such a thing.

He'd known in his heart all along that she wasn't his but still, it was funny how you could convince yourself of something just because you wanted it to be true.

And he did.

That was the part he couldn't sort out in his head. He'd somehow allowed himself to believe that there was a chance that Morgan could be his daughter and he'd liked it. *How different would life have been if Morgan was his?*

Would he have joined the army? The police force? It was impossible to know. What would it have changed now if Cam had told him that she was his daughter?

Is that what she'd meant? Morgan wasn't his, so he was free to go to college, move away and chase his dreams?

If he closed his eyes, Evan could still see the pain on Cam's face as she'd said those words to him. Which, if he was honest with himself, was the real reason why he'd barely slept in days.

Dammit.

Being alone with his thoughts on the river wasn't helping, so looking for a change of pace to at least keep his mind busy, Evan decided he might as well tackle the to-do list over at his mom's place. He still called her every few days, but it had been a few weeks since he'd popped in. It was past time to put in an appearance. He stopped at the hardware store to pick up a can of stain for the fence boards and was unloading his supplies into the driveway when his mother returned from the grocery store.

"Well, look what the cat dragged in."

"Hi, Mom." He gave her a kiss on the cheek and took her bags from her. "I thought I'd get to that fence you need stained. If that's okay with you?"

"Of course." She led the way up the walk into the old house and the kitchen that hadn't changed since Evan was a kid. "You know I always like to see you. And it's been awhile." She looked at him sideways and raised her eyebrow.

He loved his mother, but sometimes it was exhausting to be the only child of a widowed mother. "Sorry I haven't been around much. I've been busy, Mom."

"With Cam Riley?" She poured him a glass of iced tea and set it on the table, an invitation to sit.

Evan nodded and took a sip of the tea. "Yeah. She moved back to town."

"And you've been busy with her again?"

There was something in his mother's voice. He set the glass down and looked at her.

"What are you trying to say?"

Lorraine shrugged. "I'm just saying that you've been busy with her. At least that's what I assume. I don't know, since you haven't been by to see me."

"Don't guilt me, Mom." He shook his head and took a deep drink of the tea. "That's bullshit."

"Don't use that language with me."

He ignored her comment. "I thought you liked Cam," he said instead. "Why do you care if we've been seeing each other again? I thought you'd like that." Evan actually did think his mom would have liked to see him dating Cam again. They'd always gotten along so well. His mom welcomed Cam like her own daughter: having her for dinner, helping in the garden, and even shopping together sometimes. It seemed strange for that to be any different now.

"I like Cam well enough," his mom said. "I just don't think it's the right time for you to be dating anyone right now. I thought you had plans? And now that you've been accepted to school…" Lorraine shook her head. "It's not really the right time to start up with someone now, is it? You need your freedom. Nothing to tie you down."

Evan almost choked on his drink. "What did you say?"

Lorraine paused with a can of mushroom soup in her hand. "Pardon?"

"I asked you what you just said." He put his drink down, and pushed the glass away as if it held some offensive substance. "About being tied down."

His mom turned around slowly, still holding the can. "I just said that at this time of your life, it's fortunate that you're not tied down with responsibilities. It gives you a certain amount of—"

"What were your *exact* words?"

Lorraine shook her head and laughed. "I don't remember, Evan. It doesn't matter."

"It does."

And it did. Because he'd just heard the *exact* same thing out of Cam's mouth.

"Mom?" He narrowed his eyes as a thought popped into his head. "Have you seen Cam since she's been back in town?"

It was slight, and he might have missed it had he not been watching closely, but his mom flinched.

"Mom?"

"I might have run into her outside of Daisy's the other day." Lorraine turned her back and resumed putting her groceries away.

He was on his feet and next to her in the next beat. "And what did you say to her?"

She blinked up at him but didn't answer the question.

"Mom?" Evan took the can she was holding and placed it deliberately on the counter. "Tell me what you said to her."

Lorraine sighed and crossed her arms over her chest. "I might have mentioned that it wasn't a good time for you to get involved with anyone."

Evan felt as though he'd been punched in the gut. He swallowed hard. "Did you tell her that I needed my freedom?"

"Yes." She nodded readily. "You've just been accepted to college, Evan. It's not a good time for you to be tied down."

Tied down.

There it was again.

He took a step backward. Cam's voice rang in his ears: *"Leave. Just like before."*

Just. Like. Before.

The room spun and he needed to sit. Somehow he made it to the table, where he put his head on the chipped Formica. *What had happened years ago?* He hadn't told Cam he was joining the army—that was a bad decision, but he'd always intended to come home and ask her to marry him the first chance he got. When he had something to offer her. When he was worthy of her. But she'd been gone. His mother told him that when she'd stopped by the house, she was so angry with him for leaving that she never wanted to see him again. She was going to start over on the coast without him.

He'd been so heartbroken at the time, he'd never questioned his mom's story. Especially when he found out Cam was pregnant and getting married. He'd assumed it was true. Why wouldn't he have?

"Mom?" He shook his head. "What did you tell Cam?"

She sighed, clearly exasperated with the conversation. "Evan Anderson, I just finished telling you what I said. I don't know what—"

"No," he interrupted. "Years ago. When I left to join up. You told me Cam came by the house." He lifted his head and stared at her, watching her eyes. "What did you say to her?"

"Evan." She shook her head and waved her hand in an effort to dismiss him. "How can I be expected to remember what I said all those years ago?"

"Try."

It must have been the ice in his voice, because she stopped fussing and froze to the spot.

In an instant, the stubbornness drained from her small body. Her voice was small, almost pleading with him when she spoke again. "Evan. It's not…"

"Tell me, Mom. What did you say?"

His mother aged at least ten years in front of him. She shook her head from side to side, but finally opened her mouth to speak. "I told her you didn't love her and that's why you'd left."

The breath rushed from his lungs. "You told her what?"

"You have to understand, Evan. I was just trying to do what was best for you." She spoke quickly, her hands wringing and twisting together. "You were young and you were finally going to get your life on track. I didn't want to take a chance that you would throw it all away for a girl. You had a chance to finally make something out of your life."

"How could you?"

"You don't know what it was like for me," she cried. "I was alone. A single mom with no one to help me. I worked two jobs, Evan. All I ever wanted was for you to grow up and be okay. And then finally…you had a chance, Evan. I wasn't going to let you waste it. Not for a girl."

"I was doing it all for her, Mom. For *us*."

He took another moment to let everything he'd just learned absorb. Around him, he was vaguely aware that his mother was prattling on about how she'd only done what she'd done for him and for his future, but he was no longer listening. *Everything that had played out over the last sixteen years didn't have to. None of it should have happened.*

But he didn't blame his mom. Sure, he was angry. And he probably would be for a while. But it wasn't her fault. If he'd been upfront with Cam from the beginning, and told her exactly what she meant to him and what he was willing to do for her—for *them*—none of it would have happened. It was his fault.

It had always been his fault.

Finally, Evan stood and pushed the chair back.

"Evan. Don't go," his mother pleaded. "Not like this. Please."

He shook his head in response and walked to the door.

"But what about school?" She hurled the question at him. "Don't you understand? Don't you see? What about your dreams, Evan?"

He turned slowly and looked at his mother with a mixture of sadness and pity for her that she might never understand. "Cam *is* my dream, Mom. She always has been."

And it was about time she knew it, too.

THE EXAM HAD ONLY TAKEN a few minutes. Especially when Cam explained to the doctor that there was no need for any pretense. Morgan knew why they were there and she was fully cooperative.

After the blood was drawn, Cam took Morgan to a cafe across the street. The technician had told them they'd have the results in a few hours, but Cam didn't need them. She knew who Morgan's father was. She always had.

"You okay, sweetie?" Cam put their drinks on the table and slid into the seat across from her daughter. Morgan's phone, still not powered on, sat in front of her. "You still haven't turned your phone on."

Morgan shrugged in response. "I'm not sure I want to."

"Who are you avoiding?"

"Everyone." She sighed and added, "Jess. Trent. Dad."

"That's everyone." Morgan's lip twitched up into a little smile and Cam considered it a win. "Jess is probably still grounded," Cam said. "And she's probably just as scared to face reality as you." Everything she said was true. Cam had called Shelby the day before and they'd had a long talk about both their daughters, who were good kids, but had made some bad choices. She tried not to think of Evan telling her that exact thing. "And Trent…I'm sure he wants to talk to you, too."

Cam had to swallow hard. She still wasn't sure how she felt about Morgan dating, but everything she'd learned about Trent Butterfield in the last few days was pretty good. And he had come by the apartment more than once in an effort to see Morgan, so as far as boys went, he probably wasn't too bad. "As for your dad…" Cam had a lot less advice to give on that particular subject matter. Instead, she reached over and squeezed Morgan's hand. "You guys will sort it out. I know you will. Things are just confusing for him right now with the divorce and the new baby and…" She paused to collect herself. It didn't get any easier talking about Ryan and his new life, but as Morgan's mother it was her job to make it as okay as she could.

"It's okay, Mom." Morgan released her hand and picked up her hot chocolate. "I think I've decided to tell him how I feel."

"Really?"

Morgan laughed. "Don't sound so surprised. Aren't you always telling me it's not good to bottle up my feelings?"

"I do." Cam sat back, surprised. "I just didn't think you were listening."

Morgan shrugged. "Sometimes."

Cam grinned and stirred sugar into her coffee. They sat in silence for a few minutes and it was Morgan who spoke next.

"I'm okay with it, Mom. Timber Creek, I mean. It's all right."

Cam looked up. "It's all right?"

"Yup." She nodded. "I mean, I know it hasn't been easy and I just…I just wanted you to know. I'm good with it. I think

I'll like living there. And I promise to try not to screw up again."

"You promise to *try*?" Cam laughed. "I guess that's all a mom can really ask for, hey, kiddo?" Cam caught herself and added, "Sorry. I know you don't really like it when I call you that."

Morgan grinned over the edge of her mug. "Actually, I don't mind."

Cam thought her face might split from the smile she wore. She blew her daughter a kiss. "I love you."

"I know." Her daughter winked and added, "I love you too, Mom."

She didn't want to make a big deal of it, but it had been far too long since Cam had heard those words from her daughter. She looked down into her cup so Morgan wouldn't notice the unshed tears in her eyes.

"Is it okay with you if I sit out there and turn my phone on?" Morgan pointed to the deck off the back of the cafe. "I think I'm...well, I'm going to see if..."

"It's fine."

Morgan took her mug and her phone, and pushed out through the glass doors into the spring sunshine. Cam watched her for a minute and then turned back to her own drink. She glanced at her phone to check the time. Her lawyer was going to call her as soon as the results were in so she could sign the papers and put all of this behind her. Then maybe she could move on.

Whatever that looked like.

She couldn't think about it. Not yet. Just as she had for the last few days, Cam pushed thoughts of Evan and his hurtful words from her head. *One thing at a time.* She'd deal with that later.

Cam was so wrapped up in her thoughts that she didn't

notice the man standing over her until he spoke. "Is it all right if I sit down?"

Her head shot up and a million objections came to mind, but the look on his face stopped her. She glanced outside to see Morgan engrossed in her phone before she looked back to her soon-to-be ex-husband.

"What are you doing here?"

"Can I sit?" he asked again.

She had a feeling that whatever he wanted to say, he wasn't going to leave until he said it. She nodded and wrapped her hands around her mug, more to keep from reaching out and hitting him than anything else.

His actions were jerky and slow, as if he were incredibly uncomfortable. *Good*, she thought.

"I know this is…well, it's a lot of things," he said. "I saw your car outside and I just took a chance that you…" He took a breath and started over again. "I wanted to apologize, Cam."

Of all the things she expected to hear, an apology wasn't one of them.

He rubbed his hands over his face, mussing his always impeccable hair. It was then that Cam noticed for the first time how tired he looked, as if he'd aged at least ten years in the last few months.

"This isn't how I wanted everything to go down," Ryan said. "I hope you know I never meant to hurt you and especially not Morgan."

"You have a funny way of showing it. Because that's exactly what you did." Cam shook her head. "I'm not worried about myself, but Morgan…Ryan, you can't just—"

"I know." He held up a hand. "And I know she's mine. I do. Of course she's mine. I've always known. My lawyer insisted on this dumb test…I'm sorry to have to put you through it."

"It was never necessary, Ryan. That's the part that hurts the most." But it wasn't just Ryan who wasn't sure about

Morgan's paternity and if she was honest with herself, *that* was what hurt the most.

"I know." He reached out for her hand and then remembered himself. "And I'm sorry, Cam. I really am." He closed his eyes and sighed. "She was the reason you stayed."

Cam choked on the sip of coffee she'd just taken. It took her a moment to pull herself together. "Excuse me?"

"It was always him, Cam." She didn't even pretend to hide her shock of what he was saying. "I'm not stupid or blind. I was never going to measure up to him. And I stopped trying years ago."

She shook her head. "Why would you say that? I never—"

"You didn't have to." Cam had never seen Ryan look so defeated. "I knew when we met you were heartbroken. I'd like to think I didn't take advantage of you, but…well, that doesn't matter now. I was never going to be him, Cam. And we both knew it. I also knew that you'd never leave me. Because of Morgan. You're a good mother. You wouldn't have done that to her."

"That's not…" She didn't bother finishing the sentence.

"I'm sorry." He nodded. "I'm sorry I wasn't a better husband to you. I'm sorry I wasn't the husband you deserved." He dropped his head, and stared at the table top in front of them. When he looked up, his eyes glistened with unshed tears. She'd only seen Ryan cry once before, when his father died. "I'm sorry for so much," he said. "None of this should have happened." Cam wanted to say something, but she couldn't think of a damned thing to say. He was right. Even if she didn't want to admit it, even to herself, Ryan was right. She'd been in love with Evan, even on the day she married Ryan.

"I'm sorry, too," she said after a minute. "It wasn't fair of me. But I want you to know that I did love you. I mean, there was a time…"

"I know." He nodded. "I loved you too."

They stared at each other, a million things still unsaid.

Finally, Ryan sniffed and scrubbed at his face again. "Dammit, Cam. This is all such a mess and with Chastity and the baby…Christ. I swear I don't know how it all got so…" He chuckled a little. "This is all new to me and I just don't know… well, I'm trying to figure out how to balance everything and be a father to Morgan, a partner to Chastity, and a good dad to the new baby while still…well, working and…I know this is coming out of left field."

"It is." She wasn't going to let him off the hook so easily.

"I've been an ass."

"You have."

He nodded and attempted a smile. "I deserved that." She didn't disagree. "But I need you to know that I'm trying to change. I'm *going* to change. For Morgan and the new baby. I need to be the father I never was. I know that now."

"What changed?" He looked so vulnerable and sincere that more than anything she wanted to believe him, but a lot had happened between them. "Why now?"

He shrugged. "It's time. It's past time. And I know Morgan might never forgive me for not making her needs first and putting her through all this…" he waved his hand vaguely. "But I'm still going to try. She deserves better."

She nodded. It was the first thing Cam could really agree with him on. "She does."

"And I'm going to give it to her." He sat up straight, but Cam could see the uncertainty in the way he held himself. "And, well…I could really use some advice."

Cam looked at the man before her. The one she used to know so well. The one she'd shared so much of her life with. It was hard to reconcile the man she thought she knew with the one in front of her. There were still glimpses of the Ryan he'd been when they'd first married, but…he was different now. It was hard to look at him.

"I can't be that person, Ryan." She shook her head. "Not anymore."

"No, I know." He sat up and attempted a smile. "I guess I just thought we could be…well, that you and I could still be…"

"Friends?"

"Yes." Relief washed over his face. "I miss you, Cam. I miss talking to you, bouncing ideas off you and being friends. We had a lot of good times, didn't we?"

She nodded. "We did." She smiled sadly because she missed him too. Not the cheating, lying version of him but the version of him that would sit up late and binge watch Netflix shows with her, the version who would lay on the floor with their daughter and draw pictures of horses for hours, the version of him that had surprised them with a trip to Disneyland when Morgan was five. Of course they had a lot of good memories. Despite it all, you didn't stay married to someone for almost fifteen years, and not have good times. "But we can't be friends, Ryan," she said. "Not like we were. Not anymore."

His face fell. "But—"

"It can't be the same." She shook her head. "But I do hope we can stay friendly. Especially for Morgan." She glanced out to the patio where Morgan, still oblivious of the fact that her father was inside, now had her phone pressed to her ear, a smile on her face. "She's been through a lot. She really needs her dad."

Chapter Seventeen

IT HAD BEEN a long few days. After the results came in from the test, Ryan and Cam signed their papers together. They'd agreed on a fair divorce settlement that would mean money wouldn't be quite so tight anymore and while she probably wouldn't be able to quit her job, at least now there'd be a little breathing room.

True to his word, Ryan was trying to make an effort with his daughter, so Cam agreed to let Morgan spend the night with her dad. It was important for them to reconnect, and if Morgan was willing to forgive her dad for his absence, Cam was happy to allow them the time together. They had a long road of rebuilding a relationship in front of them.

There was no one from her old life in Portland she felt like calling. Besides, she needed the time alone to think about her next steps so she checked into a hotel and pampered herself with a long bubble bath and a glass of red wine, alone.

In the end, Cam didn't spend much time thinking about anything. She fell into a deep sleep and woke up late. There was one conclusion she had made, however. No matter what, Cam and Morgan were going to stay in Timber Creek.

There'd never been anywhere else that felt like home, and it was time she put down some real roots for both of them.

The next morning, after picking up Morgan, Cam took her time making the drive back to Timber Creek. It was a beautiful day, so close to the edge of summer, with a bright blue sky and the sun warming her arm through the window.

"How long till we get there?" Her daughter looked up from her phone.

Apparently Morgan didn't share her desire to take their time. "Are you in a hurry?"

"Kinda." She shrugged and looked back at her phone.

"Are you going to tell me why?" Cam kept her tone light, but didn't increase her speed.

"Well…" Morgan put her phone down. "I know I might still be in trouble, but I was kind of hoping that I could meet up with Trent for a little bit. He was really worried about me, and he actually wants to meet you properly because he feels partly responsible for—"

"What happened wasn't Trent's fault." Cam believed it, too. She'd done a lot of thinking about what Evan had said, about kids being kids. And although she didn't totally believe that all teenagers got into trouble, got drunk, and went skinny-dipping, she did believe that some did. And it didn't make them bad kids. It wasn't an easy conclusion to come to, but she was trying. And Cam knew that for all of their similarities, Morgan was a different person than she'd been when she was a teenager. For better or worse, she was going to make different choices. "And yes," she said to Morgan. "I'd really like the opportunity to meet him."

Her daughter's face broke into a wide smile. "Really? He's a nice guy. Honestly. And he's on the basketball team at school. You'll like him. He…"

Morgan chatted on about her new boyfriend, not leaving any detail out as she filled Cam in on everything she might need to know about the boy, and a lot of things she probably didn't. Cam didn't mind, though. Morgan was happy, and she was letting Cam into her life. Those two details were all that mattered.

For the rest of the drive, they took turns picking songs on the radio and singing loudly out of tune. By the time they rolled past the sign announcing their arrival in Timber Creek, Cam was happy but exhausted. All she wanted to do was pick up something for dinner and crash on the couch for the rest of the evening.

But Morgan had other plans.

"So, it's okay if I see Trent tonight?"

"It is." Cam nodded. "But you have school tomorrow, so not too late."

"Yeah. Sure." Morgan nodded absentmindedly as she was frantically tapping something into her cell phone. "Can you drop me off on Main Street? He's going to meet me there."

"Now?"

"Yeah." Morgan looked at her. "That's cool, right? Just across from the store."

"That's awfully specific." Cam stifled a yawn and shook her head in defeat. "Whatever." It would only take a minute. Besides, she could run into the grocery store and grab something for dinner. She steered the car to the right instead of going straight and made her way to the center of town.

"Just park here." Morgan jabbed her finger to an open spot. "It's right here."

"What's right here?" Cam put the car in park and eyed her daughter, who was acting stranger by the minute.

"Come on."

"On your *date*?"

Morgan didn't answer her because she was already out of the car and staring at the vacant storefront they'd parked in front of. Only it wasn't vacant. Cam's eyes widened at what she saw. *There was no way.*

Slowly, she made her way out of the car, never taking her eyes off the storefront and the display that occupied the window.

"What is…why is my…Morgan? What is this?" She looked to her daughter, who smiled wider than Cam could remember ever seeing.

"Do you like it?"

Cam's eyes floated back to the display that consisted of four oversized easels. Three of the easels held a print of one of her photographs propped up on them for the entire town to see; the fourth read: *Cam Riley Photography* . She'd never seen her pictures in such a large format before. They took her breath away. Cam's hand floated to her mouth and she took a step closer.

"How did this happen?"

Morgan ignored her question. "Do you like it?"

Cam nodded and took another step forward toward the storefront. "I don't understand."

"Maybe I can explain."

She turned to see Evan behind her. Her stomach did a weird flip thing that only annoyed her because she was still mad at him. No, not mad. *Hurt.*

"How did you…" She shook her head. There were too many questions. Too many things she needed to know about what she was looking at. But one question took precedence. "Why?" she asked. "Why did you do this?"

Evan's face transformed into a small, sad smile. "That's simple," he said. "I needed to show you how amazing your work is. I wanted to show you that your dreams can come true."

She shook her head and resumed staring at the photos in

front of her. "I don't even know what my dreams are anymore."

He held out a hand. "Maybe this is a good place to start."

———

EVAN DIDN'T KNOW whether she was going to take his hand or not, but more than anything, he wanted her to. He *needed* her to. He couldn't stand the distance between them. He'd let that distance separate them once before, and he'd be damned if he would let it happen again.

He held his hand out in the space between them for what felt like an eternity before she took it. The second her skin touched his, the cold space inside him that had been present since their argument warmed. He wrapped his fingers around hers and squeezed.

"I know you're upset," he said. "And you should be. But right now, I just want this to be about you. Give me twenty minutes and then if you want to leave, you can. But if you want to yell at me, cry, whatever…that's okay, too."

He thought he saw a glimmer of a smile. She narrowed her eyes. "Twenty minutes?"

"Twenty minutes. I promise."

She nodded and Evan didn't hesitate. He looked over his shoulder and winked at Morgan, who'd been watching and waiting. She'd played her role in getting her mom there perfectly. He owed her. But first, Evan needed to convince Cam that not only was he not going anywhere this time, when it came to her, he was all in. No matter what.

"I want to show you something." Evan led the way into the store. It had been vacant for the last six months, after the owners of the pottery studio had moved out of state. Evan had called in a few favors and with the help of Cam's friends, had somehow made a miracle happen in the last twenty-four hours.

Junky had let him into Cam's little apartment, which was breaking so many laws that Evan didn't know where to start. But he'd managed to convince him that it was important and Cam wouldn't mind. He hoped that was true.

He'd found her camera bag, which luckily she hadn't taken with her to the city, and scoured through half a dozen memory cards, choosing his favorite photos from hundreds of great shots. Christy had secured the use of some art easels from the school, and Amber had worked her negotiating skills with the property owner to let them use the space for two weeks for a few hundred dollars.

Drew sweet-talked the print shop in town into doing a rush print job on the photos and Ben had provided trays of finger foods for the event. And it *was* an event. As they walked through the doors, Cam was greeted by friends and neighbors who were all there to celebrate her and her photos, which were worthy of celebrating in their own right. Evan knew she was talented, but seeing her prints blown up, framed and hanging throughout the space, brought them to life in a new way, and gave Evan an entirely new appreciation for just how talented Cam really was.

"What is—" Cam came to a full stop and brought her free hand to her mouth. She looked at Evan. "I still don't understand, Evan. Why are all my pictures...these people...what's going on?"

"I wanted to show you that your dream *can* come true, Cam. You're so talented that your photos deserve to be seen. I know you didn't believe me when I told you that you were talented enough to do this for a living. I needed to show you."

"But this..." She looked around the space, taking it all in. The photos on the wall, the people milling about admiring them. Everything.

"This is it, Cam."

Right then, their presence was noticed. Someone started

clapping and soon the entire room joined in. Evan squeezed her hand once more before he let go. Cam needed to soak in the moment on her own. She'd earned it and she deserved it.

He took a step back as her friends descended upon her to offer her congratulations, and soon Cam was swept up in the crowd. There were no prices on the pictures, because Evan had no idea how to set such a thing up, but Christy had started making a list of people who were interested in purchasing pieces, and even more exciting, people who were requesting their own photo shoots.

"I can't believe you pulled it off." Ben walked up and handed him a beer. "Cheers." They clinked bottles and Evan drank deep.

"This is all her."

The two friends stood silently, drinking their beers and watching. Evan kept his eyes on Cam but he didn't miss the way his friend was watching Drew.

"What's going on there?" he asked after a moment.

"Same old." Ben shrugged. "She's still married to my brother."

Evan stared at his friend. Ben rarely referred to the past in such a way.

"But I think something's wrong," Ben said.

"What do you mean?"

"She seems different. Quiet."

"Have you talked to her?"

"Once or twice." Ben took a drink of his beer. "I think maybe it's time I returned my brother's call though."

Evan didn't bother trying to hide his surprise. "Really? Why now?"

"Just a feeling," Ben said. "Like I said, something isn't right."

Evan didn't push, and Ben didn't offer any more information. He knew his buddy well enough to know that he'd talk when he was ready, and not a minute earlier.

"So, what about you?" Ben asked. "You made Cam's dream come true. What about yours?"

"She is my dream come true."

Ben laughed. "Yeah, I get that. I meant what about school? When do you leave?"

"I don't." Evan glanced at his watch. "But I think Cam should be the first one I talk to about that." He put his empty beer bottle on a nearby table, excused himself and went to interrupt Cam. Her twenty minutes were up.

"EXCUSE ME." Evan appeared at her side and cupped her elbow gently in his hand. "I promised you twenty minutes," he said. "Can I borrow you for a second?"

She nodded, thanked the couple she was talking to, and allowed Evan to lead her out the back door of the makeshift gallery.

Cam's head was still spinning with everything that had happened in such a short time. Evan had created a gallery. A *gallery.* Of *her* work. It was still so much to take in and wrap her head around.

"Thank you," she said as soon as they were outside in the small alley behind the building. "I can't even imagine how much work this all was, and you didn't have to…well, it's really…thank you."

"I'd do anything for you, Cam." He took her hands and held them tight. "Anything. I hope you know that."

She nodded, because of course she knew that. In some way, she'd always known it. Even during all their years apart, she'd known that Evan would always be there for her. And even with everything that had happened between them recently, she knew.

"I need you to know something, Cam."

"It's okay."

"No." He stopped her. "It's not. I never should have asked you about Morgan. That was wrong." Cam's heart ached. "I know she's not mine, no matter how much I wish she was."

"What?" She looked up sharply. "You do?"

"Oh my God, Cam." His smile was sad. "Of course I wish she was mine. She's fantastic. And it was supposed to be me," he said. "It was always supposed to be me and you. I think I wanted her to be mine so badly because that would mean that…well, I don't know what it would have meant. But I'm sorry that I, even for a minute, let myself think that you could have kept something like that from me."

"You know I wouldn't have."

He nodded. "I know. I wish the last sixteen years hadn't—"

"Don't." She put her finger to his lips. "Don't wish it all away. It happened and I'm not sorry about that. I'm really not. Because if I hadn't met Ryan, I wouldn't have Morgan. I wouldn't be standing here right now. And if you hadn't left to join the army, you wouldn't be Officer Anderson right now." She smiled. "And you wouldn't be going back to school so you can make a difference for kids." She couldn't help but feel an overwhelming sadness at the thought of Evan leaving. After all they'd been through, it was almost unbearable to think that they still weren't going to be together. But it was the right thing. Despite the underlying sadness, Cam smiled and said, "This all happened the way it was supposed to."

"Well, maybe not quite the way it was supposed to." He took her hand and led her to an old bench against the brick wall. Evan never let go of her hand while he explained how his mother had confessed to the way she'd treated Cam all those years ago, and then again more recently. "Her heart was in the right place." He chuckled. "At least I think so.

Regardless, she never should have gotten involved. I'm sorry."

He brushed away a stray tear on her cheek that she didn't even know was there.

"So what now?" Cam said after a moment. "Where do we go now?"

"We do everything we can to live our dreams."

She almost laughed. He made it all sound so simple, but Cam knew it was anything but. "This is all amazing, Evan." She gestured to the makeshift gallery behind them. "But it's not real life. We both know that."

"No," he said. "I don't know that. Why can't it be real life, Cam? Those people in there? They love your photos. Christy has a list of people who want to *buy* them, Cam. You can sell them."

The idea of making money from her photographs was so crazy and completely overwhelming, but at the same time, it was exhilarating. "But how much money can a few pictures make?"

"And portrait sessions, Cam." Evan was getting excited now. He sat up straight. "You can charge for photo sessions, too. It's a real thing, Cam. Think about it."

She did. And she had a lot more thinking to do, but maybe Evan was right. Maybe she could actually make a living doing what she loved. It was a lot to take in. But there was more, too.

"What about you?" She looked down at her hands. No matter what had happened between them, or what could happen in the future, Evan had done everything he could to make her dream come true. There was no way she would ever stand in the way of his. "When do you leave?"

His face shifted, and he nodded solemnly. "In a few days."

A few days.

Her heart sank and she bit her bottom lip to keep from crying. She couldn't let him see how much it hurt to know that he was going to leave again. Even if it was something he needed to do, it still broke her heart all the same. "So soon?" she asked. "I didn't realize classes started in the summer."

"They don't."

Her head shot up, her eyes full of questions as she searched his face for answers.

"But I need to register for my classes and pick up my books and course materials. Since I'm going to be doing everything by correspondence, I need to get a jump on things."

He kept talking about classes and registration, but she wasn't listening. She was still trying to process one of the things he'd said. "Wait." She finally interrupted him. "What did you say about correspondence? What does that mean?"

Evan's grin told her everything she needed to know. Still, she needed him to say it.

"Evan…what's going on? Are you going to school?"

"Yes and no." Cam held her breath. "There was a corre-spondence option," he explained. "For mature students who are working and want to continue working in a related field while taking classes."

"What does that mean?" She didn't dare to hope it meant that Evan might be staying in Timber Creek. *Could it be that after all these years, they could finally be together?*

"It means that I'll be taking most of my classes from right here in Timber Creek." Cam clamped her hand over her mouth to keep from screaming. "It also means it'll take me a bit longer to finish my degree, but I'll be able to keep working and even integrate what I'm learning into town here. Which means that I should be able to start working with kids right away, maybe even set up a program to help youth at risk."

She couldn't contain herself anymore. Cam wrapped her arms around his neck and squeezed. Evan unwrapped her arms and took her face in his hands. "Mostly what it means,

Cam, is that I get to be with you. You and Morgan. If you'll have me, that is."

In response, she crushed her lips to his and kissed him hard.

"Is that a yes?" He laughed.

"No," Cam said as seriously as she could. "It's an abso-freakin-lutely." She kissed him again, and this time she wasn't ever going to stop.

Chapter Eighteen

CAM PACKED the last of the books into the box on the table and taped the box shut. They didn't have a lot of things to move from their space over Junky's Auto Shop, but what they did have was all packed up and almost loaded into the back of Evan's truck. After only a month of officially dating, Evan had asked Cam and Morgan if they'd be willing to move out of their far too cozy apartment and into his house with him.

Morgan had jumped at the opportunity for more space and more privacy. The fact that Evan lived closer to her friends hadn't hurt either. The decision had been a little harder for Cam. Not because she didn't want to live with Evan. More than anything, she did. They spent all their time together anyway, and it didn't make sense for her to keep the little apartment. Not to mention, it would be nice to have an actual bedroom again and all the privacy that came with that. But it was bittersweet, too.

Cam had come to love their home over the garage. There was still nothing special about it, except of course for the very reason it was special. It had been the first place Cam and Morgan had called home together. Just the two of them. She knew she was being sentimental, but the apartment over Junky's represented their fresh start and their coming together as mother and daughter.

She wiped a tear from her cheek and laughed at herself as she carried the box down to Evan's waiting truck.

"Is that everything?" Evan took the box from her and loaded it with the others.

She nodded as another wave of emotion hit her.

"Hey." He pulled her into his arms. "It's okay."

"It's silly."

"It's not." He stroked her hair. Cam was grateful that he didn't make her feel self-conscious for the sudden display of emotion. "This was your first place together. I get it. You're allowed to feel whatever you need to feel."

She lifted her head and stood on her toes to kiss him. "Thank you. I don't want you to think I'm not excited about living with you."

"I don't think that for a second." He held open the door of his truck for her before joining her in the front seat. "Maybe you'll feel a little better when you see the surprise I have for you at the house."

"Surprise? What is it?"

"If I told you, it wouldn't be a surprise." He laughed and Cam rolled her eyes with a shake of her head. She took one last look out the window and then fixed her eyes forward on their future.

It wasn't until after they'd unloaded all the boxes into the house that Evan finally took her hand and led her out to the backyard. "It's time for your surprise. Are you ready?"

With the busyness of the day, she'd forgotten all about it, and told him so. Evan pretended to be offended, but he smiled and led her through the yard toward the shed in the back corner by the driveway. "I've been working on this for weeks," he said. "I hope you like it but we can make changes if it's not everything you need."

Confused, Cam opened the door of the shed and stepped inside. Where she'd expected to see shelves of pots and cans of paint, there were clean walls painted a light gray. A desk sat in one corner, with a large interchangeable backdrop set up on the other side of the room.

It was a studio.

It was *her* studio.

"I know we'll still need to put in some shelves for your things, and maybe over here we can—"

"It's perfect." She silenced him with a kiss. "I can't believe you did all this for me."

"Baby, I'd do anything for you."

Cam glowed with happiness. The last month had felt like a dream, only better because she knew she wasn't going to wake up.

"Do you think you'll be able to book enough jobs now so you can finally quit waitressing?"

Cam shook her head and wandered around the small space. It was perfect and there was no doubt she'd be able to book more work now that she could offer an indoor option as well as the outdoor sessions she'd been doing. But she was still hesitant to let go of her shifts at the End of the Road. It wasn't that Cam loved her job, she didn't really at all, but she wasn't bringing in quite enough yet with her photography. "Soon," she said. "One thing at a time, okay?"

Evan came up behind her and put his arms around her. "Okay." He kissed the top of her head. "Now, what do you say we go get you unpacked in *our* house?"

She liked the sound of that. A lot.

"WHAT DO you have in this one?" Trent carried the box into Morgan's new room and made a show of putting it down on the stack. "I think you have bricks in there."

"Not bricks." She laughed. "Books. Well, photo albums really."

"Photo albums?" Trent collapsed into her desk chair. "Like, old-school photo albums?"

Morgan nodded. When she was a kid, she'd loved all the pictures her mom took. So much so that she'd beg her to print them all out so she could put them in albums and flip through them. "Mostly just family pictures, holidays and things like that." Maybe she could put together a little photo album for her new baby brother or sister? It was still going to be a few months until the baby was born, and she'd mostly gotten used to the idea of not being the only child in her dad's life, in fact, it surprised her that Morgan was actually looking forward to having a sibling. Her dad had really stepped up when it came to parenting, and while they still weren't as close as they could be. It was better. She shrugged, returning her attention to Trent. "Maybe I'm a little old-fashioned, but I like looking at them in front of me instead of a computer screen."

"Makes sense."

"It does?"

"Sure." He spun in the chair and grinned. "It's just like I prefer real books to those e-book things."

"Right?" Morgan turned around so Trent wouldn't see her goofy smile. She couldn't help it. Just being around Trent made her stomach curl up in knots and made her want to squeal, and she was so *not* the squealing type.

"Hey," Trent said. "Do you have any more boxes to bring in? I'll get them for you before I have to go."

Morgan felt the disappointment all the way to her toes. "You have to go?"

He nodded. "I have to work. First shift at Hill's Hardware

store later today." He flipped his hair back off his face. "My dad was super pissed about the whole party at the lake and more or less told me to get a job or else. It took a few weeks, but I finally convinced George Hill to give me a job. I think it's my dad's idea of keeping me out of trouble."

"But you're not trouble." She took a step toward him. "I mean, it's not like any of what happened was your fault."

"I know, but you know parents…"

Morgan nodded.

"Besides, I think I could use the extra money anyway," Trent said. "I was kind of hoping that maybe you'd be my date for the year end formal?"

"Of course." She didn't even bother to hide her excitement. Morgan's smile stretched her face. "I'd love to be your date."

He stood up so they were only inches apart. *Close enough to…*

"What's this about a real date?"

Both Morgan and Trent took two huge steps backward at the sound of Evan's voice. Morgan spun around and clutched her hands together in front of her.

"Do we need to make some rules about having boys in your bedroom?"

She was positive that her face was flaming red, but if Trent noticed, he didn't say anything. Instead, he grabbed her hand and gave it a quick squeeze. "I should get going anyway," he said to her. "I'll call you later, Morgan. Bye, Officer Anderson."

Evan nodded and let the boy past. When Trent was gone, Morgan put her hands on her hips and stared at Evan. "Are you seriously going to make him call you *Officer* Anderson? He's my…well, I guess he's my boyfriend."

"Then yes." Evan laughed. "I'm definitely going to make him call me Officer Anderson."

Morgan threw up her hands with a groan and started to unpack a box.

"Are you getting settled in okay? Your room all right?"

Her room was awesome. It was twice the size as the one in the apartment and she had her own bathroom. Evan's house wasn't huge, but compared to what they'd been living in, it felt massive. Most importantly, it felt like a home.

"It's great," she said. "Thanks, Evan."

He nodded and took another step inside. "I just really want you to...well, it's important that you..." He laughed. "This is not coming out right."

"It's okay." She looked over her shoulder and pulled a stack of books out of a box. "I get it."

"Are you okay with all of this?" he asked. "I know it happened kind of fast."

To people of the outside looking in, it might have seemed that things between her mom and Evan had moved quickly, but for Morgan, it was natural. Anyone could see that they were meant to be together. There was no point in pretending anything else. "It's fine, Evan. Honestly." She picked up an old teddy bear and sat on the bed, facing him. "Are *you* okay? Because you look a little stressed."

Evan laughed. "I'm not stressed. Not at all. But I did want to ask you something. It's kind of important."

Morgan crossed her legs up underneath her and settled in because she had a feeling she knew what he wanted to say to her.

"I know that the last few months have been kind of crazy for you," he started. "It's been a bit of a transition."

"You could say that."

"And I know I'm not your dad." He twisted his hands together. "You have a dad, and I never want to come in between that. You know that, right?"

She nodded, no longer sure of what he was going to say.

Evan swallowed hard and shifted into the seat Trent had recently vacated. "I guess what I'm trying to say is, all I want for you and me is to be…"

"Friends?"

Evan laughed. The tense mood diffused. "Of course friends, but also…I hope that I can be maybe a sort of…"

"Stepdad?"

"Well, yes, but…I'm probably not explaining it properly, but I want to be there for you, Morgan. Whatever you need, okay? You can count on me."

Evan was always so self-assured and confident; seeing this different, nervous version of him was kind of strange for Morgan. But also, it was funny. And sweet. Because she wasn't stupid—she knew exactly what Evan was trying to say. She crossed the room and stood in front of him. "You know what?"

"What's that?"

"I already know I can count on you for anything."

He stood and pulled her into a hug. Morgan hadn't really thought about how strange it might be for her mom to date, and maybe that's because it was Evan she was dating and it wasn't strange. In fact, she felt lucky more than anything that her mom hadn't chosen some idiot, but instead had found a guy who not only accepted Morgan as part of the deal, but also really liked her.

"Now," she said when the hug was over. "When are you going to put a ring on it and ask my mom to marry you?"

PUT A RING ON IT.

For the next three days, Evan couldn't get Morgan's question out of his mind. Of course he wanted to marry Cam, but maybe things were happening too fast. After all, there was no need to rush. He planned to be with her forever—he could wait.

Even if he didn't want to.

Fortunately, after some initial tension, his mother and Cam had gotten past the history between them, and although Evan knew their relationship might never be a close one, at least it wasn't going to be awkward. Despite her misguided attempts to *help* Evan, he knew his mother's heart had always been in the right place and it was a relief to him that they'd all been able to move forward and let the past go.

Morgan seemed to enjoy having a grandmotherly figure around since Cam's parents were so far away, and his mother had embraced Morgan as her own, enlisting her to help around the garden, a project Morgan actually seemed to enjoy.

Every day, it felt more like they were a family and Evan thought more about making it official.

Evan could be a patient man if necessary, but he was also a man who knew the value of being prepared, which was why he'd gone shopping to pick out the perfect ring and had been carrying it around in his pocket ever since. He had no immediate plans to ask her, but if the situation came up...well, he wanted to be ready.

It was a rare Friday night that Evan wasn't on shift, so they'd been able to accept Christy and Mark's offer for chicken wings and beer. On one end of the table, the girls were in a deep conversation about something, although Evan couldn't quite make it out. But it didn't matter. He loved watching her, especially when she was so relaxed and happy. So different from when she'd moved to town. A lot had changed.

Evan reached for his bottle of beer.

"It's pretty crazy, don't you think?"

Mark was asking him a question. Evan racked his brain in an effort to remember what his friend had been saying, but he came up empty. "Sorry," he admitted. "I was daydreaming for a minute."

Mark followed his gaze and laughed. "I can see that. I was just saying how crazy it was that you guys are sitting here, back together again. It's kind of like old times, isn't it?"

Evan nodded. "It is. Who would have thought we'd all end up like this, hey? Cam and I. You and Christy still crazy about each other." Something flickered across Mark's face, and Evan hesitated. "Is everything okay there?" He lowered his voice. "With Christy, I mean?"

Mark nodded, and returned his focus to his beer, but a moment later when the women excused themselves to go to the restroom, he put his bottle down on the table and looked at Evan. "Can I give you a piece of advice?"

Evan nodded.

"Don't let babies make you crazy."

"Pardon?" He sat back and chuckled, but Mark wasn't laughing. "What's going on, Mark?"

"No one ever tells you that trying to have a baby can actually destroy your marriage," he said with a sad shake of his head.

"Destroy? What are you talking about?" Evan vaguely knew that Mark and Christy had been trying to get pregnant, but he certainly didn't know any of the details about it. "Making babies is the fun part, right?" He winked but Mark wasn't laughing.

"So help me, I never thought there'd be a time when I dreaded the thought of making love to my wife, Evan." He dropped his head and shook it slightly before looking up again. "Wait. That's not entirely fair. I *want* to be with Christy. It's all this measuring temperatures, taking pills, injections, schedules and positions and…" He shook his head again and took a deep drink of his beer. "I guess it is what it is. But I'll tell you something, Evan. It's a total mood killer. And it's changed her. Hell, it's changed us."

Evan didn't know what to say to his friend. "I'm sorry, man." It didn't feel adequate, but it was all he had to offer, so it would have to do.

"Hey," Mark said. "Don't worry about it. I'm sorry to drop that on you when we should be celebrating." He lifted his beer. "To you and Cam. Together the way you always should have been."

Evan toasted and took a drink, but he didn't completely agree with his friend. A lot had happened, and some of it he would change if he could, but most of it, he wouldn't. They wouldn't have been any good to each other all those years ago. They needed to grow up, find themselves, have their own lives before they could fully appreciate what they could have together. And who they could be on their own.

He believed that.

He also believed that it was time to make sure Cam knew exactly how he felt.

Evan spotted the women making their way across the room. Cam stopped to talk to Ben at the bar. She smiled at something he said and her whole face lit up. He excused himself from the table and went to her, not able to wait one more minute.

"May I have this dance?"

She turned and her whole face split into a smile. "Now?"

"Of course now."

She laughed. "No one else is dancing."

"I don't care about anyone else." He held his hand out and she took it.

He thought he heard Ben say something in the background, but a moment later the song changed to a slower beat and Evan pulled his love into his arms.

"You're crazy," Cam said, but she snuggled into his embrace.

"I know it."

He spun her slowly around the small dance floor, keeping a close hold on her. "Are you happy?"

She nodded against his chest. "So much. Everything is perfect right now. Just the way it is."

"Perfect?"

Cam pulled back a little so she could look him in the eyes. "Yes. I couldn't ask for anything else. Morgan is getting settled in and in the last few months, she's like an almost completely different person. It's just…it's nice to see her happy."

"And you?" He ran a finger down her cheek before cupping her face in his hand.

She smiled and leaned into his touch. "It's all a work in progress, but yes. So much happier. Thank you."

"Thank you?"

"For everything," she said. "Just for being you. For being here. For loving me."

He shook his head softly before reaching up and holding her hands in his hands. His eyes shone, but he looked directly into hers when he said, "Baby, I love the fuck out of you."

She chuckled at his harsh choice of words.

"I know that's not the most eloquent way to say it," Evan said quickly. "And I'm sorry for the curse. But it's the truth and the only way to really say it. You mean more to me than anything else in the world." Her laughter stopped and she looked straight into his eyes.

"It's a lot, Evan. A single mom with a teenage girl—it's a lot."

"I know it."

"And I don't want you to—"

He put a finger to her lips. "I'm never going to do or be anything that I don't want. Do you understand that?"

She nodded.

"Which means, I would not be here right now if I didn't one hundred percent want all of this. You. Morgan. *All* of it."

"I know. It's just—"

"No. There's no *just*." He spun her slowly. "There are going to be challenges. It's not always going to be easy, but it's going to be amazing and I'm all in, babe. For the hard stuff and the easy stuff. All of it. I'm in."

A tear slipped down her cheek, but she was smiling.

He didn't want to let her go, so he held her close with his left arm and slipped his hand into his pocket. His fingers wrapped around the ring and he knew what he needed to do. Without missing a beat, he moved her easily around the dance floor, twirling her out gently before pulling her close again and as he did so, he took her left hand and slipped the ring on her finger.

Cam froze and stared at her hand. "What is—"

"It doesn't have to be anything." He pressed a kiss on her forehead. "Or it can be everything. Whatever you want it to be."

Chapter Nineteen

A MONTH LATER...

THE SUMMER SUN warmed Cam's little backyard studio
perfectly. She stood by the window and looked out into the
yard. Over the last few weeks, Cam had put her touch on the
space by planting a few perennials and big pots of colorful
flowers. Evan had picked up some oversized wicker chairs for
them that she'd put in the corner, where they could watch the
sun set behind the mountain in the evenings.

It was a gorgeous day, and what she really wanted to do
was sit in those chairs right now with a glass of lemonade and
a good book. But she had two photo sessions to edit and
prepare for clients, as well as selecting some new shots for a
gallery in Seattle who'd offered to show her work. It wasn't a
big gallery, but the exposure was incredible and Cam still
couldn't believe that her photographs were hanging in a gallery
anywhere. It still seemed surreal.

Everything in her life seemed surreal a lot of the time these
days. As if it were too good to be true. But she refused to sit

around and wait for her bubble to burst. That was her old way of thinking and Cam was no longer going to let herself fall into those patterns. She'd spent too many years pushing down her own desires and wants because she didn't think she could have them, or even that she deserved them.

No longer.

"Knock knock." Cam turned away from the window and her thoughts to see Christy at the door of her studio. One of the best things about being back in town was rekindling their friendship. "I hope I'm not interrupting. Evan said you were—"

"No. Not at all. I was just taking a break."

Christy's face lacked its usual relaxed smile. Cam crossed the room and took her hand. "What's wrong? Are you okay?"

Her friend nodded. "I am. I just…it's fine. I just needed to see a friendly face."

"Where's Mark?"

Christy's face crumpled. She swiped at the tears streaking down her face. "I'm sorry. I shouldn't be crying. It's just that…"

"Christy?" Cam put her arm around her friend and led her over to the chair. "What's going on? Is everything okay?"

Her friend nodded. "Everything's fine." Cam didn't believe her. "I think it's just all these hormones. I'm just so emotional. Really, I can't stop crying."

"Is Mark okay? Is everything between you…" Cam didn't want to say it out loud even though she'd known for months that there was a lot of tension in her friend's marriage. They hadn't really talked about it, even though Cam had been meaning to ask her. She felt bad that she hadn't been the type of friend she should have been.

Christy waved her away. "Yes. Mark's fine." She took the tissue Cam offered her and blew her nose. "I was just…I think this is going to be our last round of IVF and…" She started to cry again. "What if it doesn't work?"

Cam squeezed her friend in a fierce hug. Christy had already been through so much. "You'll be okay," Cam said honestly. "If it doesn't work, you will be okay. You and Mark both. You really will. I promise."

Christy nodded against Cam's shoulder. "I know. I really do. It's just…"

"There are other options, you know?" Christy sat back and attempted a small smile. "I mean," Cam continued, "you can always borrow Morgan."

That had the desired effect and made Christy laugh, because just the day before they'd been talking about how difficult raising a teenager was and how it may very well be the reason for all of Cam's recent gray hairs.

"She's a great kid," Christy said. "But she's definitely your daughter. Stubborn just like her mama."

The two of them spent a few more minutes talking about Morgan and her latest dramas, which mostly revolved around a curfew she didn't think was fair and the recent part-time job she'd taken at Daisy's since finishing up her community service. Fortunately, despite the trouble they'd gotten in together, Morgan and Jess were still close friends. A fact Cam was grateful for. The high school years were so much easier with a good group of friends. She should know.

After Christy excused herself, she tried to get some more work done but Cam couldn't concentrate on the images in front of her of the computer screen of the happy couple she'd photographed at their wedding the weekend before. It was the first wedding she'd done and she'd been so focused on getting the couple's shots just right that it wasn't until later when she was flicking through them all on her computer that it hit her.

A wedding.

What would it be like to stand up in front of all their friends and family and declare her love for Evan after all these years?

That was what Evan wanted. She'd always known that on some level, even though he'd never come right out and said it. She looked at the ring on her left hand. It was a sapphire set in white gold with tiny, sparkling diamonds around it. He'd never said it was an engagement ring. He'd told her it was whatever she wanted it to be.

At the time, when he'd given it to her, she'd been overwhelmed with all the changes in her life and was still trying to get settled and adjusted to her new life. The idea of getting married again was too much and something she'd never considered. After all, she'd been married before. It was kind of crazy to want to do it again, wasn't it?

But Evan was different. Not only that, but their *love* was different.

It deserved to be celebrated and recognized just as much as any other relationship. Maybe more.

And when Cam closed her eyes and pictured it, it no longer seemed crazy at all.

It seemed like the most natural thing in the world.

Cam got up from her desk and walked again to the sunny window. She could see straight across the yard and into the kitchen window, where Evan was at the sink, still in his uniform after his shift.

She twisted the ring on her finger one more time and, with a smile on her face, left her studio.

Cam didn't even make it into the house before Evan met her on the lawn, a tray holding two glasses of lemonade in his hands. "Hi, beautiful. I thought maybe you could use a little break."

She thanked him, but didn't take a glass. Instead, she took the tray from him and placed it gently on the table between the wicker chairs before taking his hands in hers.

"What's going on? You okay?"

She nodded. "I wanted to ask you a question." He waited, so she continued. "When you gave me this ring, you told me it could be whatever I wanted it to be."

"That's right." He turned her hands in his and squeezed. "It's a symbol of my commitment to you, Cam. Whatever you want that to look like."

She smiled and looked straight into his eyes. "When you gave it to me, there was so much going on, with Morgan and the move and…well, everything. I needed time to process it all."

"I know. It's okay."

"But there was one thing I didn't need to process," she continued. "And that's how I feel for you. And how I've always felt. I still don't understand completely why you want to take on all the craziness that is me and my life, but I believe you when you say you want it."

He dropped her hands and held her face in his. "I want all your craziness, Cam, because I love you."

"I love you, too." She grinned. "And if it's okay with you… I was hoping maybe this ring could be an engagement ring."

He shook his head and took a step away from her. Cam's heart fell.

But then right there in the yard, Evan dropped to one knee and took her hand in his. "More than anything I want to be your husband, Cam. I want to walk beside you every day for the rest of our lives. I want to fall asleep beside you and wake up to your beautiful face. Your heart is the only one that's ever captured me so completely and you would make me the happiest man in the world if you agreed to be my wife." She took a sharp breath but Evan wasn't done. "Cam Riley, you're the love of my life and you always will be. For goodness sake, will you *finally* marry me?"

She laughed but her eyes filled with tears that she swiped

away while she nodded. "Yes," she said. "A million times yes. Of course I'll marry you."

Thank you for reading, When We Left! I hope you fell in love with Cam and Evan and ALL the friends of Timber Creek.

The second chances continue with Christy and Mark's story in When We Were Us.
Marriage isn't always easy, especially when you're faced with a heartbreaking struggle that could test even the strongest love.
You can read an excerpt right after this...

For more love and happily ever afters, I have an exclusive sweet novella that's not for sale anywhere. You can read it HERE!

When We Were Us

I hope you enjoy this excerpt from the next in the Timber Creek Series, When We Were Us

Christy Thomas took a deep breath and then another.

It didn't work. She was still shaking and unable to focus on her reflection in the mirror.

With both hands planted firmly on the countertop, she squeezed her eyes shut and tried again.

One. Two. Three.

The counting technique her holistic healer had taught her was not working. Christy swallowed hard, opened her eyes, and stared at her reflection. Maybe it was the fluorescent lighting of the clinic's bathroom that made her look so puffy and old.

Maybe. But not likely. It was her.

Christy hardly recognized herself lately. *When had she become this worn-out version of herself?* The hot tears pricked at her eyes and threatened to spill over.

Again.

The worst part was she wouldn't be able to stop them. She'd always been an emotional person, but with all the hormones the doctors had her taking, it was next level, out of control.

She was exhausted.

And it wasn't over.

"Come on, Christy," she whispered to the woman in the mirror. "You can do this. Pull it together."

She tried her breathing exercises once more and pulled out her compact in a vain effort to cover the red blotches on her cheeks and the dark circles under her eyes. When she'd done the best she could, Christy snapped the compact shut, stood as straight as she could, and pasted what she hoped would pass as a smile on her face.

"There you are," her husband Mark said as soon as he saw her. He pushed up from the wall where he'd been leaning, tucked his phone into his back pocket and reached for her hand. "I was beginning to think you may have fallen in." He gave her a grin that was as equally fake as the one she wore on her own face. "Are you ready for this?"

How was she supposed to answer that question? Was she ready to lay on the doctor's examination table, like some sort of specimen, to see whether their latest round of in vitro fertilization and hormone therapies had worked, and they were finally, thankfully, mercifully pregnant?

Yes. She was ready for that.

But Mark's question was two-sided.

Was she ready to lie on that table, surrounded by doctors, nurses, and students and hear the news that once again the ultrasound revealed the treatments hadn't worked, and now, not only were they not pregnant, but they were completely out of options? Was she ready for that?

No.

Instead of saying exactly what she was thinking, Christy nodded and with cheer she didn't feel said, "Absolutely. Let's do this."

Mark's hand felt clammy in hers. Not the warm, strong support that he usually offered her with a simple touch.

When had that changed?

As they walked slowly down the hallway to Doctor Duncan's office, Christy snuck a look at her tall, strong husband. Even as teenagers, he'd always been a foot taller than her. The way he'd wrap his arms around her had always made her feel safe and protected, as if nothing bad could ever happen.

If only things were still so simple. If only she could be protected from sadness and bad news, with only Mark shielding her. But it wasn't like that anymore. How could he possibly protect her from the disappointment that radiated off him every time they found out the treatments hadn't worked? She knew he didn't mean to make her feel bad; he even tried his best to hide his feelings. After all, it wasn't her fault. Not entirely. A low sperm count and "tricky" eggs meant they carried *equal* fault with their infertility. But knowing that and *knowing* it were two very different things.

It was *her* body that continually failed to accept the embryos. It was *her* body that couldn't seem to manage to accomplish the very thing it was designed to do.

"I have a good feeling about it this time." Mark squeezed her hand. "It's different this time, isn't it?"

Different than the last two times? Only in the sense that instead of the overwhelming feeling of hope and anticipation, Christy —who was generally unwaveringly positive and optimistic to the point of occasionally being annoying to her friends and family—couldn't for the life of her find anything to smile at these days.

At least not genuinely.

"It is, isn't it?" Mark asked again.

She nodded and, like the good wife she was, smiled. "It is." She lied. Because it didn't feel any different than the last few times they'd been through the process. She didn't have any tingling in her breasts, no feeling of fullness or the miraculous twinge that signified that there was now a new life growing in her womb. None of the things that women described in her online forums applied to her. But then again, not everyone experienced a moment when they just knew. *Maybe she was one of those women?*

With her free hand, she crossed her fingers.

It couldn't hurt.

She wanted to tell Mark how scared she was that she'd let him down again. She wanted to talk about what they could do if they got bad news again. More than anything, she wanted to tell him that she loved him and they'd be okay. No matter what. But somehow she couldn't find the words.

"Do you feel pregnant?"

She opened her mouth to lie again but thankfully, Dr. Duncan's nurse, Amanda, greeted them. "Dr. and Mrs. Thomas. Welcome back." She smiled warmly, the way she always did. She'd likely been trained to always be optimistic and hopeful without giving patients a false sense of security that they would be receiving good news. "Let's take you right back and get you set up."

Christy followed Amanda numbly down the small corridor to the exam room she already knew too well. The last time she'd been there was to have their last three embryos implanted in her uterus. It seemed crazy that they were the last ones. They were the last three hopes she and Mark had for a baby.

Dr. Duncan had warned against a multiple pregnancy, but those warnings seemed a world away. Not that twins or even triplets would be anything to be warned against, but also because the idea that even one embryo would stick seemed so unlikely to Christy's battered heart there was no way she could conceivably imagine multiples.

Amanda gave her a gown to change into and left the room

so she could have a moment of privacy with Mark while she got situated for the exam that would change their lives either way.

Mark bent and pressed a kiss to her forehead. "I love you."

The tears that had been threatening all day were suddenly gone. Ironically when she would have welcomed them the most. When she would have welcomed any feeling at all, except for the deep sense of emptiness that filled her.

Mark held tight to his wife's hand, willing her to be okay. He no longer wished for a successful pregnancy, although of course he wanted that. But more than anything, he just wanted Christy to be okay. More and more over the last few months, during this last round of IVF, he felt her changing, hardening somehow. Pulling away from him.

At first, he thought it was just the stress of the treatments that was causing the shift in his usual lighthearted wife. But more and more, he worried that it was something bigger.

"Good afternoon." Doctor Brian Duncan greeted them in the same welcoming way he always did. It must be a mixed bag to be a fertility doctor, as opposed to having a general practice like his own. Sure, Brian would have all the highs of helping people get pregnant and realize their dreams to start a family. But there would also be the flip side of that coin. Breaking hearts.

The way he'd done with them. Up until now.

Mark refused to think anything but positive thoughts. *This time was going to be different. It had to be different.* Mark himself had seen it in his own practice for years. Especially with the couples he'd referred to Dr. Duncan. In vitro fertilization was becoming more and more successful. The success rates were strong. It was more unusual for it not to work.

The statistics were in their favor.

It had to work.

Especially considering this last round had eaten up the last bit of their savings. IVF was expensive, and insurance wasn't much help. Mark didn't want to tell Christy that he'd had to cash in a retirement fund he'd set up as well as take out a line of credit in order to make the final payment for this treatment. She thought they'd been able to use their savings. Mark hated keeping things like that from her and it was the only time he'd ever flat out lied to her in their relationship, but it was only to protect her.

She had enough going on with the hormone treatments and the emotional madness that cycled through her on a daily basis. He couldn't worry her about the financial side of things.

Besides, it would pay off when they held their very own baby in their arms. It would more than pay off. And there was no way she could be mad at him then.

"How are you both doing today?" Dr. Duncan looked at them each in turn, but his smile faded a little as his gaze landed on Christy. "How are you feeling, Christy? Has everything been okay this round?"

She nodded and that same smile that Mark had seen a little too often lately—the one that didn't quite reach her eyes and create the cute little crinkle in the corners that he loved so much—slid across her face. "I'm a little tired, Doctor. But otherwise, I'm just fine."

The doctor patted her hand, but he still looked concerned. "Well, it's normal for you to be tired. After all, your body is working very hard."

Christy's smile dropped away. Mark knew what she was thinking. That her body wasn't working hard. Because if it were, they'd already be pregnant. He knew she blamed herself for their infertility. More than anything, he wanted to take that away from her. As a medical doctor himself, he *knew* that wasn't true. *But deep down, didn't he blame her? Just a little bit?*

Mark shook the thought away. He couldn't let himself think that way. Besides, this was the time it was going to work. He knew it.

"Well, why don't we take a look at what's going on in there, shall we?"

It was Mark who answered with a simple nod of his head.

Dr. Duncan and his nurse Amanda kept up an easy line of conversation and chatter that Mark knew was designed to put them at ease, but he wasn't listening. He was focused on his wife's face. She'd been crying for the littlest reasons for months. Like toast that was slightly browner than she would have preferred, or just that morning the fact that there were no seeds in the raspberry jam. But now, lying on the exam table waiting for the news that they were going to be parents—or not, he had to remind himself—she was straight-faced, with no glimmer of emotion or…anything really.

He squeezed Christy's hand and she met his gaze.

I love you. He mouthed the words but she didn't respond. Instead, she squeezed her eyes shut as Dr. Duncan placed the ultrasound wand on her belly.

"It's going to be a little cool," he said despite the fact they all knew he heated the ultrasound gel, but no one said anything.

———

She'd known going in what the results would be.

No baby.

Not even one.

She wasn't pregnant.

Again.

Leaving the clinic felt final this time. They wouldn't be

back. There were no more embryos and no more money. That was it.

Her final failure to be a mother.

Christy knew Mark felt it too, the sense of finality when the glass door swung gently shut behind them in a soft whoosh that felt incongruous with how she was feeling. Thankfully, after Doctor Duncan finished his exam, she was able to get dressed and they could leave. After all, there was nothing more he could say.

And then finally, mercifully they were back in the car, driving away from the clinic and the doctor who, despite his best efforts, couldn't give them what they so desperately wanted.

"We can go…" Mark let the sentence fall away unfinished. "Christy? Are you…are we…"

Numb, she tucked her hands between her legs to keep him from reaching for them. She couldn't stand the idea of being touched. Of being loved by him when she'd just failed so completely to give him what he wanted most. Not right then.

"I love you."

She forced a small smile. "I know. I love you too."

That was the hardest part. Their love for each other. It just didn't seem fair. They loved each other so much and they'd done everything right. They'd been safe in high school and all through college, using protection so they wouldn't start a family until they were ready and able to give their child everything he or she deserved. And then it was time. After they were married and settled back into their home town of Timber Creek, with a house of their own that had spare bedrooms to fill, it was finally time to start the family they'd both dreamed about since they were high school sweethearts and barely more than children themselves.

But it hadn't happened.

And now all they had was that love that had pulled them along all these years. *Would it be enough?*

She didn't want to cry. She wanted to stay numb so she couldn't feel the overwhelming sense of loss inside her, knowing she'd never be a mother. She swallowed hard to keep the tears down. She wouldn't cry. She couldn't.

"Christy." Mark's voice was soft, almost as if he knew if he spoke too loudly she would crack and break. "There are other things we can—"

"Can we just not talk about this right now?" She kept her eyes fixed to the road in front of them and the thick pine forest that lined the highway. She unrolled the window and inhaled the pine-filled air. It was a smell that never failed to ground her. "Let's just not talk about it for a few days, okay?" She looked at him then and could see the confusion on his face. Up until a few hours ago, it had been Christy who wanted to talk about other options, and Mark who'd wanted to wait. He was so sure the IVF would work that he didn't want to entertain any other ideas. Now the roles had flipped. Maybe it didn't make sense to him, but it did to her. She needed a break. Even for a few days of not having this dominate her every waking moment.

She'd tried to use the Timber Creek High School reunion party as a distraction, but that had been over for months. Besides, even when she filled her days with business to distract her, it was never enough.

It was always there. Right under the surface.

"I just need a few days, Mark. Please."

"Okay." He nodded and turned his attention back to the road but Christy could see the hurt lined on his face. It wasn't just her who this experience had taken a toll on. Mark was hurting just as deeply as she was. It wasn't just her who'd wanted parenthood.

She knew that. Of course she did. But knowing it and doing something about it were two very different things. And even though it made her sick inside, she just couldn't bring herself to reach out to him. With every minute that passed, she hated herself a little bit more for it.

Don't wait! Read the rest of Christy's story NOW in *When We Were Us!*

About the Author

Elena Aitken is a USA Today Bestselling Author of more than forty romance and women's fiction novels. The mother of 'grown up' twins, Elena now lives with her very own mountain man in the heart of the very mountains she writes about. She can often be found with her toes in the lake and a glass of wine in her hand, dreaming up her next book and working on her own happily ever after.

To learn more about Elena:
www.elenaaitken.com
elena@elenaaitken.com

www.ingramcontent.com/pod-product-compliance
Lightning Source LLC
Chambersburg PA
CBHW021234250626
47155CB00008B/3006